NOVELS BY BURT WEISSBOURD

Danger in Plain Sight

"Here's what happens when you enter Mr. Weissbourd's world: You can't get out. You will be astonished not only by the colorful, playful, lethal characters, you will be hooked into a plot that laughs at whatever else you thought you were doing today. Callie and Cash, beauty and the beast, and the characters that swim through their world are each a gem of humanity observed."

—**David Field**, screenwriter and former head
of West Coast Production United Artists

"Weissbourd delivers a polished page-turner about terrorism, money laundering, and the price of sins rooted in avarice."

—*BlueInk Review*

"From the author of the brilliant Corey Logan Trilogy, *Danger in Plain Sight* is the latest thriller from Burt Weissbourd and his finest novel yet. Weissbourd has created an entire genre—*Seattle Noir*. Callie James and her son, Lew, are indelible characters. I devoured the novel in a single night–and I think you will, too."

—**Jacob Epstein**, writer and executive story editor
Hill Street Blues, writer *LA Law*

"A woman gets in touch with her inner action hero in this bracing thriller."

–*Kirkus Reviews*

Inside Passage

"A narrative that is relentlessly taut and exciting."

—Foreword Reviews

"*Inside Passage* hit all the hallmarks of a great read... Riveting story from the first paragraph."

—Nightly Reading

"The family dynamics and insights to human behavior had me reeling.... Juicy, fascinating stuff."

—The (Not Always) Lazy W

"*Inside Passage* is a great thriller and the restaurants you include as part of the story: Canlis, El Gaucho, Tulio, Queen City Grill, Wild Ginger, are all very sexy places. You really captured our city!"

—Scott Carsburg, James Beard award winner
and legendary Seattle chef

"I got completely hooked on *Inside Passage*'"

—Nancy Guppy, host of *Art Zone* on Seattle Channel

Teaser

"A stunning, fast-paced thriller."

—*Roxy's Reviews*

"Burt Weissbourd is such a great writer... Such a great book!"

—*So I Am a Reader*

"Weissbourd, a seasoned screenwriter and film producer, has the mechanics down pat. Teaser is a fun, action-filled ride."

—*Foreword Reviews*

"Weissbourd's stellar writing, memorable characters and an extremely well-crafted narrative never disappoint."

—*Discerning Reader*

Minos

"Original, consistently compelling...Minos is an exceptionally entertaining and engaging read from beginning to end."

—*Midwest Book Review*

"These books transcend the expectations of genre fiction to become literature."

—**Jacob Epstein**, writer and executive story editor
of *Hill Street Blues*, writer *LA Law*

"Mr. Weissbourd draws you into a world of characters and stories that keep you riveted, and you're pretty sure you are visiting people and worlds that have little or nothing to do with you. But he keeps going deeper, and by the end, he has delivered you back to yourself, a self you may not have admitted to before. Mr. Weissbourd, please keep writing."

—**David Field**, screenwriter and former head
of West Coast Production United Artists

In Velvet

"This thrilling novel has a breathless pace that combines science and nature to create nail-biting tension."

—Foreword Reviews

"*In Velvet* left me breathless, a bit contemplative, and completely satisfied."

—Manic Readers

"Weissbourd's writing reminds me of the great Raymond Chandler mysteries."

—John McCaffrey, *KGB Bar Lit Mag*

"*In Velvet* is a thrill from start to finish!"

—Closed the Cover

ROUGH JUSTICE

BURT WEISSBOURD

ROUGH JUSTICE

BLUE CITY PRESS
ISLIP, NY

RARE BIRD
LOS ANGELES, CALIF.

THIS IS A GENUINE RARE BIRD | BLUE CITY PRESS BOOK

Rare Bird Books
6044 North Figueroa Street
Los Angeles, CA 90042
rarebirdbooks.com

Blue City Press
62 West Bayberry Road
Islip, NY 11751

Cover Design by Lisa Fyfe

Printed in the United States

PAPERBACK ISBN: 9781644283097

10 9 8 7 6 5 4 3 2 1

Publisher's Cataloging-in-Publication Data available upon request.

To William Landau-Taylor

PROLOGUE

People still argue about where, or when, it started. Some, mostly the hindsighters, say it began in Hong Kong, in the complex, unorthodox mind of an aging Chinese gangster, Yu Shin Shi.

Others start it with Fanny Rose, a.k.a. Rosie, the gifted queen of the Los Angeles Immigration Bar.

The mortified high and mighty at Immigration won't discuss where, or when. Privately, they say Rosie and Yu were the Devil's own instrument. Period.

If you were to ask Him—The Prince of Darkness, that is—he'd put it in LA. He'd start it when they got together.

CHAPTER ONE

Hong Kong, 1990

"And fast outta the gate, you bet your sweet cujones...I can take you back when Rosie was yeh high." Smiling Danny "the Viper" Nash extended his hand at hip height, cracked his famous smile, and went right on, "Yes siree, she was a go-getter—you'd have the family over for dinner, she'd eat like a little lady, excuse herself, then steal the loose change right off your bedroom dresser."

Yu nodded, apparently pleased.

The smiling Viper raised a manicured hand, palm up, punctuation. "This one time, I'm with her on a plane. Now, she can't take flying, makes her sick. Well, she throws up on this fancy, well-muscled, mean-looking fella sleeping in the seat next to her. Fouls his extravagant, and I kid you not—$4,000 Loro Piana grey cashmere suit. Now I swear to God, I'm sweating bullets, my heart is pounding in my chest. I mean here's the king a cool, covered with creamed codfish, and I see how he shifts in his seat and sets his meaty hand right in a puddle of creamed cod. Next to me, God be my witness, Rosie just keeps reading some comic book, like nothing happened. Well, just then, this big fella wakes up, making a face out of a nightmare. He's snarling, staring down at this stinking, creamed cod covering—and I mean all over—his fine cashmere. Now, I'm near to passing out as he raises this dripping, cod-coated hand, a paw big enough to tear your head right off and turns toward her, eyes blazing. Well, sweet as molasses, little Rosie looks him straight in the eye, smiles and asks, 'are you feeling better now, sir?'"

Smiling Danny lifted his Stetson, raised his bushy eyebrows, then he tapped his bald head, twice, with two fingers. "I am not kidding you, son, and she was eleven at the time. Hell, I knew she'd help you. That little gal was born to be a crackerjack lawyer. Yes siree Bob."

Yu Shin Shi bowed his head ever so slightly, plainly pleased that he'd chosen this colorful, crafty man.

"Thank you, son. I like a man likes my stories," Smiling Danny nodded. He paused, contemplative, then looked at Yu, shifting gears. "So, we got business?" Danny flashed old faithful. "'Cause if you're here to soak up Jewish wisdom partner, then I'm granny goose."

Yu raised his long arms as he graciously explained, "My esteemed friend, I fear that Hong Kong will eventually fall under the unstable hand of Beijing, and, as such, cannot be a good place to hold assets... After consulting your niece, Rosie, I have determined to immigrate to the great American West. I have prepared a list of places where you may buy land for me in California. As a child of Hong Kong, I believe in land. As a student of real estate, I believe in California."

Danny smiled. "Now we're cooking." He looked heavenward. "Yes Lord, this is a fine day." Danny took the list from Yu, scanned it hurriedly. Then he read it again, more carefully. He paused, took off his ten-gallon hat, then wiped his forehead with a red bandana. "Babe, you're a friend of mine. I tell you as my friend, this is not smart. I mean you want to buy on the beach, fine. Buy it within an hour, maybe an hour and a quarter of the city. What you got here are the cheapest, least desirable beaches in the great state of California."

Yu nodded. "Precisely."

Smiling Danny frowned. "No one in LA is going to drive more than an hour to get to the beach. No way. Cambria...San Simenon...Santa Maria's the boondocks. You got bums and winos sleeping on the beach, the hippies fuck outdoors. This is 1990—LA's got never-ending traffic jams, no jet train. So even if you get sand, where's your resale?"

"I hope you are sadly mistaken, as my course is set. If you are in some discomfort—"

"Hey, hold on. We don't have to agree on everything, do we pal? I'll still look out for you. Talk to me. Tell me what you got in mind."

"Hotel and residential developments. They must be on, or have a good view of, the beach…and price affordable. That is all. You may look in Oregon and Washington State as well."

"Yu, buddy, do me this one favor—before buying, consider that I got some better properties. Wilshire Blvd. apartments…West LA condominiums…Marin County view lots…You don't have to go buying low-rent beachfront hours from anywhere."

"I have considered the many alternatives you suggest, and I agree, they are fine, sound investments. Yet they require great capital, and as you call it, 'the smart money,' it is surely already there. The competition is too fierce for an inexperienced outsider, such as myself, to take a position of leadership."

"I see. You're going for the whole enchilada, that it?"

"At my age, there are few opportunities left."

"Then listen to me. You have to think practical, think the city. If it's America you want to cash in on, for Christ's sake, you have to think like an American."

"Yes, definitely." Yu nodded agreement. "Bugsy Siegel, that great American visionary, he built Las Vegas in the desert."

Los Angeles, 1991–2003

Yu Shin Shi was five foot ten inches tall, lean and wiry, with long limbs inaccurately suggesting a mountain climber. An abandoned bastard— adopted into a family with seven older daughters—he was always polite, made a point of remembering people's names, and rarely allowed a negative word about anyone or anything to cross his lips. Cursed with the excessive caution of an unwanted child, he grew into a thoughtful, unusually deliberate man. It was said he could weigh pros and cons endlessly before arriving at a decision. Once decided, however, Yu left the company of other men. Once decided, this courteous Chinese gangster was as committed to realizing his objective as a salmon was committed to returning to its natal stream to spawn.

The immigration lawyer that Danny "the Viper" had recommended was a smart, ingenious young woman named Fanny Rose, Rosie for short. Rosie was thirty when the wiry, slow moving Chinese fella first asked her to go for a walk on the beach. Rosie thought Yu was crazy that first day, but she was smart enough to keep her mouth shut. Unnaturally ambitious, Rosie always did her homework, and she knew that Yu owned twelve Mahjong parlors and forty-five percent of a gambling house in Macau. To Rosie, that made Yu rich, and Rosie loved rich foreigners.

Rosie made an impression on Yu. For someone coming from Hong Kong in 1990, you had to wait years for a green card. Rosie got Yu his card in less than six months. Under protest, Rosie accepted Yu's suggestion of a $15,000 retainer and a $20,000 bonus when the card was actually received. Rosie's normal fee was $7,500, but normally it took many years, and normally, the applicants were not as, well, eccentric as Yu.

Once unleashed, Yu's love for the land was uncontainable. An admirer of Walt Disney, William Randolph Hearst, and in later years, Chinatown's Noah Cross, Yu stuck to the West coast. He carefully, and ruthlessly, worked his way from California to Washington. Buying property along the Pacific Coast in the early nineties was so lucrative that by 1999, Yu's net worth was said to be well over twenty million dollars.

During that time, Rosie learned the ins and outs of the immigration system so well that she became known as "Rosie–uh, you know, Green Cards." As Rosie's practice grew, she quietly introduced Yu to some of her more prominent film and political clients. Yu reciprocated however he could. By 1995, Rosie was bringing investors to Yu's beachfront developments, and Yu was bringing wealthy Chinese clients to the young immigration lawyer.

Yu loved rubbing shoulders with the film crowd. Before long, they were regular investors in his beachfront enterprises. After they made some money, they'd always invite Yu to the openings of their movies. The cautious, cynical Chinese gentleman was finding happiness in the fast lane.

Rosie, however, was an unsatisfied woman. Though she had an attractive face, with sensual lips and a slender body, she couldn't walk normally. In fact, even with a cane, her steps were chaotic and unsightly. This was due to a childhood illness that left her with a spastic gait. A gangly, unconventional LA kid knew pain, and Rosie had felt more than her share. Servicing the big shots was not, as she would say, chopped liver, but Rosie was after real power, the whole deal. As shrewd as she was unconventional, Rosie knew that her future was not in entertainment or politics. For Rosie, money, serious money, was the only path to the power she coveted.

In 2003, Yu's luck changed. A massive earthquake along the coast caused the floating escalator and the elaborate high ceiling in Yu's Paradise Point Hotel to fall into the crowded lobby. The floating escalator was seven stories high and weighed tons. The specially designed vaulted marble ceiling rained heavy marble shards over all of the guests. The wreckage from the collapsed elevator and the falling ceiling killed eleven people in the lobby and injured fourteen others. The unfortunate victims had been sipping wine at a reception for the California Bar Association.

By 2003, lawsuits were a way of life in California, and the lawyers were tripping over each other to milk this catastrophe. As one so succinctly put it—"Paradise Point?...You bet!" Apparently, the normally cautious Yu had shifted his insurance coverage to Buzz, the broker who handled insurance matters for the William Morris Agency. Buzz was a good guy and could always get Laker tickets, on the floor, but he wasn't *all over*—not even *on top of*—conservative hotel insurance.

Two months after the accident, Yu sat down with his lawyer, an LA real estate wiz, and the senior partner of the firm, a distinguished litigator. It took them an hour and forty-two minutes to figure out that even if Yu was lucky enough to settle the lawsuits out of court, he was bankrupt.

That night, Yu took a long walk on the beach. He loved Southern California. It was more than home, it was a way of life, his way of life.

He wasn't going to give it up. He thought, and he walked, and then he had a remarkable idea.

Yu's call woke Rosie from a deep sleep. What he said was characteristically succinct. "Rosie, I propose to make you rich, like Rockefeller."

Rosie's response was, characteristically, to the point, "Babe, I'm in."

Six months later, they were married…The hindsighters still can't explain why it took twelve years.

The only thing certain is that it happened in LA, had to.

CHAPTER TWO

Paris, Spring, 2019

The cafe, Le Select, was always crowded. On the busy Boulevarde Montparnasse, a stone's throw from the Raspail Métro access, it seemed to attract the younger, more bohemian crowd that Sara favored. Looking down at the irregular pattern of rectangular white and gray tiles on the floor, she bypassed the loud, colorfully dressed Parisians gathered around the bar and chose a banquette in the farthest, darkest corner. Sara sipped coffee and waited. She enjoyed the smells, particularly the espresso, and she liked watching the bartender, Jean-Louis, work the long-burnished wood bar. He'd pick a drink order out of the air, argue painters, take a bet on the soccer match, all the while mixing and serving drinks. Leaning out of a shadow, she waved and put on her best smile as Jimmy came up the Metro steps and into the cafe. With her dark curly hair, olive skin, delicate, almost fragile features, and her slender, lithe body, Sara could be beautiful.

"Good news, kiddo." He handed her a letter.

He had no idea how she felt about his nickname for her. In fact, she hated it, like she hated him. She read the letter hurriedly. "Thank you, Jimmy," Sara whispered, and studying a spot on the wall, she took his hand. The letter was from the US Citizenship and Immigration Service—she had a date for her interview.

At twenty-five, unless she was truly at ease, Sara Cambert was very shy. In fact, her timid manner hid a tough, first-class mind, and an inner life that was intense, ironic, even feisty. Sara likened herself to Lauren Bacall hopelessly miscast as a cowering, nonverbal, shrinking violet—she'd spent many hours watching old movies at the Cinémathèque Française in Paris, and Bacall was her favorite actress, hands-down.

There was an unhappy history to this dichotomy. Abandoned at birth, Sara was brought up in a primitive French orphanage. She was to learn that the French don't coddle their orphans, particularly their half Algerian orphans.

At the moment, however, she didn't want to think about the past. At the moment, she was hoping that maybe, just maybe, this would be her chance to put the past behind her, to start fresh. Sara was actually smiling, looking down at Jimmy's Dartmouth tie, as his self-assured, jovial voice interrupted her reverie.

"Sweet stuff, let's go over it all one last time. Then I'll wrap up the letter for you. Can't hurt to get it just so."

It figured. He would ruin the good news. And it bothered her that he was still so interested in the details of her past. Maybe he was just drawing it out, an excuse to keep sleeping with her. Thinking about that part was like hearing nails on a chalkboard. Feeling sad, she gave herself a little pep talk. She was never shy when it came to that. "Get with the program, gal," she told herself. "You can hardly talk to people. You've got no money, you've got no connections, and for all that, this geek just delivered your green card. Sweetie, just remember, Princess Di had to make love to that weird Prince Charles." She went over it for him, for the umpteenth time, from the beginning. He followed in his little blue book of notes.

Sara spoke softly and concisely—every word carefully, often perfectly, chosen. She began, "I was born quick and strong-willed." A pause. "Otherwise, I would have died in the orphanage."

Sara stared at the floor, then she detailed, yet again, how she'd escaped from the orphanage at ten, and finally found her mother in a mission hospital in Marseilles. She was fourteen when she snuck her mother out of the hospital. She always liked telling about, remembering, the years with her mom.

"For five years after the hospital, we lived on a boat, living off the fertile Southern Mediterranean. It was the first time I'd ever been happy. My mom, Ali, had grown up on the sea, diving for shellfish, and she taught me everything she knew. For me, it was a long-delayed childhood. For my mom, it was an opportunity to do one thing right—be a mother to her daughter—and we didn't stop talking, telling stories, until she died in my arms, peaceably." Jimmy had actually tracked down the death certificate for her file.

Six years later, Sara spoke four languages, could speak articulately to people if she felt comfortable, knew she wanted to immigrate to America, and had her hand on Jimmy's thigh. When she finally finished telling him the ups and downs of the last six years, thirty-five minutes' worth, Sara took several deep breaths. Exhausted, she looked down at the tabletop, and speaking softly said only, "Thank you."

Jimmy smiled, loosening his tie. "If the US of A doesn't have room for a gal with your kind of pizazz, it's time to rethink what I do. The letter's in the works. Sorry to make you go through it all again, but I've got to get it just right, immigration's not famous for second chances." Jimmy squeezed her hand.

Sara glanced at him, furtively. He was thirty-eight, tall, and built like he rowed crew. She had to admit that Jimmy could be charming, and he was good at selling his country. Otherwise, he was a two-faced, too-smart-by-half, overbearing, full-of-shit weasel.

"This means you could be at the trading company next month. Christ, I'll miss you kiddo." Sara counted tiles on the floor, quiet.

Seattle, Spring, 2019

Sara arrived in Seattle only twenty-six days later, on a cloudy afternoon in April. Descending through the clouds, she wasn't prepared for Puget Sound. It was the trees, they were everywhere, greener than any trees she'd ever seen. And this water didn't look like any portion of any ocean that she knew—so calm, all of those islands, the big white ferryboats, the setting sun reflecting pink off Mount Rainier. Sure, there were freighters in the shipping lanes, but look at the Cascades in the distance, the downtown skyscrapers, the sparsely populated, hospitable islands, and then they were down.

The trip had been uneventful, and then the formal immigration procedure was anticlimactic. After waiting a long time, she gave the man at immigration her sealed immigrant visa packet. He opened it, glanced at her file, then gave it to someone to send on to Arlington, Texas, where her green card would be made. He smiled, said, "Welcome to the United States," stamped her passport—"Processed for I-55 temporary evidence for admission for lawful permanent residence"—and verified the address where they would send her green card, the address that the company had given her. That was it. She followed the exit signs, not entirely convinced that she was in America.

The airport was not unlike the two or three others that she knew. There were wide clean hallways, lots of directional signs and symbols, and advertisements on the walls. It was, at least, less crowded than Charles de Gaulle, in Paris. The big surprise was the pretty, ample lady who knew her name. The lady had been waiting at the exit, right after immigration. She asked in a polite way, "Are you Sara Cambert?"

Sara nodded. The woman seemed friendly, almost folksy looking.

"I'm Susie. I'm with Northwest Traders. Jimmy asked me to be your liaison, help you get set up. C'mon, sweetie, let's take a look at your new home."

"Thank you." Sara smiled. She always smiled when she was afraid something was wrong.

"I'm sure you'll like it here with Northwest, hon, we're like one happy family. You got a problem, it's Northwest's problem too. Betcha you don't find much of that in your European nations." Susie took Sara's large duffel bag, nodding toward the door. "We've got a place for you right near the island office. Why don't we shoot right over? On the way, I'll give you the lowdown on Northwest." She looked at Sara. "Honey, am I going too fast for you?"

Sara looked away at a departing aircraft. She needed time to think about this woman, so she asked, "Lowdown?" a word she actually knew.

"Hah, that was silly of me." Susie smiled, a big one, as she put her arm around Sara. It was a strong arm. "Lowdown is the down and dirty, the truth of the matter—who wants the action, who you stay away from, that sort of thing. You with me now?" She winked. "Good. I have to say...gal like you could look pretty damn hot. I'll take you shopping, whadaya say?"

Sara nodded yes, staring at the floor.

The car ride was uneventful. Susie talked the whole way, mostly telling Sara stories about Texas. Sara had to laugh. The way Susie told it, men in Texas seemed to be big, fat Frenchmen—only with smaller penises.

They arrived at the marina in Anacortes, less than two hours later. In spite of herself, Sara realized that she was, unexpectedly, warming up to this folksy, talkative woman. Maybe in this anything-goes country, this land of cowboys, rock stars, and Disney World, this kind of lady was common. Sara didn't know.

The parking lot was almost empty. According to Susie, weeknights, before summer, were just plain dead. She punched in the code that opened the locked gate from the parking lot to the docks. The marina offered a pretty fair sampling of the overwhelming variety of contemporary pleasure craft. Every slip was in use. To Sara, all of the boats seemed sleek and new, a far cry from the fishing boats in the old Mediterranean port where her mom kept the beat-up old fishing boat that they'd bought for a song and fixed up themselves.

The Northwest Trading Company boat, *the Island Spirit*, was a handsome thirty-six-foot yacht. It had twin diesels, newly painted trim, and clearly, someone had paid careful attention to the woodworking detail. It was actually smaller than many of the pleasure boats kept in Anacortes to cruise the San Juan Islands. As Susie said, "It ain't your French Riviera, but hon, there's big bucks floating in here." Susie, obviously familiar with the boat, helped Sara aboard, and started the engine. "Sugar, this is the company's pick-up boat. Wait'll you see the boat we party on, hah."

Sara didn't respond. She was taking in the splendid sunset over the Rosario Strait. They left the marina, moving toward the islands, backlit in varying shades of pink and red.

After the sun set, some of the islands they passed were speckled with lights from the occasional home, and then, every so often, a cluster of lights marked a town. Susie pointed, "That's Port Johnston. Years ago, it was one of the biggest mill towns in the Northwest." Susie smiled. "Sweetie, I love history and geography...I bet you didn't know that the San Juan Islands are an archipelago with over 478 miles of shoreline. That's a true known fact."

Sara nodded. She'd started to relax when the boat left the harbor— the sea brought back fond memories for her, memories of time spent with her mother.

"Hon, let's go out back, see some stars." The sun had set, and Susie steered the boat between two uninhabited islands, anchoring in a dark, protected channel.

Susie led Sara to the aft deck. It was a clear, windy night. The water shone black in the moonlight. The Island Spirit was the only boat in the narrow, remote channel. Sara was looking up at the stars—more than she'd ever seen—when the blackjack came down above her head. Sara didn't know if it was her reflexes or just a lifetime of looking over her shoulder— whatever it was, it saved her life. Somehow, she sensed the impending blow—moving her head slightly to the right as the blackjack hit her. That slight movement caused the weapon to glance off her head and strike her shoulder, bruising her left shoulder blade. She screamed, turning to face her attacker.

"You scared? You should be scared, you friggin' mousey raghead." No more drawl, no more understanding smiles. Susie circled, slapping the blackjack on her left palm. Sara was in pain, and she moved warily away. Susie, if that was her name, was no longer folksy nor even feminine. Her movements, her voice, everything had changed. She was a predator stalking her prey.

"What do you want from me? I don't have money." Sara was buying time. Backing toward the edge of the deck. She felt the adrenaline starting, then the familiar physical rhythms that went with responding to pain, danger.

"You've done your bit, honey." Susie nodded, then she moved closer, swinging the blackjack at Sara's face. Sara jumped away, and timing it perfectly, grabbed the swinging arm with both hands, accelerating Susie's momentum. Holding tightly, she leapt backward with all of her strength, pulling both of them into the icy water.

As a diver, Sara was no stranger to cold water, and she didn't panic. Sara guessed that the water was maybe sixty degrees. She knew that cold water was her ally, her edge on this killer. Susie was thrashing, swinging her blackjack at Sara. In the water, staying away from the weapon was no problem. Sara tread water, moving just far enough away to tire Susie out. Still, Susie was a strong swimmer and clearly dangerous. Sara was starting to feel the throbbing pain in her shoulder grow stronger. She realized that she'd have to take her best shot, soon.

Suzie's voice was deep, masculine now, "Ready to die…bitch?" She swam toward Sara. That's when Sara took a deep diver's breath and disappeared under the water. She surfaced behind Susie, grabbed her hair with her good arm and, after taking another deep breath, Sara dove, pulling Susie under. Sara's kick was strong, and she pulled Susie down with her. The water was colder than any Sara had dived in without a wetsuit. Susie panicked as soon as she was pulled under the cold water. She flailed at Sara, losing the blackjack, unable to hit the strong swimmer that was relentlessly pulling her down, backward. Sara could hold her breath for almost two minutes, but she only needed forty-five seconds. Before drowning, Susie swallowed a great deal of water.

Sara burst through the surface of the water, gasping for breath. As soon as she could, she used her good arm and legs to swim for the boat. She had the presence of mind to drag Susie by the hair with her free left hand. At the boat, she tied Susie's wrist to the stern line, then climbed aboard. Dropping her clothes as she went, Sara turned on the shower below. She stood under the hot shower for a long time, crying. It was not the pain in her shoulder but an overwhelming sense of loss. She'd been in her new homeland less than twelve hours, and already, it was just like everyplace else. She cried until she felt better, then Sara forced herself to make a plan.

Taking what she needed from the first aid kit, she stopped to look at her shoulder in the cabin mirror. It was badly bruised but not broken. Naked at the mirror, she turned away. There was a no-nonsense, almost graceful, quality in the way this shy, awkward woman moved. She dressed hurriedly with what was available in the cabin, took whatever supplies she needed, including her own large duffel bag, and went up to the aft deck. Setting her supplies in the dinghy, Sara lowered the inflatable into the water. Next, using a winch, she hoisted Susie up.

She swung the body back into the boat, pushing it down the stairs and into the cabin below. Thinking a moment, Sara took more food and clothing, a flashlight, toolkit, and Coleman lantern and added them to the pile of supplies in the dinghy. Sara went back down and tied off a long rope to the galley stove. She found a USGC approved, secured gas tank, poured gasoline over the galley and the cabin, then she soaked the rope in gasoline. When she was satisfied, Sara took the rope up the stairs, across the aft deck and back to the dinghy. Next, she found the gas tank and opened it, splashing gas around it. After lighting the gasoline-drenched rope, Sara stepped into the dinghy and rowed her little inflatable into the darkness. Several minutes later, she saw the fire light up the dark, hidden channel. Sometime later, the thirty-six-foot yacht, *The Island Spirit*, blew up, creating a brief, dazzling light show against the northern night sky.

Sara rowed until she reached a distant uninhabited island. The island was one of the 768 fragments of the dying mountain range known as the San Juan Islands. There are only 457 at high tide. Sara's island was one of those 457. Sara set up camp on the wooded, isolated, deserted island. She lived on the island for four days—thinking, recovering, rethinking. A week before she died, her mother had given her a letter from her father that she'd saved. It was twenty-six years old, faded, but readable. Sara read it over and over. After, she tried to remember the things her mother had told her about him. At the end of that time, she had just one good idea—find her dad.

CHAPTER THREE

Seattle

Callie and Cash sat at their favorite table, secluded, in the far corner of the bar upstairs. From their spot, they could look down over the dining room then out the picture window to the street. It was the very same window that had exploded into her dining room a little more than a year ago when Daniel Odile Grand, Callie's ex, came crashing through the glass after he was viciously struck by a truck. Callie touched Cash's forearm, a thing she did more often lately, thinking that it felt like a lot longer than a year since then.

It was just after eleven, most of the diners downstairs had finished their meals and left. Jill, who was tending bar upstairs for several people who were still drinking, brought their dinners up from the kitchen. Callie had Copper River Salmon, considered the world's finest salmon with its silken texture, deep red color, and an incredibly rich, almost nutty flavor. The salmon gets its unique, distinctive character from making a three-hundred-mile journey up the glacial-fed waters of the Copper River to spawn.

Cash had the cassoulet with game sausages, a new preparation that Andre had invented and named for Doc. Doc, an old, close friend of Cash, had been killed here, in Callie's restaurant, about a year ago.

Cash put his hand over Callie's. They looked at each other, smiling warmly. Then they each raised a glass of wine, a toast to Doc, without a word said. They kissed then, appreciating the moment. They were wildly in love. Neither of them understood how it had become so intense, but it was lovely, and they were learning to enjoy it.

"How'd it go tonight?" Cash asked.

"Good night. Nice energy, lots of regulars. You were missed."

"I'll be here this weekend. I'm still putting this deal together."

"Do I want to hear about it?"

"Probably not. It's legal, but complicated."

"Is the Macher in it?"

"Maybe, we'll see."

"Then it's probably better if I don't know."

That's when Will, Callie's maître d', came up the stairs to their table. "Sorry to bother you, but Cash, there's a young woman downstairs who insists that she has to talk with you. She says you don't know her, but yes, you'll want to hear her story, and it won't wait. She said she's been looking for you for several days."

"What's your take?"

"She doesn't look at you. She stares down at the floor, takes time choosing her words. But she's intense, she's plainly worried, and there's someone home. Short answer, she got me upstairs."

"Let's meet her."

Several minutes later, a tentative young woman with dark curly hair, olive skin, delicate, almost fragile features, and a slender agile body stood beside their table. She wore a black leather jacket and a scarf around her head. She placed a large, well-worn duffel bag under the table.

Cash stood, then pulled another chair over to their table. "Please sit down. My name is Cash Logan. How can I help you?"

She sat down, stared at the table. "Please bear with me." She looked away. "If I feel comfortable, I can be articulate, but with new people, it takes time for me to choose my words."

Cash and Callie waited, aware now that she was from another country, though her English was good, flawless.

"I'm not sure how to say this, but I need help, and you're the only one I could turn to."

"Why me? I don't know you."

She took off her scarf, showed her lovely, curly black hair. "Yes, you don't know me, but I need to tell you a story. It will take some time, but you have to hear the details before you can understand why I came to see you." She offered her hand. "My name is Sara."

First Cash, then Callie shook her outstretched hand.

Sara spoke slowly, softly—every word carefully, often perfectly, chosen. "I grew up in a frighteningly primitive French orphanage," she began. She went on, looking away. "I was born quick and strong-willed." A pause. "Otherwise, I would have died in that orphanage." She twisted her finger through a lock of black hair.

Cash and Callie leaned in, listening carefully, unsure why they were hearing this.

Sara nodded to herself, then continued. "At five, I decided I was going to outwit the nuns." She stared at the floor. "You see 'Little Sara,' the abused toddler, saw that the autistic children on the ward weren't beaten as often. She figured out that because of their debilitating disorder, they weren't expected to function at the same level. And, she saw that they were not supervised as closely. It was only logical, 'Little Sara' concluded, to become autistic."

"Are you saying that at five years old, you actually decided to make yourself become autistic?" Cash asked, uncertain.

"Yes, it was one of my first good ideas…After careful observation, 'Little Sara' slowly developed the mannerisms of an autistic child. She would stare at the wall for hours, chew off her fingertips, and neither speak nor acknowledge the spoken word. Sudden outbursts of gibberish were not uncommon for 'Little Sara.' At seven, she was diagnosed as untreatable. At ten, she escaped, taking her file with her."

"And this really happened?" Callie asked, incredulous. "This is all real."

"It did. It is…" Sara nodded again, pleased that they were listening, paying attention to her. She was still speaking carefully, but more easily now. She looked up. "The orphanage was in Bordeaux and 'Little Sara's' destination was Marseilles…Her file indicated that her mother had given birth to her at a Catholic hospital there. 'Little Sara' simply walked onto a train to Marseilles and disappeared into the Algerian ghetto…Cute, and half Algerian, she found a café where she volunteered to work for food scraps and a corner to sleep in. 'Little Sara' worked hard, learned the Algerian dialect of Arabic fluently, and searched for her mother.

"Everyone who knew her remarked on 'Little Sara's' ingenuity and tenacity. At twelve, posing as a janitorial assistant, 'Little Sara' stole the hospital file…This showed her mother's Algerian name, Khalil. This, in turn, led to meeting many Khalils, a trip to Algeria, and finally getting an old picture from a third cousin. 'Little Sara' learned that six months after her pregnancy, her mother had become HIV positive. She hoped to leave her baby with her own mother until she got a job and was back on her feet. Her mother, Samia, finally agreed to take the child, but only after harshly criticizing her daughter for her lifestyle, her sexual promiscuity, and a laundry list of past mistakes committed before she ran away from home at seventeen. They fought, bitterly, before she went back to Paris.

"The baby was born three months later, and, in part, because her mother had been on antivirals, 'Little Sara' tested negative for HIV. Samia took the baby from the hospital as promised. But before returning to Algeria, she left the baby at the orphanage. No one ever knew why. Soon after, before Ali was ready to pick up her baby, her mother sent her a letter, saying that her baby had been given to an Algerian family going to South America. She didn't know where. Not surprisingly, given her mother's illness and promiscuity, Ali was disowned from the family. Her mother died a month later.

"'Little Sara' eventually found her mother, using her real name, Ali Kahlil, in a mission hospital, run by the nuns. A distinctive birthmark on her right cheek made identification certain. 'Little Sara' was fourteen when she walked up to the bed and looked at the frail, emaciated woman. From this point on, she had an easier time telling her story, and she always stopped calling herself 'Little Sara.'" She was looking at them now, more confident.

Both Cash and Callie noticed the shift in perspective, and it just added to their interest, their unexpected fascination with this woman.

"'Mother, it's Sara, it's me.' I spoke Arabic, the woman on the bed just stared at the ceiling. 'I've come to take you away from here.

I've saved money.' The woman on the bed showed no sign of hearing her. She coughed and let the spittle run down her chin. Sara gently wiped it off and said, 'We have time, I'll tell you all about me.'

"I came to the dreary room every morning and stayed all day. There were eight beds in the long narrow room. I never stopped talking to the woman on bed number six from the moment I came in to the moment I left. I recognized my mother's condition—it was not unlike my own at the orphanage, and I knew that on some level my mother could hear me. One day, when the nun came to tell me that it was time to bathe number six, the bed was empty. We were gone.

"For five years after the hospital, we lived on a boat, living off the plentiful Southern Mediterranean. It was the first time I'd ever been happy. My mom, Ali, had grown up on the sea, diving for shellfish, and she taught me everything she knew. For me, it was a chance to be outdoors and enjoy a long-postponed childhood. For my mom, it was her opportunity to be a mother to her daughter. We didn't stop talking, telling stories, until she died in my arms, a happy woman.

"Six years later, I spoke four languages, knew I wanted to immigrate to America, and against all odds, I got my visa. I'll tell the visa story later–I know you'll want to hear it. For now, suffice it to say that a woman met me at the Seattle airport when I arrived, ten days ago. She took me to the San Juan Islands on a boat. We were going to my new job at the Pacific Trading company. We stopped in an isolated inlet to look at the stars. She came from behind me and tried to kill me with a blackjack. I'm agile. I sensed her coming and swerved. She missed my head and hit my shoulder. I grabbed her arm, and I was able to pull her into the icy water. Because of my time diving in the cold Mediterranean with my mother, I was able to dive under and come up behind her. I pulled her by her hair deep underwater. I can hold my breath for two minutes underwater, and I drowned her. Later, I put her in the boat, set fire to the boat and blew it up."

Cash just looked at her, plainly unsettled, disconcerted. Callie held her hands tightly clasped on her lap.

"I hid on an uninhabited island for four days, trying to figure out what to do. I had one idea. Before my mother died, she gave me a letter. This letter was from the young man who got her pregnant, though he never knew that. She looked at Cash for the first time. "The letter was from you. Cash Logan. You are my father."

Cash's mouth dropped, wide open. He was dumbstruck. "There has to be some mistake…Has to be…"

Sara took out the letter, handed it to him.

Cash read it carefully, then again. "Yes, I wrote that letter…I remember writing it…I knew your mother as Charlotte Cambert. We were together in Paris for maybe five weeks." Cash took a beat, pensive. "How old are you, Sara?"

"Twenty-five."

"Yes, it was about twenty-six years ago, 1993. I was coming back from my first tour in the army. One of my army friends was older. He'd lived in France and had an Algerian girlfriend. She knew Charlotte and introduced us. I met Charlotte and stayed on with her until I had to leave. I wrote this letter maybe eight or nine months later, because I hoped to see her again, but she never responded."

"She was HIV positive, and her mother told her that she had given her baby away to an Algerian family that moved away to parts unknown, somewhere in South America. My mother was heartbroken about losing her baby, then she was disowned and her mother died. During this time, she grew ill, severely depressed, then finally completely withdrawn. My mother never knew that her mother put me in the orphanage."

"I'm in shock, absolutely stunned…atypically, speechless…Sara, I can't undo what's happened, and I have absolutely no idea what to do now or even what to say. But yes, it's possible that you are my daughter. Was she certain, absolutely positive, that I was the father?"

"Yes…Yes…You were the only man that she was with for a long time before the pregnancy. She worked out the dates. She told me that you were absolutely, without any possible doubt, my father."

"Your mother was a smart woman, and I remember her as being honest. I liked how important that was to her. Sara, I believe her if she told you that."

"She had no reason to tell me if she wasn't sure. She wanted me to know before she died. Still, will you take a blood test with me? That should give us proof."

"I will…Yes, of course…Tomorrow morning…Truthfully, I'm still in shock…Nonetheless, as hard as it is to imagine, part of me is just beginning to think, and to worry, that I might have a daughter."

Cash stood, took his daughter's hand. Before they knew what was happening, Sara began to cry.

Sometime later, Callie stood and gently touched Sara's arm. "You must be exhausted. Our apartment is upstairs. We have a spare room. You can stay with us tonight. We'll go see my friend Mary, a good doctor, tomorrow morning."

Sara nodded. "Thank you. Thank you for listening, for trusting me, and for your generosity. I had no idea where I'd stay tonight."

"You'll be safe here. We'll talk more tomorrow morning. Come with me." Cash took Sara's bag, then led her as he followed Callie down the stairs, through the kitchen, then out the back door to the landing. At the landing, they went up the adjacent stairs to their warm, welcoming apartment. Inside, Callie led Sara to their guest room. "My almost sixteen-year-old son lives here with us. This is his room." She pointed to another door. "He's out of town on a school trip." She showed Sara to the guest room.

At the door, she turned. "Thank you again."

Both Cash and Callie nodded. "Our pleasure, Sara." Cash added.

When she'd closed the door, Callie looked at Cash, took him in her arms. "You're a good man. I don't know what I would have done as a man in your shoes." She stepped back, took his hand. "You believe her story don't you."

"I think I do. How do you make up something like that?"

"It changes everything for you. Doesn't it?"

"Yes, everything."

"She reminds me of you, Cash Logan. She broke the mold intended for her—on her own. She's one of a kind, an original, very brave and very smart. She's likely your daughter."

"It's possible, and if that's actually true, I'm just beginning to sense what it means…"

"She's strong and capable, like you, but she has to be lonely and very frightened. Ours has to be a complicated world to understand, harder still to be part of."

"You're right and ahead of me. At the very least, let's try to help her find her way…"

"Easier said than done."

"Worth trying."

She nodded.

"Just know one thing. I couldn't do this—I couldn't even imagine being a father—without you. I've never loved you more than I do at this very moment."

Callie took him in her arms, then whispered, tenderly. "What you just said, it's true for me, too.

♦♦♦

By eleven the next morning, Callie, Cash, and Sara were back at the same table near the bar. They'd gone to see Callie's doctor friend, Mary, early in the morning. She'd taken blood from Cash and Sara, and they were waiting to hear the results. While they waited, Cash asked Sara questions. He wanted to learn more about what happened after her mother had died.

Sara told him again how a week before she died, her mother had given her his letter. She went on to explain, "It changed my life. I had learned to talk again—really talk—with my mother. When she died, I didn't have the courage to talk with anyone else. The French treated me like dirt. So I'd steal some money and go to the movies. I finally got a job cleaning up at a theater. I watched movies absolutely every night after work. I saw *To Have and Have Not*, *Key Largo*, *The Big Sleep*, over and over, three or four times each. I couldn't get enough of Bogart, Bacall, the whole American deal. I mean those people could talk. In my twenty-one-year-old head, you made me a part of all of that." She told her father how—on the second anniversary of her mother's death—she'd made her big decisions. "I was drunk, alone in my attic room, reading *Rolling Stone* magazine. I decided my life was stupid. That night, I gave up cigarettes. Half an hour later, I decided to immigrate—and from that moment on, in the same way I knew I'd survive the orphanage, knew I'd find my mother, I knew that I would become an American citizen—the only question was how."

"Likely doable for a girl who fooled the nuns at five."

"Just another good idea," Callie shrugged, feigning detachment.

"Well yes, exactly." Sara smiled. "My immigration program began simply—I had to learn fluent American English. Equally important, there was the lesson my mother had drilled into me on the boat—basically, to do anything, an Algerian girl who was nobody had to be tough, a fighter. I took this literally, and killing two birds with one stone, I found an American martial arts instructor. He was soon my boyfriend, and besides love making, fighting, weapons training, and a handful of lucrative smuggling gigs, I learned American usage. I was, of course, interested in language. And from the start, I chose my words carefully. He'd spent two years in prison, and I eagerly developed a command of the language that would make even a crude cop blush. After two years, his new friends thought I was American. Privately, they'd ask him where I'd done time."

Callie and Cash watched her, impressed yet again, as she looked at a spot on the ceiling.

Sara went on, "Anyway, this one night, we got stoned, and he wanted me to have sex with a friend of his while he watched. I said no. He hit me, then I broke his arm and three ribs. I was really pissed. I never looked back."

"How old were you?" Cash asked.

"I was twenty-three when I beat up my boyfriend. I spoke French, Arabic, and English. Without intending to, I'd become an advanced student of American language and culture. That same year, I was hired as a translator by a marginally corrupt American freight company, operating out of Marseilles. The only good thing about that job was that I had to learn Spanish, which by then, came easily for me.

"At twenty-three, feeling almost American, I went to see the immigration man at the consulate. I was told unequivocally that my application for an immigrant visa could not even be considered without labor certification. 'And really,' the immigration man told me, 'It's not possible that a woman without a sponsor, not to mention a father or an education, could be issued a labor certificate. Not possible.' Furthermore, this full-of-himself guy explained, 'the quotas are such that in the unlikely event you could accomplish the impossible, little missy, the wait would still be three years.'"

Callie guessed her answer, "Doable…Right?"

"Well, I was no stranger to difficulties, and these seemed, to me, insignificant. I wrote a letter to the consul explaining my situation, and three months later, I wrote again to follow up. At twenty-four, I was contacted by Jimmy, a lower level guy at the consulate."

"Tell me about Jimmy."

"Three weeks after sending my second letter, he called with a question, and a suggestion for my application. He was in Paris and wanted me to meet him at the consulate. I was there the next week to see him." She paused, nodding.

"I met with him on a rainy Wednesday morning. I knew right away that this guy was up to something, and that I was smarter than he was. Slowly and carefully, I responded to his questions, elaborating on bits and pieces of my past. He seemed particularly interested in the part about no family. Pretty soon, I figured out what he was looking for, and I improvised from my history to meet his needs. With frequent pauses to carefully organize my words, I told him how I had difficulties making friends, no current relationship with a man, and no living relatives, even distant ones. My shyness combined with my sensitivity to my part Algerian, half-caste racial identity made life in France unbearable for me. When asked, I candidly admitted that French men often approached me. However, my history made a relationship with a Frenchman impossible. With just a hint of tears in my eyes, I confessed that I wanted to start a new life, cut all my ties to my miserable past. From that day on, he treated me like I was some sort of diamond in the rough that he alone could bring to its natural brilliance."

Here, Cash interrupted, "You mean some consular guy actually chose you, even helped you?"

"Yes, it was like the movies. He took care of everything."

"Took care of what? Please walk me through it."

"Well, first, he got me a sponsor, the Northwest Trading company. The way he put it, they had this all set up—labor certificate, priority date, everything—for a lady who got married, and at the last minute decided to stay in France. He said my language qualifications were better than hers, and the system lets you make a switch." Sara paused here, organizing her thoughts, then she went on, "Anyway, Northwest hired me and got me a labor certificate. Then, they used the other person's priority date, and within three months I had my interview and my immigrant visa number, Jimmy called them A numbers. There were no problems, ever. I thought it was because I was sleeping with him."

Callie shook her head. "You're unstoppable."

Cash nodded. "Go on. What happened next?"

"I get to the airport in Seattle, and someone's waiting for me. This lady says she's from the company and they've set me up with a place to stay. She's got all the right info, and Jimmy said there'd be someone to meet me, so I go with her. She takes me on this fancy company boat, friendly, folksy even, and then she tries to kill me. She was a professional."

"How did you know that?"

"Not my first rodeo, bucko. My boyfriend's prison pals—never mind the details."

"What happened?"

"What I told you last night. I killed her instead. Then I blew up the boat with her on it."

"I see." Cash was thinking, worried now. Someone was carefully bringing in immigrants and then killing them. That was a lot of effort. Someone must be paying a lot of money for new identities. He'd bet they were replacing the dead immigrants.

Sara interrupted his thoughts. "I parked on this island for four days, then I rowed to a town, caught the ferry, and began looking for you. I thought it over and decided that I needed some help. You were it."

"How'd you find me?"

"Let's just say that I've had some experience with this kind of thing. I checked out every Terry Logan—that was the name on the return address on the letter—in Seattle. None of them, except you, left a message on their voicemail to suggest a restaurant phone number and ask for Cash. My mom said your friend called you Cash when she met you. She wasn't sure why. Her English was just okay, and some words were hard for her. She also explained to me that you were unusual— what was her word—uncommon."

Cash gave her a thumbs-up. "You're brave, able, and smart. But Sara, before we go any further, there's something on my mind, something worrying me. Look, these people are heavy hitters. You should probably go back to France. If they know you're alive, they'll kill you."

"I won't go back."

"Why?"

"In France, I'm nobody. No mother, no father, nobody. In France, when you're nobody, they take advantage of you."

"Then go somewhere else for a while. Disappear."

"No, I'm going to be an American citizen."

"Think about that. The people that brought you in want you dead. With any luck, they think you are. So long as they think that, you're okay. The minute they know you're still alive, you're uninsurable."

Sara frowned. It had never occurred to her that she might die.

"I'd bet that someone's making a lot of money for your visa, for your identity. It only works if you're dead. I'm impressed with how far you've come, but it's not a movie, and if you fool with it, they'll try to kill you, for sure. And this time, they won't underestimate you."

"Maybe." Sara sighed. "I'm staying, anyway."

Cash looked her in the eye. The phone rang on the bar. It was Will buzzing them from downstairs. Cash took the call. He said hello to Mary, the doctor. He listened to her, then he thanked her.

He faced Sara. "We're father and daughter," he announced. Then Cash smiled wide. He took Sara's hand with one hand, Callie's with the other. He turned to Sara. "Again, after thinking carefully about the very real danger, after considering that there are many unknown risks, are you still sticking with your decision?"

Sara got a determined look they were starting to recognize. Her mind was made up. "Yes, I'm staying, period, or, put plainly, in the vernacular—come hell or high water."

"I'd bet that you know precisely what that means, too?" Callie nodded.

"Yes. Truthfully, that was the title of a movie I liked with Jeff Bridges, so I looked up the meaning."

"Come hell or highwater. Okay." Cash put his arm over her shoulder. "Then I'm going to help you…my strong-minded, unexpected daughter. You see, I lost my daughter once. It's not going to happen again."

CHAPTER FOUR

Beverly Hills/Seattle/Malibu, Spring, 2019

Rosie's office complex was in Beverly Hills, on Camden, one block west of Rodeo Drive. The outer office had large mahogany double doors. In the crowded waiting room, it was not uncommon to hear five or six languages being spoken at the same time. To get from the waiting room to the inner offices, the receptionist had to buzz you through a stunning second door. This second door, and the wall it sat in, was made wholly of glass. The actual door was three-inch-thick clear glass, perfect and unblemished, and the glass surround was five-inch-thick black glass. When opened, the transparent glass door slid into a pocket in the black glass surround, disappearing.

The door opened into a wide corridor with a Cabernet designer carpet. At the end of the corridor sat Rosie's office suite. Decorated with gifts from grateful clients—Chinese jade, African ivory carvings, a rare Iranian silver sculpture, and a beautiful French impressionist painting, it inspired confidence. Sitting behind her teak desk, Rosie was preparing for her day.

For Rosie, the day-to-day practice of immigration law was part savvy, part patience, and part servicing relationships. At the end of the day, however, the status of any immigration lawyer was determined by his or her clientele—and Rosie was very particular.

She'd designed her firm in five tiers. At the bottom were the routine green card cases—nannies, housekeepers, gardeners, dishwashers, etc. This was a volume business, and it paid the overhead. Her office staff included carefully chosen paralegals, fluent in a variety of languages.

The second tier handled those cases that required specialized visas, a French cinematographer coming in to shoot a movie, a Japanese businessman opening a branch office in Seattle. Higher up, the third tier, was the corporate tier—multinational corporations with offices all over the world transferring employees and their families. The fourth tier handled government business. Each of the other junior partners was responsible for one tier. At the top, the fifth tier, sat Rosie.

Rosie only handled those cases that: one—would improve her relationship with the service; two—be a favor to an important asset (e.g. a senator or a movie star); three—were important assets themselves—the Shah of Iran's nephew, the CEO of Mercedes Benz US (a rare stroke of luck), etc.; four—would enhance her standing in the profession. Her services were so sought after that Rosie could pick and choose her clients.

Furthermore, since meeting Yu, Rosie had worked hard and systematically to become the standard of quality in her business—the gold standard, if you will—to the point that she now cochaired the ethics committee of the immigration bar. Yu had been emphatic on this point. She was a student of immigration law and her practice conformed to the letter of that law.

Every morning, Robert, Rosie's reliable assistant, prepared a summary of the day's events for her. The routine was always the same. First came calls to return. Out of 150 to 200 calls received each day, she returned perhaps ten. Robert, or one of the junior partners, handled the others. She would then meet prospective clients. She never saw more than three in any one morning. Lunch was always with Yu, and she devoted her afternoons to existing clients—one client per day with an appointment, and two with unexpected problems. She was hard to get to, but unlike so many of her colleagues, if you got to Rosie, you got her undivided attention. This morning she was seeing a French movie producer, then a Saudi multimillionaire who wanted to raise cattle in Texas.

The morning was, all in all, routine.

◆◆◆

Lunch with Yu was at the El Padrino room at the Beverly Wilshire Hotel. Decorated in a Mexican rancher motif, Yu favored it because it was down the street from the William Morris Agency. He said that he liked the "buzz" that the agents made, and it reminded him of his big mistake. In his curious way, whenever he thought of the insurance blunder, Yu felt good. Good because it had been the beginning of everything else. Today Yu had his regular corner booth, and he was "kibbitzing" with a movie director and his agent when he saw Rosie come in. Always the perfect gentleman, Yu got up and pulled out her chair.

"Thank you, babe." Rosie kissed him on the cheek, smiled at the film people, then sat down. Yu excused himself then sat down opposite her.

When they were alone, Rosie asked, "Babe, did you see the morning paper?"

"Electrical accident, wasn't it?"

"He fried that dirtbag troublemaker in the pool at his club—that ratty, old place on Motor Avenue. Can you believe it? The guy's an artist."

At that moment, lunch came. It was always the same. The elderly headwaiter, Jack, prepared cold salmon off the buffet for Yu and the cheese blintzes for Rosie. Jack knew that Yu couldn't eat the potato salad because he was watching his cholesterol, so he got green bean salad. Rosie always got extra potato salad and high fat extras. Because of her elevated metabolism, she was always trying to gain weight. As she ate, he went on with business, "It was prudent to settle with Mr. Weinberg. He was a potential sore point."

"Sore point?…Hon, he could have eaten the whole enchilada." Rosie was talking between bites.

"Eaten the whole—"

Yu didn't need to finish, Rosie knew just when to break into his slow, deliberate rhythm. "The guy was the deputy regional commissioner for the internal investigations branch of the INS…He could have set us on fire, burned down our whole deal."

"My dear, I doubt that. In eight years, he's the first to even ask an intelligent question."

"Tell me something, how'd he come up with an intelligent question?" Rosie always worried after the fact, after they'd asserted themselves.

She worried that they'd left some stone unturned, that they'd forgotten something. It was a nearly perfect criminal combination—the obsessive Chinese who couldn't make a decision without examining every aspect of it, and the tough, scrupulous Jewish woman, who, when they finally did decide, made sure that the path behind them was spotlessly clean. She was fast in putting forth option, he was careful in evaluating them. He never looked back, and she was careful that they'd left no trail. As casual, even nonchalant, as they might sound, between them, they painstakingly covered every detail.

"I can't say. Somehow, he became curious about Pacific, the Hong Kong Bank, and, to his credit, used the powers of his office to make the Northwest connection. Then he ran Northwest through the INS computer, and he got Sara Cambert's A number. That certainly won't happen again, if I understand you."

"Count on it." Rosie was almost finished with her lunch and Yu was just starting. Normally, she had two double espressos and a piece of extra rich, creamy cheesecake as he ate.

As it was Monday, Yu had brought over the figures from the trading company. Every Monday, the computer ran a summary of the various financial transactions that the company was involved in as well as the report of International Capital Management, an offshore shell corporation that had wholly owned subsidiaries, all offshore shell corporations as well. The result was that all of these entities could do business worldwide, many of them had investment portfolios, and no one would ever know the true beneficiary of the transaction or the investment. On Mondays, Rosie would drink her coffee, eat her cheesecake, and review the financial statements as Yu finished his lunch.

This week was particularly interesting as their bank in the Cayman Islands had opened a new account. The account was opened by a shell corporation, The Cayman Co. The Cayman Co. then made a substantial deposit to a new account at their bank in Hong Kong. The bank was a subsidiary of the Pacific Trading Company. The deposit was for $5,000,000. The Cayman Co. also opened a new investment account in ICM, the initial deposit was for $35,000,000. Each new account was identified by an eight-digit number.

Rosie was sure that this was the new accounts for Sara Cambert. She reviewed what she knew about her:

Her name was Pierrette Fleurie. A French woman, she was an officer in a bank in San Francisco. She married her boss, the bank president, and was promoted to head of the safekeeping department. Soon after her marriage, she became an American citizen. A year later, Pierrette stole $40 million in bearer bonds. She forged transfer orders—a request from the customer to move the bonds from one account to another—and then sold the bonds out of the new accounts. Curiously, as she knew so well, the transfer orders were not picked up on the monthly statements. She knew, however, that her deception would be uncovere?d in the biannual count of securities. Just before the regular accounting, the body of her new husband, ten years her senior, was found. He'd died of an apparent heart attack. She disappeared with the money, hiding, using a fake identity, in New York City. The money had not been recovered.

"How did she get to us?" Yu asked, reading her intense expression, guessing accurately what she was thinking about.

"Early on, Pierrette had contacted a friend in a Panamanian bank in her efforts to get the best help to move the vast sums of money. The Panamanian banker had done business with us, indirectly, and he knew how to discretely contact one of our people. After we agreed on the financial terms, Pierrette was gently routed to the Bank of Hong Kong. Once the money was safely on its circuitous way, the trail impossible to follow, they consulted with her on disappearing and found her a new identity—Sara Cambert. She picked up her new visa at the office in the trading company on the San Juan Islands, and then was sent off on a long undisclosed assignment elsewhere. In fact, 'Sara Cambert'—having discovered a taste for Latin men—has left Washington State and is living happily in Miami, Florida, as Sara Cambert. Pierrette Fleurie is wanted for the theft of $40,000,000. Though Police suspect that she somehow killed her husband, they found no proof of that."

With a pencil, Rosie underlined the two numbers then showed them to Yu.

"Sara Cambert," he said.

Seattle

Cash, Callie, Sara, and Detective Ed Samter were in the kitchen of Callie's restaurant, Le Cochon Bronze, sitting around the long maple prep table. Olives, sausages, and fruit were spread out on the table, and Callie had served espressos, cappuccinos, and lattes all around.

About a year ago, the detective had become a regular customer in Callie's restaurant, and, before long, a good friend. Their relationship had taken a good turn somewhat earlier, when Cash and Callie helped the detective arrest Amjad Hasin a.k.a. Salim Azar, a notorious weapons dealer and money launderer, a little over a year ago. Everyone had thought that Amjad was dead until Callie was able to find him, as part of a trade she'd put together to save Cash's life. Detective Samter had been promoted to lieutenant.

Cash had called Ed Samter this morning to ask him questions about what happened to Sara. Ed, in turn, had called a detective in LA that he'd worked with and liked. Later, he called Cash back with more info and the good news that his friend from LA, Sergeant Lincoln, was on his way to Seattle. He didn't tell Cash that he'd promised to take Lincoln salmon fishing, one of Lincoln's passions. Rather, he said that Lincoln suspected that Sara's case was connected to the death of an LA immigration officer that he was investigating, which, incidentally, was true. The important thing was that he'd be here, in Seattle, this afternoon.

It was two-thirty and for the last half hour, the detective had listened to Sara's story. When she'd finished, Detective Samter turned to Cash. "I can't get used to the idea that this brave, articulate young lady is your daughter." And to Sara, "Your story is chilling. But I can tell you that you're in good hands with these people. I have no idea what Cash will be like as a father. But I can assure you that he's very able to protect you."

Then to Cash and Callie. "You two are trouble magnets. What are the chances of encountering yet another stolen identity operation within a year?"

"When it rains, it pours." Cash shrugged, straight faced.

"Life is a tale told by an idiot," Samter retorted, adding, "Or an insufferable smart ass."

"Lest you forget, we live in a rainbow of chaos," Callie scolded, sternly. Then unable to resist, "So, detective, act well your part; there all the honor lies."

Sara looked at the three of them, uncertain what was going on, guessing that this was banter. She decided to join in. "Baby, the rain must fall!" And, an afterthought. "Let the revels begin...Let the fire be started..."

Callie put her arm around Sara. "You and I are going to be friends."

Malibu

The problem with West Los Angeles, Yu was thinking, came down to this one thing—there was no shared history. Yu was in the steam room, thinking. Every day, after lunch, he went back to his Malibu home and reflected on things in his private steam room, the steam room he had imported, tile by tile, from a bankrupt hotel in Hong Kong. Today he was thinking about how he could best make a contribution to the quality of life in his beloved city. Yu was considering a rare books library when Union Gedony came into the hand-tiled steam room, stark naked.

Union never entered a room unnoticed. Since he'd turned twenty, 270 pounds was his personal best. Extremely well-muscled, six feet, five inches tall, he looked like a stronger, extra-large version of the Michelin Man. Moreover, this out-sized man consistently marched to his own different drummer, a percussionist with a singular worldview. To Union's way of thinking, everything was concrete. There were no intangibles. If he saw a painting, it was red or big or well-framed. A woman was never moody or sweet, she was flat chested or needed dental work or lived on Wilshire.

If he had a weakness, Union's Achilles heel was with anger management. As a child, he occasionally had angry outbursts. Aware that it was an unacceptable liability, he worked very hard and learned techniques to control his temper. By the time he was an adult, Union was extra careful. In truth, he was more than careful. He was meticulous—obsessively meticulous—which appealed to Yu. Even his detractors admitted that his annoying attention to detail worked well for him. The guy never got caught. In fact, as a strikebreaker, Union had no criminal record. Yu first met him when Union was recommended to help Yu settle a hotel worker strike at one of his beachfront hotels. Fascinated by his odd name, Union Gedony, Yu had asked him how he came by it. Union had replied simply, "Trouble wid da Union, ged Donny...I was Donny." Yu hired him that very day, and now, Union was in charge of security for the Pacific Trading company. He had a staff of eight.

Every Monday, he met in the steam room with Yu. Today, he was angry and confused about Susie. "Chief, it don't cut the mustard. Susie don't have accidents." Union grinned his grin, a technique he used to manage his anger, then went on, "She was always getting the clothes right—designer outfits, just so—working out a plan...You know, she enjoyed her work, checked out the details, a pro's pro."

Yu nodded, accustomed to Union's precise, colorful descriptive style. "I understand your concern. I want you to stay on it. What do we know about this girl?"

"Twenty-five, just a kid. No sweat." Union laughed.

Yu put it together easily and nodded appreciatively. Union was sweating himself, like a pig on a spit, so the big man had found his choice of words funny. "Perhaps there was some freak accident. I suggest you inquire after the bodies. Right away...Take one of our planes to Anacortes. I've arranged for a small jet. Please spend whatever time and money it takes to ensure the success of your inquiries."

Union nodded, hosed down the wall, creating more heat. He was turning pink, and waves of sweat rolled off his flesh as he handled the hose.

"I must compliment you on the swimming pool incident. Well-conceived, perfectly executed."

"I got some problems in that department, too. Some fancy cop is asking questions about the immigration guy."

"Who?...Why?"

"I'm not sure why. He's a well-dressed, Black LA cop, Sergeant Lincoln. I saw him at that shabby old club on Motor Avenue. He's not interested in green cards."

"Have Lennie find out who he is. Precisely who he is." Without a word, Yu went out to shower, barely nodding at Union.

◆◆◆

Rosie's museum benefit evolved into a weekend event. Friday night was a fancy dinner party put on by the Russian consulate. The ambassador had flown in from Washington, and in an inspired effort to transform their dowdy image, the representatives of the Russians had taken over a trendy show biz "eatery," Wolfgang Puck at the Hotel Bel-Air.

Saturday evening was a series of small fundraising cocktail parties preceding the main event, the following evening, a formal dinner dance at the museum. The most prestigious of these was at Yu and Rosie's Malibu home. To be invited to this event, you had to be either a "golden donor" or a celebrity. Golden donors were those who had given more than $25,000 to the museum. There were over 200 golden donors coming to mix with the kind of celebrities that only Rosie and Yu could produce. This afternoon the celebrities included Julia Roberts, Leonardo DiCaprio, Ellen DeGeneres, George Clooney, Natalie Portman, Scarlett Johansson, Johnny Depp, Jennifer Lawrence, Hailie Berry, etc. It was rumored that Mikhail Baryshnikov might be making a surprise appearance.

Yu, elegant in a tuxedo, touched Rosie's hand and led her out onto one of the balconies. He put his arm around her waist and asked, "Can you spare me for an hour?"

Rosie looked at her husband. It was not like him to leave her before a big party. "Problem, babe?" she took his hand.

"I don't know. Union set up a call with Lennie for six fifteen, so I thought I might listen in."

Rosie nodded. Union never called unless there was a specific reason.

"Party starts at seven. There's plenty of time." Rosie kissed her husband, then shifted gears to ask, "This Sara Cambert, what's she—net, net—to us?"

"Perhaps $14,000,000. However, at the moment my darling, we could have a small problem. It seems that they've found the remains of Suzie's body, but Union said there's no sign of the other girl." He touched the tips of his long wiry fingers.

"That's the ocean out there, babe. They'll never find her."

"Yes, that was my first thought. However, the curious tidal patterns of the area tend to wash everything in the channel where the boat exploded into a certain enclosed area, a certain bay. Union reported that they dredged the bay. They found debris—bits and pieces—from the boat, remains of Suzie's body, and that's all."

"Maybe a fish got her. She couldn't stop Suzie. It'd take Rambo to beat Suzie." Rosie sighed, knit her brow. "Still, we can't be too careful."

"I'm going to have Union stay on it."

"Yes, that's a good idea, babe." She nodded, whispered, "You look great."

◆◆◆

They were still seated around the maple prep table in the kitchen. They were five now, since Sergeant Lincoln had joined Sara, Callie, Cash, and Detective Samter. Lincoln was slight, agile, dressed like an ad in *Fortune Magazine* for private banking, and quick to smile.

He'd began by detailing how much he was looking forward to the salmon fishing. After, he told them the other reason why he'd come. He explained that a highly regarded immigration officer, Sammy Weinberg, had died in a so-called accident—electrocuted while swimming in the pool at the Picwood Racquet Club.

After befriending and buying some Cuban cigars from Jaime, the entrepreneurial illegal Mexican locker room attendant, Lincoln had leaned on him to open Sammy's locker. Inside, he found Sammy's appointment book, and now, he took the book out of his pocket and lay it open on the table. He turned to a marked piece of paper. On the paper, in his all caps style, Sammy had printed PACIFIC TRADERS… NORTHWEST TRADING CO. (SUBSIDIARY)…A40671286. The rest of the page was covered with his doodling, mostly circles of all sizes.

Sara winced, then said, "That's my A number, and Northwest Trading Company is where I had my job."

"Yes, I found your name associated with that A number after Detective Samter called to explain the situation. You've surely upset some very powerful people, disrupted their well laid plans. So you're in far more danger than you could imagine. Let me tell you what I know."

Callie served more latte for Lincoln. He sipped, nodded, then began. "Unfortunately, you're dealing with considerable power, local as well as national. The Pacific Trading Company, a.k.a. Pacific Traders, is owned and operated by Yu Shin Shi and his wife, Fanny Rose. Pacific Traders have several subsidiary companies, such as the Hong Kong Bank, The Northwest Trading Company, International Capital Management, The Cayman Co., and others. Many of them, such as ICM and the Cayman Co. are directed by a shell corporation, so the beneficiaries are untraceable. In short, these folks are extremely well-organized, very sophisticated heavy hitters."

Lincoln let this sink in. "Moreover, Rosie and Yu are world-class fundraisers and contributors to everything from the symphony to Cedars-Sinai Medical Center to the Firemen's Home. An astonishing number of important national candidates, Democrat and Republican, fill their campaign coffers at their fancy Malibu home. Rosie runs a high-powered law firm, donates time to the ACLU, sits on the board of the Dorothy Chandler Pavilion, and chairs the ethics committee of the immigration bar. Yu runs Pacific Traders, cochairs the fund drive for the AIDs research foundation, and sits on the Time Warner board.

They're model citizens, community-minded and responsible. You have no chance against them. None at all. Don't even try."

"Did you say immigration bar?" Cash's eyes were narrow, focused.

"I did. But don't jump to conclusions. There are thousands of immigration lawyers in LA. Rosie only handles the prestige cases, and she's known to follow the letter of the law."

"Anything on file?"

"There was nothing active. On a hunch, I had my computer jock check the dead files. No reference to Yu, Rosie, or the trading company. Then I ran federal cases, looking for anything from immigration. I came across this follow-up on Sammy, the immigration investigator that died in an accident. The investigating officer was convinced it was an accident as were his superiors. The Pacific Trading Company was on the investigating officer's gas chit. Nothing more. The cop's recently retired."

"Cards to the gamblers, buddy, we got a game." Cash raised his palms. Proof positive.

"Detective Samter warned me you'd say something like that." Lincoln handed Cash the file and went on, "This is going to be volcanic. I'll help."

"I'm in." Detective Samter announced.

"As am I," Callie added.

Sara looked at each of them in turn. "Cards to the gamblers?... My God, you people, all of you...I love this country."

◆◆◆

At precisely six fifteen p.m., as promised, Union called from a pay phone in Anacortes. Lennie said, "Union, Yu is here with me, he's picking up the other phone."

"Good," was all Union said. There was a pause as Yu picked up the phone.

"Go ahead Union, I'm listening," Yu said.

"I checked around at the ferry terminal in Anacortes, one of the security guys identified Sara Cambert from the photo Lennie gave me—"

Lennie interrupted, "The one from the original visa packet."

"Yeah, I show this picture to him. She's a pretty foreigner, distinctive face. He says yeah, that looks like her. I ask around, another ferry worker IDs the girl, too."

"Well done, Union. I want you to have our people find her— wherever—whatever it takes. Report to Lennie every six hours. Do your best, this is critically important. Time is of the essence, thank you."

Yu went on, "Lennie, what have you found about Sergeant Lincoln? Union, please stay on the line."

Lennie opened a file. As he spoke, he rebuttoned his vest, properly. "Maverick, not a team player, Black, very good record. My man says his performance is so strong that they have to put up with his eccentricities." Lennie opened a notebook, checking something. He pointed at it. "I found Lincoln's name in the Cuban investigator's notebook. Apparently, Lincoln and the Cuban, Antonio, had an appointment. It looks like he and Lincoln met the day before his accident."

Yu frowned. "That's unfortunate, for Mr. Lincoln. Union, find him and follow him. Considering he is quite an accomplished police officer, following him will be difficult. Money is, therefore, not a constraint. If he's out of town, track him down."

"I'll have our people find him tonight."

Yu went on, forcibly. "Take whatever precautions you feel are necessary to ensure that no one can tie you or your people to the operation. Thank you both." Yu left.

Lennie stayed on the phone. "Union, he's unhappy. Call in all the help you need."

"I'm on it. Call you in six."

"Okay, I'll be—" Lennie stopped. Union was gone.

◆◆◆

Rosie was in their room putting on her final touches of makeup when Yu came in. She saw instantly that something was wrong. "What was it?"

"There's reason to believe Sara Cambert is alive. Union's after her."

"Union will handle it. This is what he's paid for. Even if she's dumb enough to go public, no one would believe her. There's no paper on her. She's not Sara Cambert. Hon, the bitch is dead, any way you cut it."

"I know you're right, darling. Still, this is unsettling." Yu smiled, then whispered in her ear, "I'll worry later, my dear. Let's enjoy the party."

◆◆◆

"Cash, are you aware that your daughter's forty-two years old, born in Bordeaux, and her whereabouts are unknown?" Lincoln asked, sipping espresso on the maple prep table in Callie's kitchen.

Cash turned to Lincoln, "What?"

"I talked to my guy over at immigration. I had him run her through the computer. They got a Sara Cambert that came in April 1, port of entry, Seattle. So far so good, right?"

Sara looked up for the first time, nodding.

"Only this gal's born in Bordeaux, back in January of 1977."

"So, where is she?" Callie asked.

"Here's where it gets tricky. The computer only gets the name, date of birth, place of birth, and file number. So, I ask the INS guy to pull the file, and he can't find it. He goes to his boss, the head honcho says it must be in transit, someone must have requested it. Bottom line, it's gone, unavailable. So I try another idea. You delightful people told me that Northwest Traders were Sara's sponsor. Ever resourceful, the Black Sam Spade pretends he's an INS investigator and calls Northwest. Nice, sharp lady, named Betty, answers the phone, listens, and tells me she'll have the information in an hour. Okay, I call back in an hour, she tells me this Sara Cambert showed up for work, picked up her green card, then two days later the company put her on an important assignment. She'll be traveling—Betty doesn't know where. Betty did confirm, however, that Sara was forty-two years old. I'll bet Betty's on the team, taking orders."

Lincoln paused, thoughtful. "Here's where I come out. These folks are your money players—they don't miss a trick. Sara could go in and demand an investigation, but I don't see what that would accomplish.

Some INS internal investigator would get about as far as I did. Frankly, he's likely to have her deported. To a cop, she's just another fruitcake. There's absolutely no evidence that she ever got her immigrant visa. There's no record of her application, and she certainly never received a green card."

"What about the French end?"

"I called the head of the immigrant visa section in France. Same deal. Only records they have showed this forty-two-year-old Sara Cambert born in Bordeaux and a file number. That's the missing file."

Lincoln nodded, took a moment, then went on, "Remember, anyone in the system, from the airport inspection supervisor to a file clerk in the processing facility, could process a new place and date of birth into the computer. But in this case, that's just the beginning. Somewhere between the officer at the airport and Arlington, Texas, I'd guess the contents of your file were replaced. If they eventually 'find' the file, and they will, everything—pictures, prints, supporting documents, birth certificate—will describe the other Sara Cambert. Your green card was issued—I confirmed that—and it was sent to Northwest Traders. The particulars, however, must have been adjusted to fit someone else: the woman that disappeared. I'd guess one of their inside people borrowed the file from Arlington after the card was issued."

Finally, Cash said, "These people are smart. No question, this other Sara Cambert's out of reach—too much planning back a this deal. So, we got no choice." Cash patted Samter on the shoulder. "Detective, we're gonna have to step outside the law here."

Samter winced. "Right. I saw this coming. Be careful what you tell me."

Lincoln nodded. "Me, too."

Cash stood, walking around. Something was nagging at him, trying to break through to consciousness. He couldn't quite get it.

Lincoln went on, "Okay, stands to reason that the Cuban investigator put Sammy Weinberg onto the trading company before his so-called accident."

"What exactly happened?" Callie asked.

"Car accident," Lincoln explained. "His body was found in the hills above Malibu. The police report hypothesized that he'd been drinking when the royal blue mustang blew a rear tire. The report speculated that he lost control of the car. The car certainly went over the cliff, caught fire, then exploded. The man was dead, unidentified. I put it together several days later, when he didn't show up at our second meeting."

"How much did he and Weinberg know?" Cash asked.

"From what he told me, they were following the stolen money, so they probably got as far as the bank in Hong Kong, then made the Pacific Trading Company connection. I'd bet Sam Weinberg had nothing except big bucks going into some little bank owned by a California corporation. Using his INS muscle, it was no big problem getting from Pacific to Northwest. But that still gets them nowhere. At a loss, he runs the Pacific Trading Company, and Northwest Traders, through the computer. A smart guy, he checks out all the applicants they've sponsored in the last year. For reasons still unknown, he got interested in Sara—maybe it was as simple as the others checked out fine. Sara's probably got nothing to do with the Cuban deal. If I'm right, she's new business. But Sammy, unknowingly, had gotten further into the operation."

Lincoln took a beat, thoughtful, then continued, "Sara's number in and of itself was no big deal. But Yu and Rosie couldn't risk having a smart INS investigator poking around their business. Sooner or later, he's likely to ask questions about Sara Cambert. We have to suppose that she's part of another big important deal that's going down, separate from whatever the Cuban investigator is after. So, they arrange for Sammy to have an accident and hope that it stops right there. When it didn't, killing the Cuban investigator became necessary. It was also smart—it erased any trail to Weinberg's information."

Callie frowned. "Damn, I'm starting to get this."

They went to the bar and talked for another hour. Cash wanted to get more aggressive. Lincoln cautioned him to go slow. Samter expressed stern disapproval with an outstretched forefinger and thumb and his unmistakable expression. Still uneasy, they went over everything they knew and tried putting it together different ways. Sara, confused, finally turned to Cash and asked, "What do you think is going on?"

Cash thought a moment, then put it simply. "These people are laundering money." He scowled. "And people." Once he'd said it everyone knew he was right. And he said it in less than ten words. Sara loved that.

♦♦♦

Callie turned to Cash. "I never thought I'd say this to you. But Babe, as you would put it, 'It's time to play offense.'"

"Yes, my dear, yes exactly. If we're not already too late." Cash turned toward Lincoln. "If these people are anything like as good as you describe, they're tracking you down as we speak. They'll be here tonight, easily, and if we're not ahead of them, they'll find you and Sara. So we need to hide her right away, safely." Cash turned to Samter. "Do you have a reliable, safe place?"

"Yes, a house we rent for our undercover people is empty. We can put her—and you and Callie—there tonight."

"Set that up, we should leave soon. When we get there, we should talk about next steps. I also want to call two men to help."

"Andre and the Macher?" Callie asked.

"Yes, we'll need Andre, and the Macher will help us however he can."

"So this is escalating very fast…"

"I don't know how else to protect my daughter." Cash caught her eye. "We'll also need a safe place for Lincoln. He has to be someplace else."

"Whoa. I'll be okay," Lincoln said. "I have an old friend here who will put me up. No one will know him or find me."

"Please just listen to me. You're in my wheelhouse now. In my world, none of your normal rules apply. You're obviously an excellent policeman, but you probably think they won't kill you unless they have to. Think again. They don't want to find you just to find Sara. If I'm right, by now, they know that you asked about Sara at the Northwest Trading Company. They know that you were asking questions about Sammy Weinberg at the Racquet club. They know that Sammy, and then you, talked with the Cuban investigator about their missing money in Hong Kong. You've already led them to Sara in Seattle. If we don't get ahead of them, they'll find you tonight and kill you. Do I need to go on?"

Samter answered before Lincoln could get a word in. "You don't want to know how he knows this, but he's right. As much as I hate to admit it, he's usually right. Shit, Lincoln, I told you he was like this."

"Jesus, is he in charge?"

Samter grimaced. "*Both* he and Callie are in charge. Sorry. We're going to get all of you safely hidden, then we're going to learn just what Cash means by 'offense.'"

Callie stood behind Sara and put her hands on her shoulder. Sara took one of Callie's hands then took Cash's hand. She turned to Cash and looked him in the eye. "So we're going to war?"

"I think so."

Callie added, "It's like Helen of Troy. People going to war over a beautiful young woman. In this case Sara, that's you."

Sara turned to Cash. "That would make you Zeus, Helen's father."

"No one's ever compared me to Zeus. I'm flattered."

Sara raised her eyebrows, then her palms. "Until you learn a little bit more about Zeus, I'd go slow with that."

Cash watched her. "Fair enough. How do you know about Zeus and Helen of Troy?"

"My mother loved to tell me the Greek myths. The Trojan war always interested me. So violent, so passionate. I always envied Helen, said to be the most beautiful woman in the world. And loved by so many men."

"You're a multifaceted woman."

"I'm no Helen of Troy, I promise you that. But I will try, with all of my heart, to make you proud of me."

"He's already proud of you," Callie answered. "More than you can imagine."

"It's unexpected, unusual, and undeniably true." Cash smiled, then he stood and looked down toward the door as three men came into the downstairs entry. Callie saw them too. She moved toward Cash "Those men have never been in my restaurant, not ever," she whispered.

"They're ahead of schedule. Let's go out the back." Then to Samter and Lincoln, "All of us should leave, right away." He took his daughter's duffel. "Follow me."

Cash led them around behind the bar to the back stairway. They hurried down and then out into the alley. Outside, he turned to Samter. "Please get at least two cops to the restaurant right away."

Samter was already on the phone, giving orders. When he finished, he said, "Four police officers will arrive shortly." Then he quickly told Cash where the empty house he suggested was, an old town house just off Pike. They agreed to meet there later. They watched Samter and Lincoln hurry down the alley to a side street, then Callie and Sara were in Cash's truck and off toward the Pike/Pine corridor.

CHAPTER FIVE

Rosie and Yu were in their office, a stunning sleek triangular building, actually built into the hillside, overlooking the ocean. It was 11:30 p.m. and they were sipping Marc, a strong French eau de vie made in Burgundy, feeling good about their party. They were sitting around a lovely teak conference table looking out through the essentially invisible glass front of the triangle. As such, they were facing the moon over the water. Lennie sat facing them, his large back to the ocean. He was giving them an update.

"Earlier tonight, we found that the cop, Lincoln, had taken a flight to Seattle this afternoon. We had two men showing his picture to taxi drivers at the airport. It took a while, but we were lucky, one of them picked him up from the airport and took him to a French restaurant, Le Couchon Bronze, in Belltown, on the water. At nine fifteen, we asked Union to meet our people there. Our people got to the restaurant fifteen minutes later, around nine thirty, and learned that Lincoln had been there, but he was already gone. No one could tell us who he was with or where he went when he left. When Union arrived, only fifteen minutes later, he took the dishwasher into the alley and showed him Sara Cambert's picture. After Union broke his forefinger, the dishwasher admitted that the young woman had been there, and that she left with the owner and her boyfriend. When Union threatened to break his thumb, he admitted that a Black man, presumably Lincoln, had been with all three of them. Before he could learn more, four police officers arrived in the restaurant. Union broke the dishwasher's thumb, then led all of our people out the back way."

"How did the police get there so quickly?"

"We don't know. Union guessed that Lincoln, an able cop, saw the others coming into the restaurant, and called the police as he left."

"What else do we know?"

"Here's an old photo of the owner, Callie James, from an article. We don't have a photo of her boyfriend, a fella named Cash Logan." Lennie showed them Callie's photo. "We've done some preliminary background on both of them. I just received it." Lennie opened a file, reread it, then passed it over to Yu and Rosie. They read it together.

The file had the particulars about Cash and Callie, though the information about Cash was vague. Callie was clearly a well-known, successful restaurant owner. Cash was characterized as a self-employed international trader. The report speculated that he did many kinds of trades such as rugs, medical equipment, and precious stones, though they couldn't be certain or prove that. The report also described Callie's fifteen-year-old son, Lew, a local high school student, and included bios of Cesaire, her chef, and Will, her maître d'.

Yu looked up, unhappy. "How is it possible that this young woman Sara knows these people? Call our man in Paris who did the research and preparation on her. I expect you to scare him as only you can do that. Remind him that he was paid very well to be sure that she had no connections, absolutely none, in the United States. This kind of mistake is unacceptable. We'll deal with him after."

Lennie nodded.

"Call Union now please. I want to talk with him."

Lennie put the phone on speaker and called Union. When Union picked up after the first ring, Lennie explained, "I have Rosie and Yu with me on the phone. I'm going to turn this over to Yu."

"Do you know anything further since texting me at ten tonight?"

"No. They disappeared. We weren't able to search their apartment because the police arrived so quickly."

"Keep looking. Later tonight, search the apartment, and tomorrow latest, go back and lean on people at the restaurant. See what we can learn about how this carefully chosen, supposedly solitary girl could possibly know them. In the meantime, see what you can find out about the restaurant woman's fifteen-year-old son, Lew. Then report to me."

"Yes, sir." Union replied.

"Thank you," Yu said, then he hung up. He turned to Rosie, who was ready to unload.

"God damnit," she snapped. "We don't make mistakes like this. Can you fix it?"

"Yes, first, let's see what we can learn about how this so-called friendless, unconnected, orphan girl, Sara, happens to know two prominent people in Seattle."

◆◆◆

Callie, Cash, and Sara were in the alley, going in the back door of the house Samter had provided. It was just off Pike, several blocks away from Toys in Babeland, the flagship nationally well-known erotic store. When they passed by, Sara asked Cash if he'd ever been in that place and before he could reply, Callie said, "Zip it, Sara. Just don't say another word about it."

"Never." Sara touched Callie's arm beside her, her expression solemn. "Not one more word."

Callie had to smile.

They'd left Cash's truck parked in the beat-up garage in the alley behind the small two-story town house. They were expected, and an armed man let them in.

Inside, they settled into a barely adequately furnished living room. Callie quickly called the restaurant. Cash was listening, his ear on the other side of her phone. As she listened to Will, Callie grew livid. "How many?" she asked. "Three and then a fourth joined them... He looked like a giant...He did what?...Broke Jean-Luke's forefinger... And his thumb...So they know Sara is here...They don't know her connection to Cash...He also gave up Lincoln...And where we live upstairs...You think they'll be back?....Damnit! I'll call you back."

Callie took his hand. "They scared Will. That's hard to do."

"They're fast and able," Cash commented, squeezing her hand before taking the phone. "I'll call Ed Samter. I have an idea."

"I was afraid of that," Callie muttered, and to herself. "Déjà vu."

Sara turned, interested. "So you guys have done this before?"

"Honey, this tune is getting painfully familiar."

"Well, okay then."

"Buckle up, young lady. We're about to take off at light speed."

"Hmm." She looked at her dad, who was dialing the phone. "My dad is a lot like me." She whispered to Callie. "No kidding."

"I was afraid of that." And before Sara could respond, they both turned to Cash.

"Ed," Cash started right in. "They broke two of our dishwasher's fingers before your officers arrived…Please just listen. They know about Sara, they know about Lincoln, they know where Callie and I live… They're smart and capable…I believe they'll be back tonight to break into our apartment…How do I know that?…It's what I would do…Ed, try not to ask me that every time I'm about to suggest something that makes you uneasy…About everything I suggest makes you uneasy?… Right about now, I'll bet you're glaring at me, like the terminator… Yes, I'll try to live with that…Meet me at the restaurant in fifteen minutes. Bring Lincoln…Come in the front door…No, I don't want any more cops…I'll get my own weapon from the apartment…I'm sorry, but this is not law enforcement…It's offense."

"Can I help?" Sara asked.

"You just killed someone, professional killers are out to kill you, I just met you. Do you think you might take a night off?"

"Is this a guy's only—what's that word—'male macho deal?'"

"I don't want to put you at risk again before I have to. Besides—"

"Sara," Callie interrupted. "Be thankful for that. And just let it be. You'll have plenty of chances to rescue our male macho guys, I guarantee that. And between us gals, I'm guessing that before this is over, you'll be telling them what to do."

"You're a pistol, Callie James, the goddamned genuine article."

Cash parked his truck in a lot a block away, then opened the front door with his key. He sat in the dark waiting for Samter and Lincoln. Five minutes later, he opened the front door for them, then he locked it behind them. "Follow me to the kitchen. No lights." Once there, Cash motioned for them to sit in the dark at the long maple prep table. Cash opened the Dutch door that opened down to the landing and the back door. At the landing, another stairway went up to their apartment. "They should be breaking through the back door soon. Since our goal is to arrest them, not kill them, I'd say this is where you guys take over."

Samter took charge. "Our best case is if we take them in the apartment. Cash, you and I should wait upstairs. Lincoln, you stay right here in case one of them stays down to keep an eye on the back door. If one of them stays behind, Lincoln, you disable him. Cash, how many men are they likely to bring, would you guess?"

"Two, three max. But I'm guessing the big guy will be here, so be careful."

Cash showed Lincoln the concealed spot in the Dutch door where he could watch anyone who came into the landing while remaining unseen, then he led Samter up the stairs and unlocked, then opened, his front door. Inside, he locked the front door, then Cash pointed out two hiding spaces off the living room. Samter took the closet just off the front door. Cash went back into the bedroom where he took a locked gun from a closet. He loaded it, set it down, and left the door open. He looked at Samter, who gave him a thumbs-up.

◆◆◆

Thirty-five minutes later, Union brought two men with him to the back door in the alley off the restaurant and the apartment. Lincoln watched them easily break into the alley door, then, as Samter had anticipated, they left one man guarding the closed back door. The giant, Union, led the second man carefully upstairs to the apartment.

Lincoln waited until they reached the door upstairs, then came behind the man below with a chloroform covered towel that he silently pressed over the man's nose and mouth as he held a gun to his head. As the man passed out, he could hear the two men at the top of the stairs work to open the front door to the apartment. Lincoln carried the unconscious man into the kitchen where he cuffed him on the floor to the cast iron stove then gagged him securely. Lincoln was back on the landing as he heard the door upstairs open and close.

Upstairs, soon after the front door closed, Cash came out of the bedroom softly. He had a short barrel shotgun out when he turned on the light. Union reached for his gun as Samter came out of the closet, firing a shot above Union's head. Cash covered both of them with the shotgun. "Put your guns down and your hands above your head," Samter ordered. "This is the Seattle Police. You're under arrest." As he talked, Lincoln came through the door, stepped to the far side of the room, his gun drawn.

That's when Union charged at the door with surprising speed. Lincoln put a bullet in his shoulder. It didn't even slow him down. As he tore out the door, Cash fired both barrels of the shotgun into Union's legs, blowing off most of his calves and his lower thighs. The big man fell down the stairs unable to use his torn legs. Cash and Lincoln followed behind him. Cash held him down with the shotgun at his head while Lincoln cuffed his hands behind his back. Quickly and ably, they used towels and tourniquets on both legs to limit the bleeding. Samter cuffed the man upstairs, then they went down the stairs, called the police, and ordered an ambulance.

"A shotgun?" Lincoln eventually asked.

Samter answered. "I told you about this guy. Didn't I?"

"It's worse than what you said."

Samter just glared at Cash.

"Did it work?" Cash asked.

Both men nodded, yes. Lincoln added, "I could have put two more slugs in this giant, and he'd still be long gone. You did the right thing."

And that was that.

Cash, Samter, and Lincoln came back to the safe house where Sara and Callie listened carefully to what had happened. After Callie asked, "Well then—so we won, right?"

Cash looked at her, said, "We just started. This is going to heat up very quickly."

"Do we want to try and make a deal? Can we negotiate a truce?"

"Unlikely," Samter responded. "But Lincoln, why don't you make contact with their accountant. You said his name was Lennie? Let's begin a conversation first thing in the morning."

"Lennie, yes. I can tell him what happened, what we're prepared to do if they don't back off." Lincoln paused, thoughtful. "I'll threaten a police investigation. And let them know, in no uncertain terms, that Sara's safety is imperative, that we'll stop at nothing to insure that."

Cash nodded. "All good, though they'll deny any involvement. Still, it will put them on notice. Whatever you and they say, at the end of the day, they'll try to kill us all, as soon as they can figure a way to do that so it won't be possible to connect our deaths to them."

Callie smiled. "Ah Cash, I'd almost forgotten how quickly you jump to a positive outcome. So what are you suggesting?"

"I haven't had time to think it through. There's one thing, though, I know that we need to do right away. We need to get all of us to another place, a safer place. I have two ideas. I have access to an isolated cabin in the woods off Toe Jam Hill, on Bainbridge Island, that I can open up. No one will find us there, but we'll be isolated. My other idea is familiar, but Ed, I'll need your help to do it. I need a good, fast boat, maybe thirty-five feet, able to go thirty or thirty-five miles per hour, sleeps at least four. Does the department have one I can use?"

"No, but I have a friend who does. I'll ask."

"We'll pay all expenses and a reasonable fee. Make sure it's well insured."

"He owes me, so he'll loan it, no charge. No disrespect Cash, but given your character and your history, I'll budget extra insurance. We'll have to pay for that."

"Spoken like a true admirer. But that's fine. We'll work that out."

"We? I should have anticipated that, too."

"Last time we worked together, you were demonstrably unhappy about everything I did. In the end, we got the guy you couldn't find, and you got promoted. Didn't you learn anything from that?"

"I give Callie the credit. She made all of that happen in spite of you."

"Is that true?" Sara asked, unconvinced.

Callie touched her arm. "Let's say that there are two distinct points of view about that. I share Cash's version…But thank you, detective."

"You're welcome. Also, it's probably a good idea to open up the Bainbridge cabin, too."

Cash shook his head. "You're still an incorrigible, ungrateful, n'er-do-well. But I'll have someone open the cabin in the morning." He took a minute, thoughtful. "One more thing. If they don't have powerful spyware already, I'm sure they'll have it soon. Companies like Circles, Boldend, and NSO have been making extremely powerful tools like Pegasus, which was developed in Israel. It can infect and pretty much take over your phone remotely. They'll be tracking your calls, reading text messages, accessing the video, pretty much everything. So get another phone—the newest upgraded Android with the latest security updates. Use it rarely, only between us. Let them trap the old phones, just use them on other business."

Samter nodded. "We've had a lecture about Pegasus. It's only sold to authorized states to fight terrorism and crime. How do you even know about it?" He raised his hand before Cash could answer.

Lincoln laughed out loud. "You're right to worry about it. Let's get the new Android tonight."

"I already have them for Sara and Callie and I."

Callie nodded. "Of course."

Sara was walking in circles, frowning, thinking about something. She eventually turned, "Thanks for the phone…Okay. There's something that's been bothering me, and I'd like to talk about it now if we're done with phones."

"You're up," Cash said.

"Here's what's concerning me. So now, there are quite a few very smart, very capable people here, working hard to protect me. As frightened as I am, you don't need to do that. I've thought about an alternative—if you let me go to any big city with an immigrant population, I could easily find a place where I could disappear. I'd like to do that. It would be better, safer, for all of you. I'm worried that one or more of you will get hurt, and I know I won't be able to protect you if things go bad."

Cash took both of her hands. "Sara, there's something I want to explain, and it's important that you understand and trust that it's absolutely true. Unexpectedly, you've become part of our little family. For me, and I'm sure I speak for Callie, it's a gift. Nothing could convince us to let you go forward without all of our help. All of it."

"Truthfully, what you just said, I don't understand it. I can't make it real…It feels like a dream…"

"You're in very real trouble. You know that's true. Sometimes, though, good things happen at unexpected times. Your arrival is a very good thing for all of us."

"What if my presence, and your efforts to help me, leads to some or all of you getting hurt? I don't know what to do about that."

"We've signed on, and we're all experienced adults who know the risks."

Callie put her arm around Sara. "And your dad is the best at protecting against the worst."

Sara hugged her close, then started to cry. She cried for a long time, a measure of so many years of fear and loneliness. She eventually turned and curled up on the shabby old safehouse couch. She lowered her head into her hands and cried again, openly—large tears flowing freely done her cheeks. When she finally moved her hands away and slowly raised her head, her eyes were sparkling, and she was hopeful through her tears. She spoke carefully, purposefully, "In the orphanage, they never noticed my birthday…Today, I feel like I'm five years old, and I'm having my first birthday party."

CHAPTER SIX

Malibu

Rosie and Yu were in the kitchen, drinking coffee, when Lennie came in. He'd called ahead, so he was expected. But Rosie and Yu were concerned because Lennie rarely asked to come into this room. They suspected he had very bad news, and he was here because he knew they'd want to hear it right away, in person.

Lennie sat his wide bottom in a large chair they'd set out for him. He took an offered glass of water, adjusted his vest, cleared his throat, then started right in. "Unfortunately, there's no nice way to tell this. First, two of our people in Seattle are in jail, charged with breaking and entering into Callie James and Cash Logan's apartment. Further, Union is in the hospital. He was shot in both legs with a double-barreled shotgun. He'll never walk again. They're operating on him right now."

"Union?...Our Union Gedonny?...How is this possible?" Rosie asked, uncharacteristically soft.

"Here's what I was able to find out. They were arrested by two experienced police officers—Sergeant Lincoln, the LA detective that you know of, and Lieutenant Ed Samter, a highly regarded Seattle police lieutenant. The man who shot Union was Cash Logan, the international trader you just learned about yesterday. They were waiting at the apartment and the capture was well-planned. Logan shot Union as he tried to escape, which is generally possible for him. Unfortunately, we underestimated these people. Sara Cambert has excellent, expert help. Sergeant Lincoln, the LA policeman, called me just before I came up here. He basically confirmed what I knew, said they're prepared to escalate, including a police investigation, unless we back off and leave

Sara Cambert alone. He even suggested we meet. I ignored his request for a meeting. I told him I had no idea what he was talking about."

"This changes everything," Rosie announced. "Every damn thing."

Yu listened, stone-faced, then took his wife's hand, a sure sign that he was very upset. He stayed silent, digesting this.

"How would you like to handle this?" Lennie finally asked.

Rosie stood, looked straight at Yu, who read her mind and nodded. She replied to both of them, "Kill Sara Cambert...Soon." She went on directly to Yu, "Babe, I need you to figure out how...And it's up to you to decide what to do with the others."

Yu eventually spoke very softly, the sure tell he was absolutely furious, awash in a red-hot rage. "We'll need expert help, right away, the very best people we know, people we can trust utterly. From Miami, I'll want my brother, Johnny Green. I'll also want Eddie King, Johnny's brother-in-law from Las Vegas. He won't be afraid of this."

"He owes me a favor," Rosie added. "I fast-tracked visas for three international dealers to work in the high-stake casino at one of his client's hotel."

"Even with a favor, he's still among the most expensive in the world," Lennie reminded them.

"That's because he's the best and that, my valued friend, is why I suggested him."

"Then I'll get him today."

"Fill him in on what we're dealing with. Of course, both of them can bring any help they need."

Rosie turned. "Between Johnny, Eddie King, their people and ours, we're ready for an all-out war...Take a careful beat first babe. There will be costs and consequences. Are we certain we want that?"

"This is already a war, my dear. What they did to our people in Seattle was a flat-out declaration of war. We can't ignore that. Let's wait until our people are here to finalize our plan. For now, Lennie, call Lincoln back. Tell him, you'd like to 'redefine' the relationship.

Explore our mutual interests. Take a pause, consider a possible ceasefire. You know what to say."

Lennie nodded. "No problem. I'll get their attention."

"In the meantime, these people who dared to go up against us need to learn exactly who they've gone to war with. They need a heart stopping, bone-chilling message."

Yu went over to Lennie's chair. Put his hand on his shoulder. "Lennie, what have you learned about Lew, Callie James's son?"

"He's on a school trip, in Washington, DC."

"Have our best two men take him right away, tonight latest. Hide him in our warehouse basement security room in New York City."

Yu left the room. No one had ever seen him quite so angry.

◆◆◆

Samter's friend's boat was moored at Elliot Bay Marina, a straight shot into Elliot Bay in Puget Sound, bypassing the Lake Washington Ship Canal running through Salmon Bay and out to sea through the Chittenden Locks. The boat, a 1962 forty-two-foot wooden Chris Craft Conqueror was well maintained, slept four comfortably, and was beautiful to look at. It had a top speed of 25 knots or 28.7 mph.

After buying, loading, and storing supplies for a week, Cash, Callie, and Sara took the boat past Bainbridge Island's Restoration Point, the 230-acre unique communal property, with eighteen stately homes, called the Country Club. Beyond the southern tip of Bainbridge, they went southwest to the far side of Blake Island, which was uninhabited. There, they moored their boat to a buoy not far from the beach on the northern tip of the island. They packed up what they wanted for dinner and rowed the dinghy to shore. On the island, Sara gathered wood and Cash built a fire. As they sat around the fire, sitting on two logs they managed to haul over, Cash took out a bottle of Glenmorangie single malt scotch. Callie supplied real whiskey glasses for each of them.

"This whiskey was a gift from my old friend Doc, who died about a year ago. I've kept it for a special occasion," Cash announced. "This qualifies." He poured for all three of them.

"I've never had any alcohol quite so fine," Sara explained. "Anything I need to know?"

"Go slow," Callie cautioned. "It's an acquired taste."

"I'm not sure what an acquired taste is, but I'll learn slowly."

Cash raised his glass, the others followed.

After clicking their glasses, there was a quiet moment, then Callie turned to Sara. "I've never seen Cash so happy." She raised her glass, again. "Bravo to you, young lady."

◆◆◆

Rosie, Yu, and Lennie were sitting in the veranda just outside of the living room, along with Yu's adopted brother Johnny Green. Johnny was standing, overlooking the railing looking out at the ocean. The six-foot-three-inch Chinese man was agile as a gymnast, and Johnny still moved like a mountain lion. People tended to give him a wide berth and once they were safely away, often remarked upon his huge upper lip, the broad facial scar that ran from his eye down under his collar, and his generally savage countenance. Tonight, he was gentle as a lamb as he watched the dear couple holding hands on the veranda. Johnny and Yu had both been adopted into the same family in Hong Kong, a family that had seven daughters and no sons. As young boys, they were both tormented, relentlessly, often tortured in the basement by their seven older sisters. When their adopted parents died in an accident, before leaving, Johnny and Yu, young teenagers now, burned down their family home with all seven sisters locked in the basement.

As far as Johnny was concerned, Yu and Rosie were his true family. "I understand that this is not a festive occasion, but it is nevertheless, a special event whenever I see both of you," Johnny bowed.

Yu smiled warmly. "It's always the same for me, whenever I see you, my brother." He stood, embracing Johnny, then he sat back. "It's time, however, for business, as time is of the essence. Lennie told you about our situation. As he said, we are kidnapping Callie James's fifteen-year-old son this evening, in fact, as we speak, and that should be a chip we can bargain with. Beyond that, we need to find where she and Cash Logan, our primary adversary, are, and where they're hiding the girl. We need to eliminate Cash, Callie, and the girl and neutralize the others, possibly including a Seattle Police Lieutenant, who's also quite able, and appears to be helping them. Your brother-in-law, Eddie, and his people will work with us. They're already in Seattle. But frankly, I'm not sure how to do this discreetly, thoroughly, without leaving a trace. As much as I'd like to eliminate them all, we can't simply kill five people including two policemen, a Seattle lieutenant and a LA sergeant who's asking questions about us, without considerable risk to our thriving, off the radar business, and our personal well-being. Even a tragic accident will draw unacceptable attention to us, raise too many questions that will point smart police officers to scrutinize our affairs."

"With your permission, I will call Eddie. When we have the boy and know where everyone is, we'll decide how to take decisive action. I'm sure you already have some thoughts about that and having the boy can only help. In the meantime, I'll fly to Seattle. Can you arrange that?"

"I anticipated that, and the plane is waiting. And, of course, call Eddie." Yu put a hand on his brother's shoulder. "After, spend another half hour with us, then I'll have someone drive you to the airport."

"Excellent. Not to worry. We will take care of all of this."

Rosie stood, put her hand on Johnny's arm. "Johnny, it's comforting to have you here. When this is over, we'll talk. There's quite a lot to catch up on."

"My pleasure, dear Rosie." Johnny gently kissed the back of her hand.

♦♦♦

Lew was with Lisa, a girl he'd gotten to know during the school trip to DC. She was sixteen, almost a year older than he was, though that didn't seem to bother her. She was tall, blond, thin—very attractive in an unaffected, not self-conscious way that Lew really liked. This evening they'd been out to dinner and now they were walking back to their hotel. They were holding hands and stopping from time to time to share a leisurely kiss. Four or five blocks from the hotel, they stepped into a dark entryway on a quiet side street. Lew kissed her deeply, leaning her back against the wall. That's when the guy grabbed his hair and pulled him off of her. He was a big well-muscled guy, and he had another strong man, though smaller and thinner, with him. The smaller man forcibly sat Lisa down on the ground, tied her hands behind her back and gagged her with duct tape. The bigger man grabbed Lew's arms, one on each side, and walked him out of the entryway into a dark alley nearby, where a four-door, inconspicuous, Ford sedan was waiting. Together, they bound his hands behind his back, then put duct tape on his mouth. One of the men opened the trunk, then both of them put him inside.

That's when Andre, an Afro-Caribbean man with a buzz cut and a prosthetic leg, stepped into the alley. It was a sports prosthetic leg—gracefully curved black metal attached to the thigh with perforated leather. He had a cane, though the clean geometry of his black metal leg allowed him to move quickly. He wore a blousy black silk shirt under his short leather jacket. He approached the men preparing to lock Lew in the trunk.

"Excuse me," the peg-legged man, Andre, said.

"Get the Hell outta this alley you one-legged freak. Now!" The taller man barked, an order.

Everything next happened very fast. Andre ferociously hit the taller man on his face with the heavy steel handle of his cane, a handle that he'd designed with ultra-high carbon steel for maximum impact. It was an expertly delivered blow. The big man fell to the ground, in agony, his jaw and cheek smashed in multiple pieces. Without missing a step, Andre kicked his metal leg into the smaller second man's groin, driving him to his knees, leaving him barely able to breathe. Then, with his left hand, Andre took a loaded syringe out of his leather jacket pocket. Quickly, he injected a shot of Etorphine, a synthetic opioid, used to tranquilize large animals, in the neck of the shorter man. Unconsciousness was almost instantaneous. The larger man was still on the pavement in excruciating pain, disoriented, his face ravaged. Andre hit him again with the cane handle, breaking his nose, then he pressed the sharp point of the cane against the man's temple while he injected the remains of the dose of Etorphine into his neck. When he, too, was unconscious, Andre lifted Lew out of the trunk.

"Andre!" Lew yelled when he saw his friend. "Jeez…Thank you! Thank you! How—"

Andre interrupted, "Your mom doesn't know. Cash called me last night and asked me to keep an eye on you."

"This was bad—"

Andre interrupted again. "Let's get these guys in the trunk, then get away from here where we can talk."

"First, we have to free my friend Lisa. She's tied up around the corner."

"I know. That will be the next thing we do." Working together they were able to put both men into the trunk. Andre tied their hands behind their backs, then used their duct tape to gag each of their mouths. When they were satisfied, Andre took the car keys, then they locked the trunk. Finally, Andre parked the car in an isolated corner of the alley.

Next, Lew led Andre to Lisa tied up in the entryway. She was still crying, very afraid. Andre helped Lew free her. "You're safe now," he told her, when she was free. "Hold on to one of my arms and one of Lew's until you get your balance. Working together, they walked casually into the street.

◆◆◆

A third of the Glenmorangie was gone, and Callie was preparing to cook steaks on the grill. Sara was singing a sad song from Willie Nelson's album *Red Headed Stranger*. It was the first song on the album. She was at the part where the yellow-haired lady touches his lost wife's pony, and the stranger kills her with one shot.

Cash and Callie were mesmerized by Sara's lovely, lyrical voice and her appealing rendition of the song. When she finished, they cheered and clapped.

"I love that album," Cash announced. "And I love the way you sang that song. How did you learn to sing?"

"My mother taught me, though she didn't know this song."

"I remember that your mother liked to sing, and she, too, sang well. How did you learn about Willie Nelson?"

"Several years after my mother died, I decided to immigrate to the United States. Long before I got my visa, I listened constantly to American music. I loved some of the country singers—Dolly Parton, Garth Brooks, Reba McEntire, but Willie Nelson was—is—my favorite. I love his voice, his lyrics. He's so strong, so unsentimental, and at the same time, he's also gentle."

"It's uncanny how much you're like your father," Callie observed. "Cash likes to sing Willie's version of 'Crazy.'"

"I like 'Crazy' too."

That's when Cash's cell phone rang. He stepped away listening carefully. When he stepped back, his face was serious. He spoke directly to Callie, "That was Andre. He's got Lew, and they're on their way here."

"Lew, oh God, is he okay?"

"Yes, he's fine. He's with Andre. I took the liberty of calling Andre last night. I didn't want to scare you, babe, but I was afraid that these people would try and take Lew, after what we did to their people yesterday. I was being very cautious, but I was right. Andre just stopped two men who were trying to kidnap Lew. He left them locked in their car trunk, unconscious."

"Oh, Cash, you know I don't like how you anticipate the worst." Callie started to cry. "But thank you, babe. I never would have even thought about that. Never."

"We're okay. Lew's fine, and he's safe with Andre. I'd like to call Samter and Lincoln, make a plan."

"Whatever you say. I'm still unsteady"

Callie was still crying. Sara held her hand.

◆◆◆

Johnny, Yu, and Rosie were catching up when Lennie came out onto the veranda, visibly unhappy. "Sorry to interrupt, but they found Charley and Ralph locked in the trunk of their car, unconscious. Whoever did this injected some kind of powerful knockout drug. Our people are bringing them to the hospital now. I only knew where to find them because that policeman, Lincoln, called me. He said this is the last time they'll be so considerate."

"Who are these goddamned people?" Rosie cried out, loudly. "Are they just lucky?…Could they be that good?"

"We've got our best people finding out about Cash Logan. Our people say that the woman, Callie James, has no history in this type of conflict before she spent personal time with Cash a year ago. She's not likely a principal player. We know that both policemen are capable, but this isn't their kind of work. Cash is a smuggler and a capable adversary. He's likely the man orchestrating this. I'll have a more detailed report about him in the morning."

Yu stood. "This is simply, totally unacceptable." He walked across the veranda, lost in thought. When he'd made up his mind, he spoke again, more forcibly, "We need to reassess. They are surely more experienced than we thought. For the moment, we must buy time, and I'd like to know how Sara knows Cash Logan. Johnny, you go ahead to Seattle, right away. Help Eddie find out where Cash, Callie, and Sara are. He and his people are already on it. They have a tech phone man who runs sophisticated spyware. In the meantime, our next step is to delay. Lennie, why don't you call Lincoln now, tell him we've reconsidered. Propose a meeting with him tomorrow. I want them to bargain with us. Tell them tomorrow that we can work this out if Sara will change her name and identity, then leave the country. If she does that, we'll let her go, we'll go our separate ways." Yu put his hand on Johnny's arm. "I have a job for you, Johnny. Tomorrow, during Lennie's meeting with Lincoln. I'll drive you to the airport, and we'll discuss it on the way."

Johnny replied, "Yes, I'm already guessing where you're going."

Lennie added, "I'll call Lincoln now to set up a meeting in Seattle tomorrow."

Johnny stopped at the door, putting on his coat before leaving. Yu was beside him, putting on his coat as well. Johnny turned back to Rosie. "You can sleep well tonight. This entire episode will be behind us in a few days."

◆◆◆

Cash, Callie, and Sara were sitting on the logs around their fire, finishing the simple, delicious dinner that Callie had prepared: steaks cooked on the grill; grilled onions, mushrooms, and potatoes; even a Mexican street corn salad that she'd put together herself. When she was ready to take a break, Sara set down her plate and looked around carefully—to the south, she could see Mount Rainier, the sun reflecting on the snow, and the Cascade Range curving around behind the cityscape of Seattle rising in the east, in the distant to the west the Olympic range above the Olympic peninsula, and straight ahead, to the north, stately Bainbridge Island. "This is like a fairy tale." She declared, then added, "And eating around a fire on the beach reminds me so much of living on the boat with my mother."

"In the Mediterranean, right?"

Sara nodded to Callie. "Yes, south of France."

Cash turned to her, thoughtful. "It's a different landscape and, I'm guessing, it's another state of mind, a different sensibility than Puget Sound?"

"Yes. There were many beautiful places, but it was always different than this. I've never known anything quite like this."

"How so?"

"There's something very special about the Sound. The Mediterranean was lovely, sunny and blue. This is more mysterious. It's often so vividly green. The lush green colors are everywhere—trees in every direction, on the mountains, covering all of the islands, surrounding the shore, and of course, the dark green water. And then unexpectedly, to me, at times it turns gray. The skies grow cloudy, light gray, making the water almost black. And when you can see it, there's all of the white—on the snow on the tops of the distant mountains, on the ferry boats cruising by. And the fresh new city on the near shore. The way it all changes is very beautiful, even dreamlike."

"Very well put. For a young girl who pretended to be autistic, who didn't speak for years, you're very articulate."

"When you spend years thinking about what you want to say, but rarely saying even a little piece of it, becoming articulate happens in your head without you knowing it's happened. With my mother, I started to see, then understand that. I talked, paid attention, and little by little got the pieces in my head out of my mouth. Later, I spent my days and nights at the movies. That's how I really learned English. And also, I had an American boyfriend. Truthfully, that's where I learned to use bad language. Now, when I'm around people who I trust, people who don't scare me, I love to talk. But that rarely happens. In fact, it's exciting for me to be with you, comfortable talking. It's as though I've been waiting years—since my mother died—to really talk. Now, it just pours out."

Cash's new phone rang. It was Lincoln. Cash put him on speaker.

"They want me to meet with Lennie, their accountant and right-hand man, tomorrow morning. They're apparently wanting a cease-fire. They've suggested a public place, a small restaurant at the Pike Place Market. Samter says he can be there with two other men to ensure my safety. What do you think?"

"Take the meeting, so long as you're covered by Samter. Let's hear them out."

"We agree."

"Is Samter with you, now?"

"He is."

"Please put him on."

"Hello, my very capable international smuggler, my nefarious black marketeer."

"I can see you detective, glowering like the Terminator...Never mind...Here's what I'm thinking. I asked my friend Andre to call you. Do you remember—"

"I do remember him, fondly. I remember how he shot a man, a killer, who was planning to kill Callie. I believe he shot him off the roof—one shot—across the alley behind her restaurant."

"That's Andre—he'll soon be in Seattle with Callie's son Lew. When he calls, he'll give you a time and place where you can pick them up. He'll communicate that with a coded message that you'll recognize. The rest of this call will be nonspecific in the unlikely chance they've managed to tap the new phones already. Could you please pick them up with an escort and get them to a place we both know—the drop off for the cabin we discussed—where I can pick both of them up tonight?"

"Done."

"Thank you. I'll give Andre more details on another phone."

◆◆◆

An hour and a half later, Cash tied up the *Conqueror* at a dock at Bainbridge Island's Eagle Harbor. Samter, Andre, and Lew were there, waiting. Andre wore his signature, blousy black silk shirt. Lew was in jeans and a navy-blue crew sweater. Cash and Callie exchanged a relieved smile. Their expression communicated that Lew looked good, relaxed, given what he'd been through.

Cash and Callie had big hugs for Lew and Andre and warm thanks for Samter. Cash surprised everyone when he said "Come on board—let's spend tonight on the boat. We'll be safe there, and it's a lot more comfortable than the cabin. And most importantly, there's someone on board I'd like you to meet. Especially you, Lew."

Lew liked his mom's boyfriend, Cash, a lot, so he was interested. "How about a clue?" he asked.

"Imagine the sister you never had."

"What?…What are you talking about?" Lew made a confused face.

Callie put an arm around her son. "You know how Cash is full of surprises. Does things his own way, and truthfully, doesn't always know as much as he thinks."

Cash shook his head, grinned reluctantly, then took her hand.

Andre had a hunch. "Lew, this could be sweet. Just hang on, bud."

Cash turned to the detective. "Are you set up for the meeting in the morning?"

"It's a safe spot—They'll know we're there looking out for him. And at least this part of this cockamamie deal is normal detective work."

"Please keep me posted. And thanks, as always, for your help." Cash led Callie and the others back on the boat.

He led them to the spacious aft deck where Sara stood, looking lovely. She wore a gray pullover sweater on top of a colorful blue, yellow, and brown light summer dress. Cash put his hands on her shoulders from behind then said to Andre and Lew, "I'd like you to meet Sara, my daughter."

In the stunned silence he said to Sara. "This is Lew, Callie's son."

Lew was speechless, his eyes wide, his mouth wide open. "Hello," he finally managed. "Is this true?…Really true?" he eventually asked her earnestly, as only he could do it.

Sara smiled. "It is, Lew, though it's a long story. There's no one, however, that I'd rather tell it to."

Lew nodded. Her warm smile, her words, had won him over.

Cash turned to Andre. "And this is my old, dear friend Andre. Be careful with him, Sara. He'll be wanting to show you the tattoo on his chest."

Callie couldn't resist. "When he was tending bar for me at the restaurant, he used to open the top buttons on his silk blouse and show his bawdy tattoo to my guests. This tattoo has two naked Vietnamese women dancing, or some believe getting ready to make love, making enticing gestures. It was a crowd-pleaser at the bar, though I hated it and constantly forbid him to show it—to no avail."

Andre nodded, paying tribute to Callie with a hand gesture, fingers saluted from his temple.

Sara raised her palms. "Well, I'll look forward to seeing that tattoo."

"My pleasure." Andre bowed. "This is an unprecedented occasion, definitely a cause for celebration, for toasts." He moved to the bar.

"Allow me to make drinks for all. I don't have the ingredients for my specialties—the drinks I learned in Vientiane, Marseilles, Tangier, Port-au-Prince, and so on—but I'm sure I could manage the lovely cocktail I introduced at Callie's own restaurant—"The Bronze Pig." People came to call it "The Pig." Andre took a little sack out of his bag, which was attached to one of the ancient ivory carvings, erotic Japanese netsuke, that Cash had smuggled into Callie's restaurant a little more than three years ago.

Callie laughed out loud. "I'd love a Pig, Andre. In fact, I think all of us should toast to Cash and Sara with a 'Bronze Pig.'"

"Me, too?" Lew asked.

"Absolutely," Andre replied for Callie.

And as Sara said, "I wouldn't miss it," Andre moved behind the bar.

◆◆◆

Yu and his brother Johnny were in the back seat of the limo. The driver had closed the partition so that they would have privacy for their conversation. Yu was explaining, "Here's what I'm thinking. I'd like to present the whole plan, then I'll welcome your thoughts."

Johnny nodded. "Of course."

"Good. First, tomorrow morning, I'd like you to kidnap Will, the maître d' at the restaurant, Le Cochon Bronze, and Cesaire, the restaurant's chef. Eddie and his people will help if you need extra men. This is a distraction, a ploy, as I will explain later. Once we have these two hostages, we will be in a position of strength to negotiate a deal whereby if Sara changes her name, her identity, and leaves the country, we'll return both hostages. This should be a relatively simple deal to make. Once we've made that deal, returned the hostages, given Sara a new identity, and seen her leave with her new passport, we'll go to the Caribbean, take the cruise on your boat that you've offered to take us on so often. We're hoping that you'll join us. We'll plan on two weeks at sea. We'll make them believe that this incident is over. This is only, in fact, the end of phase one."

"I'm following, and if I'm understanding, I'm liking your plan. What's phase two and when does it begin?"

"When we've been on the boat for four or five days, and it can't be connected to us, we'll unleash the world-class contract killer, Jose. We've already contacted him to kill Sara and Cash Logan, who will surely be with her. He's one of the best in the world, and if they think they're safe, they shouldn't be hard to reach. Soon after, we'll ask Eddie and his people to kill Lincoln and Samter. Once the contract killer has eliminated Sara and Cash, we'll send him after Callie James. Within several days, all five of our problems will be solved, by different people, and untraceable to the three of us, cruising in the Caribbean." Yu nodded, finished. "Your thoughts?"

"Bravo, maestro." Johnny simply said. "One suggestion, a detail, if I may?"

"It would be welcome."

"I think it would be prudent to tell Jose that however he disposes of Sara and Cash Logan, they should not be found. Ideally, Jose can go after Callie before she knows what's happened to Sara and Cash. As such, she will not be on guard."

"You are right. That's a good modification, an improvement."

"Directly after that, Jose can make Samter disappear in Seattle while simultaneously Eddie eliminates Lincoln in LA. Again, the bodies should disappear, never to be found."

"I think that notion and that timing is excellent. The way I'm seeing it, while we're still on the boat, all five of the people we're concerned about will simply disappear. And since the only people who can connect them are the five of them, no one will be able to see the pattern. There will be different killers, in different places, while we are thousands of miles away."

◆◆◆

Callie, Andre, and Lew were on the back-deck drinking Pigs. Callie watched, pleased, as Lew and Andre got to know Sara. Cash had gone below to speak privately with someone on the phone. Sara was holding forth. "I'm feeling too good," she said, matter-of-fact. "Here I am in a new country. Some dangerous people are trying to kill me. They almost succeeded when I arrived. They've taken away my identity, my visa, my job, given them to someone else. I've been expertly erased. I'm sure they've got professionals looking for me now. I should be scared out of my mind. Instead, I'm drinking weird drinks with people I hardly know and talking nonstop."

"Your dad has this impact on me, too," Callie admitted. "It's unsettling."

"Nothing in this family is normal," Lew added. "I mean I'm the only kid I know who actually talks, even tells the truth, to his parents."

Before anyone could respond, Cash came in, raised a palm, shushed them, then changed the subject. "I was on the phone with the Macher, the second time today. I'm convinced that pretty soon, we're going to need his help. He's already sent his plane to pick us up. Sara, how'd you like to see New York City, tonight?"

"Tonight? New York City?" She raised her hands high. "Fantastic!"

"Okay. We'll leave Boeing Field in two or three hours. Callie, I hope you'll join us. Andre, will you please take charge of the boat and look after Lew? You guys can use a night off."

"My pleasure."

"Yes, please," Lew agreed. "A night off would be good."

"Sara and the Macher?" Callie smiled. "Wouldn't miss it. I'm in."

"Drop us near my truck—It's on the water in Elliott Bay," Cash explained. "I'll show you exactly where."

Callie took Sara's arm. "The Macher—his name is Itzac, or Izzie—is one of my favorite people. He's nothing but old-world charm, a soft-spoken gentleman with a startling, colorful dash of Jewish street pizazz. You're going to love him."

"I've never heard this word—Macher? What does it mean?"

Andre answered, "It's Yiddish, that's a German derived language with many elements taken from Hebrew, historically spoken by

Ashkenazi Jews. It originated in central Europe. The word, Macher, is used to describe a powerful person, a person of influence who gets things done."

Callie explained, "Our talented friend Andre is our very own linguist, in five languages that I know of." She nodded at Sara, who was wide-eyed, "No kidding. Put simply, a Macher is a big shot."

Cash chimed in, "However charming he is, Itzac is one of the largest buyers and sellers of diamonds in the world. He's a broker in the biggest, most complex, sometimes illicit, transactions. He has a large network of international—including underworld—contacts, and he's feared and admired throughout the world of international trade. Although you'd never guess it, he's 'tougher than woodpecker lips'"

"What?' Sara interrupted. "I don't know those words either— 'tougher than woodpecker lips.' What is that?"

"As tough as nails, tougher than anyone can get. A woodpecker's beak puts holes in a tree. Its head strikes with at least one thousand times the force of gravity. Any human who experienced a hundred G impact would surely die...And the Macher's even smarter than he is tough."

"I never met anyone like that."

"I hope not...Still, he's an old, dear friend, and I know he'll like you."

"You guys live in a world I've never seen, never heard about, even in movies."

"It took me a while to understand it," Callie said. "At first, I thought Cash and his friends were solely expert, hardened criminals, and they frightened me."

"I get that it's part of it, but the level of accomplishment, the quality of the relationships, the unlikely closeness, it's rare, way outside of what I know."

"You're right. Andre, the Macher, and a handful of unexpected others, will do anything for your dad. He won't talk about it unless you ask, but he earned those friendships. I'm also absolutely sure that he wants you to be part of it."

"I'm going to cry again." She took Cash's hand.

CHAPTER SEVEN

New York City

They landed at JFK at 8:30 a.m. and since they weren't scheduled to see the Macher until 11:00, Callie suggested Katz's Deli for breakfast. She proposed Katz's both because she and Cash had a colorful history there—the last time, he'd been kidnapped in front of the restaurant—but more importantly, because she knew that it would be something new, a treat, for Sara.

Katz's Deli was on the Lower Eastside. Choosing it was a tip of the hat to the Macher, who was a regular. Sara just looked around, mesmerized, like Dorothy getting her first look at Oz. Unmistakable deli smells and sounds—heavy plates with hot pastrami and corned beef, lox, gefilte fish, chopped liver with onions, knishes, and so on, hurriedly set on tables, loud, brassy, all-business waitresses, busboys clearing quickly, people clamoring at the take-out counters, or lined up to be seated—all contributed to the bustling, aromatic din that made Katz's a world unto itself.

After taking it all in, Sara turned, wide-eyed, then she actually cried out, "My God…Oh my God…I know this place." She waited impatiently, plainly excited, as they sat at a table, then burst out, "This is where they filmed the scene from *When Harry Met Sally* where Meg Ryan faked," she whispered, "*an orgasm*—no kidding—while sitting with Billy Crystal. That was right here!" She pointed. The spot was well marked now—a sign hung from the ceiling with a red arrow pointing down to the infamous table, which sat in the middle of the busy room.

"All true," Callie said.

"This is way better than seeing the Statue of Liberty…And by the way, I've never seen, or smelled, so much food in one restaurant."

A waitress approached, pad ready. "Whadda ya wanna ordah?"

"Order for us please, babe?" Callie asked. "Okay?" she asked Sara. "Deli food is about the only food that Cash knows more about than I do."

"Then yeah, sure." Sara was reading the menu. "There's enough food on this menu to eat for a year. I don't even know what most of these words are."

"I'll handle it." Cash nodded. "We'll have three lox and onion omelets, please, and we'll split two matzo ball soups then finish with the noodle pudding kugel. Oh, and three vanilla egg creams to drink."

"Vanilla egg cream?" Sara asked.

"Vanilla syrup, milk, and a spritz of Selzer. As Izzie puts it, 'Heaven on earth.'"

"So you've been here often?"

"Izzie's a regular. He taught me deli food." He raised his big palm, moving it in a gesture that included the sprawling deli, "And all about this."

"He likes you…"

"Cash saved his life." Callie said. "But that's a story for another time."

The waitress brought their matzo ball soup. Cash cut off a piece of the large matzo ball with a large soup spoon, then scooped up some broth. He handed the spoon to Sara. "It's okay to slurp."

"Not me. No way." Callie gracefully managed it. "Lovely," she exclaimed, and took another spoonful.

Cash was already working with another spoon. Callie winced at his slurping.

"I love this," Sara said, eagerly slurping. "What are matzo balls?"

"Matzo balls are Jewish soup dumplings made from a mixture of matzah meal, beaten eggs, water, and a fat such as oil, margarine, or chicken fat." Callie looked around, fondly. "I'd guess that here they use chicken fat."

"I don't think I've ever eaten Jewish food, or actually been introduced to a Jewish person."

"That's all about to change. The Macher is Jewish."

"Unmistakably Jewish," Callie added.

"Okay then. I'm excited."

Their omelets arrived, and they dug in, famished.

◆◆◆

They arrived at a warehouse in the Diamond District at 10:55 a.m. Cash paid the taxi, and then they were in the nondescript door and up the stairs to Itzac's large storage area, which included his office space.

The door was open, and Itzac was waiting warmly. He bowed to Callie, then took both of her hands and asked, "A beautiful girl like you could have any man in the world. Why are you still with the *schlemiel* who dresses like a homeless person?"

She drew him close, kissing each of his cheeks before saying, "Itzac, just seeing you and hearing your voice, takes my breath away. And as to your question, I love the homeless schlemiel more every day. I didn't know that kind of love was even possible."

Itzac smiled. "You deserve that, and he's perhaps the luckiest man in the world." He turned to Sara. "Please forgive my slowness in introducing myself."

Callie jumped in, "Please allow me to present this exceptional young woman to you." She took Sara's hand and brought her closer. Sara was taller than Itzac. "Her name is Sara Cambert, and please bear with me until we tell you the whole story...For now, what we've just learned... proof positive... She's Cash's daughter."

The Macher turned to Cash, raised both hands in the air. "Mazel tov! Bravo!...This is wonderful." He turned back. "Sara, young lady, he will be a splendid father."

"He already is." She put out her hand. "Pleased to meet you."

"I can see that already you have brought great happiness." Itzac took her hand with both of his, shaking warmly, then he kissed the back of her hand. He raised his head, "It is my honor to meet you."

Cash put a big hand on his friend's shoulder. Izzie, the Macher, was five foot three, bald and wiry. He was eighty-one. He wore a stunning Kiton gray two-button Vicuna sport coat over a black lightweight turtleneck, with black slacks and Italian black leather shoes. It was 11:00 a.m., and they were at his office—a small room in the back of a warehouse in the diamond district. In the warehouse, containers were stacked floor to ceiling. Izzie took Cash's big hand in both of his little ones, looked up at him. "I am happy for you, *boychik*...In spite of your many shortcomings, you're a fine man, a good friend, and you have earned this great good fortune."

Seattle

While Cash, Callie, and Sara were with the Macher, Johnny and his brother-in-law, Eddie, visited Will, Callie's maître d' and Cesaire, her chef. When Will opened his apartment, expecting to receive a package, Johnny and Eddie entered forcibly wearing masks and showing guns. Within five minutes, Will was bound, gagged and locked in the trunk of their rental car. They went from there to a small house on Capitol Hill that they'd rented. There, they locked Will in the basement, where he was chained to a ring they'd anchored on the wall. His mouth was covered with duct tape.

Their next stop was in Cesaire's Belltown apartment. He, too, opened his door for his package, and thirty minutes later, he was chained against the wall opposite Will. Cesaire was also gagged with duct tape across his mouth.

First, Johnny called Lennie, who was on his way to meet Lincoln at a well-known coffee shop near the Pike Place Market, the Seattle Coffee Works on Pike Street. When Lennie picked up Johnny simply said, "Mission accomplished." Then he hung up.

Next, Johnny called Yu who was with Rosie, having coffee on the veranda. Yu saw the number and picked up the phone. "I'm curious about your morning," he said to Johnny.

"Mission accomplished," Johnny said, and hung up.

Yu hung up the phone, turned to Rosie, "Johnny, as always, brought us good news."

"It's about fucking time we caught a break." Rosie took a slow breath, took her husband's hand. "Let's take charge of this. No one is better at that than you."

"Lennie is meeting soon with the policeman, Sergeant Lincoln. The course, indeed the nature, of our relationship with these people will turn in our favor momentarily."

◆◆◆

Lincoln was sitting at a table in the Seattle Coffee Works on Pike Street, listening to Lennie. He could see Samter, standing by the door and two uniformed Seattle Policemen sitting at separate tables nearby. Lennie sat on a bench he'd brought over because the small chairs were uncomfortable, even unsafe for his width and weight. He held forth, "There's clearly been a miscommunication, an unfortunate misunderstanding. As such, we'd like to reconsider. We'll discuss a temporary cease-fire, a truce. Let's put aside our differences. Between us, privately, if we can agree, we can put this misunderstanding behind us. Suppose Sara Cambert changes her name and identity, then leaves the country. Under her new identity, she will be wanted in the US. This is our way of ensuring that she won't come back. You're free to choose a country that won't extradite her, so she will be safe from prison in the United States. If she does that, our misunderstanding is over. We can go our separate ways."

Lincoln nodded. "A cease-fire, a truce, is in both of our interests. But why would Sara ever consider changing her name and leaving the country as a wanted criminal?"

"I can help you answer those questions. Call your colleague Callie James, and ask her to talk to her maître d', Will, and her chef, Cesaire. She will not be able to reach either of them. If that answers your question, and you'd like to pursue our suggestion, please call me, and we can set a time later today or tomorrow to continue our conversation. At that time, I will give you a more detailed offer, with all of the specifics, including her new identity."

"I'll let you know either way, today," Lincoln got up and left the coffee shop, without another word.

New York City

Sara was finishing an abbreviated story of her history, focusing on the woman who met her at the Seattle airport then tried to kill her on the boat. The Macher was listening with his undivided attention, laser focused, as only he could do it.

When Sara stopped, sitting back in her chair, the Macher turned to her. "You are smart, capable, resourceful, and very lucky, clearly Cash's daughter. You're only alive because of all of those things. If you are right that Yu Shin Shi and Fanny Rose are behind this, you are facing formidable adversaries."

Cash's phone rang. He picked it up, said "It's Lincoln, he wants to talk with you Callie. Can I put him on speaker?"

Callie nodded, plainly nervous. "Go ahead Lincoln," she said.

"Before I report on their proposal, they told me to ask you, Callie, to try and reach Will, your maître d', and Cesaire, your chef. I'm sure they've both been kidnapped, but you should try and reach them, in case it's a bluff, right away."

Callie took out her own phone and tried calling both of them. She was upset, fighting back tears, when she turned back to the others. "I called both of them on the private lines that we set up specifically for me. I'm able to page them from those lines, so give them a few minutes."

Cash took her hand, then said to Lincoln, "We're giving them a few minutes to call back, but I think it's safe to assume that they have them. For what it's worth, I don't think they'll hurt them, they're likely bargaining chips in whatever deal they hope to make. So what do they want?"

"They want to give Sara a new identity, then have her leave the country. Her new identity will be wanted by the police and the FBI, for serious criminal charges, so she can't come back."

"And that means going to a country that won't extradite, so Sara, with her new identity, can't be sent back?"

"That's my guess. They've promised if Sara does this, they'll leave her alone. They will go to sea for several weeks, cruising in the Caribbean, and they never have any intention of finding her again. His phrase was 'We can go our separate ways.'"

Cash looked at Sara. "If this is true, whatever we do, Sara, you have to agree."

"You know how I feel about leaving, but I will leave if it saves your friends."

Callie checked her phone. "No messages. That's never happened since we set up this system. Let's proceed on the assumption that they have them."

Cash spoke, "I agree. Sara, we'll come back to you. Okay?"

Sara nodded.

"Lincoln, my very good friend Itzac, also known as the Macher, is with us. He's more experienced at this than any of us. Given the new situation, I'd like to ask his opinion."

"Of course."

"Itzac, Lincoln is a trusted friend. You can be candid with him. He's also an accomplished police sergeant, so discretion in certain matters is appreciated by him. Put simply, there are some things he'd rather not know about."

"Very well." Itzac steepled his fingers. "Unfortunately, you have no choice. Unless Sara refuses, you should agree to their demands and get your friends back. I agree with Cash, if you do what they ask, they'll let your friends go. But make no mistake. Sooner or later, wherever she is, they'll try to kill Sara. We have to figure out how we can keep that from happening."

"Yes, I agree," Cash said. "And we will. To begin, let's choose a safe place for Sara to go. Itzac, you should think about that." He put up a well-worn hand. "But first, Lincoln, could you please tell your contact that you'll meet with him again today to negotiate terms. Several conditions:

First, we must be free to choose the country she goes to. Second, Will and Cesaire must be released safely before Sara leaves the country with me. We'll provide proof that will satisfy them, when we know where she's going. We'll work that out. Finally, tell them that we'll want reassurances about her safety. This will mean nothing, but it's important that we ask so that they believe we think this deal will hold."

"They'll want to know where she's going."

"We can give them that information when we know. Even if we refused, or lied, they'd be able to track her from her new identity."

"I'll call their man now. Set up a meeting today."

Callie joined in. "Please make it clear that we will go to war if anything happens to Will or Cesaire. Anything at all."

"I will. I'll also fill in Samter. He'll want to cover me at the meeting. I'll call you after. Before I make this call, I'd like your agreement, Sara, to this course of action."

"Thank you for asking, but this is, as you Americans say, 'a no brainer.' Let's figure out where I should go, and how we can keep me from getting killed after I get there."

"Okay, I'll sign off and call you later. You can figure that the meeting will be at the same place an hour and a half from now, that's one fifteen my time, four fifteen your time, unless you hear from me otherwise." Lincoln broke the connection.

Itzac spoke up. "I have some ideas about where to go and how to protect you once you get there. I'm going to recommend Cuba. I know reliable people in powerful positions there. It's also close, and I can ensure that Sara won't be extradited. Finally, I have a notion about what we can offer the Cubans to get their full attention on protecting Sara and eventually getting her identity back. But first, I have some research to do. In the meantime, I think we should wait on the results of this meeting."

"Okay, let's reconvene as soon as we hear from Lincoln. Why don't you plan on joining us sometime after four thirty p.m. In the meantime, Sara and Callie, can I take you to Cipriani Dolci, one of my favorite restaurants in Grand Central, for a late lunch. Cipriani sits two levels above The Saloon at the Oyster Bar, my first real date with Callie. We can stop by the Saloon if we're still waiting after, for a quick drink."

Callie looked at him. "You sentimental fellow. You're taking your daughter to the place where we had our first real kiss!"

"Wow." Sara was excited, "I do want to see that. *Cash and Callie discover true love!* That's right up there with *When Harry Met Sally.* Callie, I'm imagining your version—"

"Sara, stop right there. Don't even think about it. Not one more word." And an afterthought, "You've got your dad's distinctive, unconventional sense of humor. And his abiding joy in suggesting inappropriate shenanigans."

"Please give me an example of my dad doing that? Just a taste, what's your word—a nibble?" Sara asked, plainly interested in this. "I mean you may be right about me, but it never occurred to me that I might have gotten some of my ill-chosen, off-color humor from my dad."

"Okay, you asked for it…Before I was with him, your dad brought his twenty-three-year-old French girlfriend, Justine, to dinner at my restaurant. He'd picked her up while he was working at my bar. I'd told him at once to leave her alone, that this was an upscale French restaurant, not some May-December dating site. He sighed, a twinkle in his eye, then explained, 'I can't help it if your fancy French clientele finds me attractive.' And, of course, he ignored me. So, when he brought her to the restaurant, I reluctantly, but politely, came to their table after dinner and asked how she'd enjoyed her meal. Justine complimented me and the restaurant in French, then she surprisingly asked, 'Why is it that you disapprove of me dating this man'?"

"I replied honestly, 'He's the bartender here, and he's old enough to be your father.' Justine answered, coldly, 'Ma chère madame, he's also one of the most interesting and thoughtful men I've ever met. And how dare you judge him or me for our sexual preferences?' I was speechless. Then, and I'm not making this up, she turned to your dad, batted her eyelashes and smiling a coy, little-girl smile, asked, 'Can we have dessert…pretty please, Daddy?'"

"I blushed, mortified, spots the color of beet-borscht appeared on my cheeks. Your dad thought Justine's quip was funny. He actually laughed."

"It is really funny, Callie. You have to admit." Sara was smiling now.

Cash took her hand, trying to keep a straight face. Before long, they were grinning, then laughing together.

Callie looked at both of them, then again. Eventually she offered, loudly, "Okay, I may be old-fashioned, prim, even puritanical, but I am not ever, ever, going to fake an orgasm, like Meg Ryan did, at a restaurant. Never. Period!" Callie's face tensed. She looked like she couldn't decide if she was going to scream or cry.

Sara suppressed a smile, making an effort. "I understand," she said, then looked at Callie, serious. "I admire you Callie. You're honest and unafraid, and by the way, I wouldn't fake an orgasm at a restaurant either. Never! No way!…Truthfully, this is my inexperienced, obviously clumsy way of having fun with people I'm becoming comfortable with, a thing I haven't felt since my mother died."

Callie started to cry, little wet tears of relief, then she took their outstretched hands and began laughing with them through her tears.

◆◆◆

Cipriani Dolci is in Grand Central terminal. It is located on the West Balcony level overlooking the beautiful Main Concourse. Cash had called to request a table right at the balcony. From their table, they could look down on hundreds of people hurrying to catch trains or simply strolling through Grand Central's main concourse. Sara was mesmerized. She thought that this was one of the most spectacular buildings she'd ever been in. She especially loved the Station's Celestial twelve story ceiling, painted with 2,500 stars and zodiac constellations, and the giant windows straight ahead across the concourse. She looked around the restaurant—the simple, stylish tables and leather chairs, the marble floors out on the balcony, the light-wood floors in the main area above, the long light-wood, blond-colored bar against the wall.

Everything was carefully, tastefully done. Never too much. Never not quite enough. It was an oasis of comfortable, calm, elegance in the chaotic, tumultuous train station.

Sara made a tip of her hat gesture to Callie and Cash. "I love this place, and I love seeing it for the first time with both of you. I can't really explain it, but a place like this simply takes my breath away. I know there's great danger, and lots of things we have to sort out, but could I please have a few minutes to take it all in?"

"Of course," Cash said. "May I order for you? The pasta, the risotto, the veal piccata are all excellent. I especially like the free-range grilled chicken."

"Please choose your favorite pasta. Callie, make sure you agree. I may have my dad's sense of humor, but I'd rather rely on you for food choices, outside of the deli. Don't ask me how I know this, but I just do. No kidding." Then to Cash. "No offense."

"No one will ever accuse you of not saying what you think, child," Cash replied. "No offense, taken. Likely a smart decision." The phone rang, Cash picked it up. "It's the Macher," he said to the others. "No word yet from Lincoln…We'll meet you downstairs, in the Saloon. Thirty minutes, say five fifteen."

◆◆◆

The sun was directly above the pool when Yu found Rosie at the four-foot marker, sun-bathing on her clear plastic raft. The raft was oversized, especially designed to hold snacks, beverages, and reading materials. Today, Rosie was lying on her stomach, reading her law firm's quarterly financial statement and nursing an egg-enriched butter pecan milkshake. Yu came out feeling good, pleased earlier by Lennie's report of his first meeting with Lincoln, and now, satisfied further with Lennie's report of the follow-up meeting. In short, they'd come to terms on their proposal.

He watched her now and smiled. She was his great good fortune, the love of his life. Yu gently called her, "My angel, I'm sorry to disturb your rest, but I had good news from Lennie. It looks like Sara Cambert and her people have accepted our offer."

Rosie turned, smiling at Yu from the pool. "Is it locked?"

"Lennie thinks so. We promised to send the new identity right away. After she has her new identity, as soon as they get their friends back, she'll leave the country. They've agreed to let one of our people watch the girl and Cash get on the plane. If they leave illegally, they'll provide proof that we'll accept, whenever, wherever they arrive. They also want assurances that Sara won't be harmed later. I had Lennie tell them that we'll be at sea for several weeks, cruising in the Caribbean, and we have no intention of trying to find her again. Lennie said they'll agree to that."

"Is Jose ready to go?"

"I told him we'll get him started when we're on our Caribbean cruise. I'll give him the location as soon as she gives it to us. I told him we'd provide technical help if he needs any kind of travel permits or documents. He's top dollar, $250,000, but he'll get the job done."

"Excellent. This is money well spent if it puts this nightmare behind us. Tell Jose I owe him a favor. He'll know what that means and what it's worth."

"I already did. He's standing by…Now, have you thought about the new identity for this young lady?"

"Yes, I have an idea about that. It's a nice touch, you'll appreciate it, and most of the work is done."

"Go on."

"A little over a year ago, we did a favor for Johnny's brother-in-law, Eddie. Eddie had a niece in Florida, who was the principal in a massive real estate fraud scheme. She and her husband were targeting immigrants, luring them to invest in real estate that they didn't own. They also resold land that had been previously sold without the knowledge or consent of the owners. They created approximately a dozen Florida corporations that issued fraudulent deeds and other documents to investors and buyers. Long story short, they amassed over $7 million, and they needed new identities to disappear. Lennie put Eddie in touch with a guy who would sell new passports, new names, and new documents for $100,000 per person. It was low cost, just average work, but good enough to get them out of the country, and they left to someplace in South America. Soon after, warrants were issued for both of them, but they were long gone.

I called Eddie yesterday, and as I suspected, he was able to buy back his niece's identity. Her name is Ellen Laslow, and she's twenty-eight years old. She'd be a good fit for Sara Cambert, and she's on the FBI's Wanted List so she won't be able to come back. Eddie's sending someone with Ellen Laslow's passport, driver's license, social security card, etcetera today. I think it could work."

"Well done. Have Lennie communicate the information to Sergeant Lincoln. We'll get her the documents when they tell us where she's going and when. We should be able to begin our cruise in two or three days. I'll have Johnny set it up, my dear. This unfortunate episode will soon be over, an inexplicable footnote."

Rosie turned on her raft. "Footnote my ass. Make it an inexplicable, nasty stain. I hate these people."

Chapter Eight

New York City

The Saloon of the Oyster Bar is in the lower level of Grand Central Station. Sara was paying close attention as they led her downstairs. She looked carefully then announced, excited, "Unbelievable! This is the place where Otis goes down to Lex Luther's lair in the 1978 *Superman*."

"Sara, how did you know that?" Callie asked. "I didn't know that."

"Great movie. I saw it maybe three times. No kidding."

"That's my girl." Cash put his arm around her.

At the lower level, Callie introduced the restaurant to Sara. You had to know how to find it. First you look for the six metal-framed glass doors under the marble arch at the bottom of the ramp on the Vanderbilt side, opposite the train tracks. In the arch itself, bold brown letters spell out OYSTER BAR RESTAURANT. All six doors open into the sizable restaurant. In the older, north side of the restaurant, people sit at serpentine white counters eating every known variety of seafood. The new bar sits in the middle, and to the south, there are scores of square tables with checkered tablecloths. The Oyster Bar Restaurant, which first opened in 1913, is a vast, lively room that is often crowded and always, always smells like fish. Its best feature—the beautiful vaulted ceilings—are covered with Guastavivo terracotta tiles set in a herringbone pattern. Once inside, you have to turn north and hike to the right rear corner of the large, fish-scented space to find the simple wood swinging saloon door. Cash bowed, extended a long arm, and ushered Sara into the Saloon.

Sara flashed an enthusiastic smile when she stepped inside the tavern—red and white checkered tablecloths; warm, dark wood; chairs trimmed with rustic brass nail heads. To her right, a handsome, winding mahogany bar made an L along the north and east sides of the restaurant. Models and photos of sailing ships hung from the walls. Cash found four seats at the bar in the far-right corner—under the mounted tarpon at the very top of the L—and ordered three Bombay Blue Sapphire Gin Martinis, extra dry, with olives. The Martinis arrived, each one with an extra inch of a refill in a glass tumbler. "The angel's share," Cash explained. Cash picked up his phone. It was Lincoln. He stepped back away from the bar into an alcove for privacy.

Sara saw the Macher first. He was moving purposely toward their corner. They'd saved the fourth chair for him, and Sara pulled it out beside her. Itzac took a moment before sitting down to bow, to kiss the back of Callie's hand, and then, after getting her permission, to kiss Sara's cheek. He took Cash's Martini as if it had been ordered for him, then raised his glass to "the two beautiful women beside me."

Cash reappeared from the alcove, took one look at the Macher drinking his martini, signaled the bartender to order another, and started right in. "That was Lincoln. We have a deal. Sara, you will get your new identity, including documents, passport, and a brief historical summary. They just called Lincoln to give him the basics. Her name is Ellen Laslow. She's twenty-eight years old. Lincoln did some homework on her—she's wanted by the FBI for a massive real estate fraud scheme in Florida. She got away with about $7 million. You will have her name, passport, etc. But once you get to wherever you'll be going, you won't be able to return until we can get your true identity back. Itzac, does this change your thinking about where she should go?"

"On the contrary, it confirms it. First, Cuba is easy to get to. We can smuggle you in on a boat. I've spoken to my man in Cuba, and they'll receive you, take care of your documents, and look after you until we sort this out. If Yu and Rosie will be cruising in the Caribbean, that will also be in our favor, but more about that later. One of the things I looked into was the Cuban investigator who was killed. Let's get Lincoln on the phone to go over what he knows."

Cash called him. "Lincoln, Itzac is here with us. He's recommending Cuba for Sara. We're at the very beginning of this, but if you could tell us what you learned from their investigator, it might help us get to the next steps."

"The Cuban investigator, Duardo, was looking for very large sums of missing money, maybe $75 million. What he told me was that Javi Garcia, a senior Cuban military officer put together a deal involving Belarus and North Korea. Cuba traded $35 million worth of cigars and $25 million of blood diamonds to Belarus in exchange for missiles. The Cubans then flipped those missiles to North Korea for $75 million. Presumably, the missiles were a little more sophisticated than what North Korea already has and would be good both to add to the arsenal and reverse-engineer for research. The Cubans are livid, crazy upset, because after Javi closed the deal, he unexpectedly disappeared with the money from the North Korean sale. Duardo believed that Rosie and Yu gave Javi a new identity and helped launder his cash. Duardo had reason to believe that Javi wound up in Mexico City."

Itzac took over. "That's exactly what I needed. Javi is precisely what we can deliver to the Cubans to motivate them to protect Sara then get her identity back. We'll come back to that later. Here's what I'm doing to protect Sara independently. First, I've discretely reached out to my most trusted people to find out if any high-level professional has a contract on Sara. There are a limited number of people that Rosie and Yu would trust with something like that, and we know who they are. Sergeant Lincoln, I think that it's best if you sign off before I explain the rest."

"Yes, I was going to suggest that. Just let me know if you need more from me and if there are things that I can do legally."

Cash answered, "Thank you, Lincoln—You've already been a great help. I'll keep you informed as it's appropriate. Itzac, it's your show."

"Okay. Our ultimate goal has to be to deliver Rosie and Yu to Cuba. If we can do that, the Cuban government can lean on them to find Javi—and whatever of the Cubans' money he hasn't already spent. It's a straightforward deal—They help the Cubans catch Javi and the money, and they restore Sara's identity. They, in turn, get a lesser punishment than life in prison or being executed. The problem is to get them to Cuba."

"What are you thinking?" Cash asked. His expression made clear that the Macher had an idea.

"It's bold, and not fully formed, but since they'll be cruising in the Caribbean, I propose that we hijack them with a ruse, that is to say, before they actually realize what we're doing. Let me elaborate. First, we recruit a band of pirates—I have an excellent group in mind. They'll be posing as a Haitian coast guard crew, patrolling on an old Haitian coast guard ship that we obtain and outfit to look convincing. We'll have them hail Rosie and Yu's yacht over the radio, saying that they're looking for a potentially dangerous fugitive and they'll need to board right away. Once on board, they'll unexpectedly show their weapons and take over, put simply, kidnap them. Our pirates will deliver them to Cuba. The Cubans will love that. Once we deliver Rosie and Yu to Cuba, the Cuban government can lean on them, negotiate with their lives, to find Javi—and whatever of the Cuban's money he hasn't already spent, and return Sara's old identity."

Cash raised his thumb. "Good, very good...I'm confident that we can recruit good Haitian crew members, create a workable old coast guard vessel, and more difficult, but still possible, stop the contract killer from going after Sara."

"Time is of the essence. I have to learn if there is such a person, and contact the professional if he is, in fact, contracted to kill Sara. I'm guessing I can persuade him to slow it down until we have Rosie and Yu, then I'll pay him the rest of his fee to walk away."

Cailie let loose an uncharacteristic, sharp whistle, then added, "I never swear, but I'm forced to say—Well goddamn done! You guys never let me down. This is so audacious, so unlikely, so inconceivable that it just might actually work."

Cash nodded agreement "It's risky and will require careful planning and considerable work. I, for one, think it's our best shot. For me, the goal has always been to give Sara her life back. That's worth taking a risk. Let's get started. Itzac, you're in charge."

"Let's begin by recruiting our crew. I've always imagined that you and Andre will be our pirate captains. You'll be traveling with our Haitian coast guard crew. You will be a high-level Royal Bahamas Defense Force on a joint operation, who need Haitian coast guard help to capture a fugitive who has fled to Haiti. With Andre's help, I have recruited five other men, all of them Haitian, four of them with actual Haitian coast guard experience, who I would trust completely to join you. I've taken the liberty of asking all of them to call in tonight."

Itzac went on, "I talked earlier with Andre, and he's already acquiring the boat. His friend located a suitable boat in Miragoâne, a town on Haiti's western coast. It's a major port for the trade in used and stolen goods, known as a 'pirate's paradise.' He found and acquired a Cape Light, a boat used, among other things, by the Canadian coast guard. Interestingly, Canada has donated Cape Light boats to the Haitian coast guard in the past, so once properly adjusted, this boat should fit right in. Andre's friend has brought it to the boat house in Port-au-Prince, so with any luck, we can have it properly set up within a week. We'll also need to camouflage it so it's not recognizable as a coast guard boat until we need it to be."

"Good." Cash nodded. "Being caught masquerading as a coast guard vessel is no joke, so Haiti is a good choice, we won't have to travel far, and being able to disguise it until it's needed is an excellent idea. I'll be traveling with Sara to Cuba, so when we're ready, I can easily meet the boat at Port-au-Prince. Lincoln said he thought that they'd be cruising south from Miami into the Caribbean. We need to confirm that, and we still need to know their itinerary. Any ideas on that?"

"I've had my best technician place high-level hacks on Johnny's, Rosie's, and Yu's phones, as well as Lennie's. It's Johnny's boat, and I'm sure he'll send out their itinerary before they leave. We'll get it from that or sooner if he files it as he should in Miami, before they leave."

Callie added, "I'll go to Haiti to help Andre with the boat as soon as you, Cash, and Sara, go to Cuba. I want to be on that boat when we deliver these bastards to Cuba."

Sara raised her martini. "This is—I dunno…Way better than the best movie I ever saw. You all leave me speechless, and breathless… Truthfully, you make my well-worn, troubled heart soar."

◆◆◆

Lincoln sat down for the third time that same day with Lennie. They were at their table at the Seattle Coffee Works. It was 7:00 p.m. PST.

Lincoln began, "Sara will be leaving to live in Cuba. She'll leave soon after she gets her proper documents. Because of the identity you've given her, she's not planning to take an airplane. She will, however, send you a picture when she's safely in Cuba. You should specify where she should take the photo and where to send it."

Lennie nodded. "That should be fine. I'll give you the specifics of the photo tonight." He handed a large envelope to Lincoln. "Here are all of the documents we discussed for her new identity and her new passport."

Lincoln looked at each document carefully. There was a driver's license, a social security number, a birth certificate, a written history, and more. Most importantly, Lincoln focused on her passport. It was a recent picture, except her name and specifics were for Ellen Laslow. Lincoln had to admit that they did good work. He wasn't surprised. "We should be ready to go in two days. They will not leave until Will and Cesaire are released safely."

"Your people will be delivered to the restaurant when we have your destination, confirmed departure, and timing of the approved photo."

"You will have that tonight."

"My principals will plan to leave on their cruise tomorrow. We want to confirm that we'll go our separate ways thereafter."

"Of course."

◆◆◆

It was 10:30 p.m. ET and Cash, Callie, and Sara were all at Itzac's stunning loft apartment, a two-story penthouse on the twentieth floor of an old West Greenwich Village building. Andre and the Haitian coast guard crew had all called in. After sorting through plans to get whatever gear they'd need, and going over their schedule, they signed off. Lincoln had called, and he was flying in tonight on Itzac's plane to bring Sara's new passport and documents. He'd delivered to Lennie all that they needed to release Will and Cesaire.

Cash had spoken with Andre who had a good Cuban friend with a fast boat, who had done this trip often, and he would take them from Miami to Cuba tomorrow night. Itzac had spoken to one of his Cuban contacts who had told them where to land in Cuba. He'd also agreed to be there when they arrived and prearrange their paperwork. He reiterated that Sara was most welcome in Cuba.

Lastly, and vitally important, Will and Cesaire had just called Callie from the restaurant to report that they were safe and unharmed. Callie had been hugely relieved.

◆◆◆

Though no one could have told you exactly how it happened, now that their work for tonight was done, Itzac was playing the piano, accompanying Cash and Sara who were improvising a rendition of a song, actually singing Willie Nelson's version of "Crazy."

Sara and Cash had somehow worked it out, and they sang surprisingly well together. It was as if they'd done this before. Callie was beyond being surprised by how naturally these two people communicated so easily without even talking. She smiled at Itzac, who nodded, feeling the same way. It was a brief respite, a moment of joyfulness, genuine sweetness, amidst the deadly gamble they'd entered into.

When the song was over, both Callie and Itzac clapped loudly, celebrating this little moment of father and daughter finding something in common that they'd each come to love separately, then making a connection, unexpectedly, when finding each other after so many years.

They all sat around Itzac's antique French country coffee table. When Sara asked about it, Itzac explained that it was from Arles, France circa 1890. When, without hesitation, or even a touch of embarrassment, she asked what "circa" meant, Itzac apologized and said it meant "around that time." Sara went on to say that what she especially liked about his coffee table was the color and texture of the solid cherry wood.

Looking out the vast windows to the west, they could see the Hudson River. They were quiet, pensive, when Sara finally broke the silence, "I need some help," she explained.

"How so?" Cash asked, simply.

"Well, I'm going back and forth—feeling at one moment like I'm in some wonderful dream, then the next, I'm suddenly scared, terrified actually—a thing that hasn't ever happened quite like this for me."

"How could you not be terrified?" Callie asked. "Think about what you've been through in the last—what is it?—just four days since we met you, maybe another week before you found us? And think about what's coming up for you in the next two days."

Cash underlined that. "San Juan Islands, Seattle, New York City, tomorrow Miami, and then a boat ride, in the dead of night, to Cuba? On top of that, you just met your dad and already you're singing 'Crazy' with him. It is like a dream."

Itzac took her hand. "Child, you're brave, smart, and articulate, an absolute pleasure to be around. All of us already admire you...The one thing I've been genuinely worried about is that you haven't been more visibly afraid, even overwhelmed, not to mention totally terrified. I'm sure you're regularly holding back, suppressing those feelings. It's certainly better for you to acknowledge them, share them with us, your friends, learn to ride them out. Powerful, smart people are trying to kill you. It's okay to be mortified, heart-achingly scared, insistent about developing strategies to manage that."

Sara put his hand to her cheek. "My dear new friend. My entire life, except for my young teenaged years with my mom, I've been on my own, suppressing all of my fears, certain that something terrible is about to happen. Imagine a child in an orphanage pretending to be autistic, biting off my own fingers, finally escaping and living on my own at ten years old. I've never been able to allow myself to experience fear. I made it my archenemy. My nemesis."

"I understand why you did that." Itzac nodded. "But you've paid a high price for it. An important part of your emotional life is not even accessible to you."

"Accessibility isn't always so good. Now, just when I have true, very able friends helping me, the terror is breaking through my carefully constructed barriers. Truthfully, the thing that scares me the most, the idea that I can't bear, is that somehow my dad will be hurt or killed."

"Sara, that's part of loving someone. If you didn't worry about that, you wouldn't be able to feel the depth, the intensity of that feeling. I lost my wife—she had a heart attack five years ago. At some moment on many of the days she was alive, I worried that she'd get sick, have an awful accident, that one of my enemies would hurt her, and so on. But we had forty-seven unforgettable years. Years that wouldn't have had the depth, the resonance, the heart-warming love that we felt if I hadn't allowed the fear, the worry, even the irrational dark foreboding, to be part of the fabric of my emotional life, and then of our emotional life together. I think that since your mother died, you haven't had people like that to love, and now that you do, and now that there's real-life threatening danger at the same time, it's hard for you to tolerate those powerful, contradictory feelings coexisting."

Callie made a bemused face at Itzac, then said, "Itzac is one of the largest buyers and sellers of diamonds in the world. He's a broker in the biggest, most complex, sometimes illicit, transactions. He has a vast network of international—including underworld—contacts, and he's feared and admired throughout the world of international trade. He's also the only man I know who could come up with an idea like turning us into contemporary pirates, and then convince us to hijack a luxury yacht. Unbeknownst to me, this same man is also a psychoanalyst...this very same man, a psychoanalyst?...Unbelievable!"

"What's a psychoanalyst?" Sara asked. "Is it like a psychologist or a psychiatrist? I never heard of that word."

Cash was laughing, grinning wide. "Yes Sara, a psychoanalyst is a specially trained therapist. They're trained to understand and interpret complex, often contradictory, emotions to treat disorders or to simply help someone be more aware of their inner life, the emotional forces, often unconscious, that affect them. They work with patients to use that awareness, that understanding, to positively influence their decisions. I only know about this from Itzac, who has tried at length on long plane rides, to make me more like that, that is to say more conscious of my feelings. I'm hopelessly inept at it, but he hasn't given up. What I did learn is that Itzac has an analyst's way of approaching knotty things. He thinks clearly, but equally important, perceptively, about surprising options to resolving hard problems."

"What does that mean?"

"To explain properly," Itzac nodded. "I have to go back fifty years when I was thirty-one years old. That's when I began my psychoanalysis— on the couch, five, then four times a week, for four and a half years. No kidding. It's when I started to work on, then to slowly learn, how to solve problems imaginatively, unexpectedly. To do that, first, I had to work out what mattered most to me, and at the same time, what I could do without. I also had to learn to walk away from things that were unrealistic for me, that I simply couldn't do. Eventually, with that understanding, with those parameters, I learned to assess complicated issues in my own creative way."

"I don't understand the last part of that. What does it mean to assess complicated issues in your own creative ways? How do you do that?" Sara wanted to know.

"It starts by being able to identify, then separate, real needs from imagined needs, things that might not be so important. Sort them out, then decide for yourself what you really care about most. For example, I learned that having high status in the conventional business community was for me, an imagined need, not a real one. By contrast, I knew that

I wanted to be able to make hard, big-stake decisions with serious consequences. And to do that, I'd need to evaluate risk in particular ways, ways that allowed me to take outsized risks, but only for what I cared most about. Being able to take oversized risks, often stepping outside the law, when it really mattered, was a real need."

"Such as?"

"Like capturing, then trading, a pair of identity thieves and expert money launderers for the greatest Cuban criminal mastermind of his time. To kidnap Rosie and Yu, to make them find and deliver Cuban's very own Lex Luther, Javi Garcia, a man who stole $75 million. And to find and return that stolen money. We decided to take those risks with one purpose: to get back the stolen identity of a certain lovely young woman, to give her the chance to live a life free of overwhelming fear. To allow her to be able to go forward wherever she chooses, however she decides, and never have to look over her shoulder for fear of her life."

Sara took Itzac's hands. "A psychoanalyst, an ingenious, thoughtful advisor, a stirring poet, and though unconventional, a true friend."

Itzac kissed her hand.

Callie smiled wide. "What Sara said is right to the point." She turned to Itzac. "You absolutely do things in your own thoughtful, carefully considered way. I remember how you helped me when I kidnapped a woman to trade her for Cash's life, and how we both knew that it was worth the risks. And now, I mean we could all go to jail for masquerading as part of the Haitian coast guard."

"That's precisely what Itzac, rightfully called the Macher, taught me," Cash explained. "By his example, he showed me that there are simply some things that are worth risking everything for. Sara, you're one of those things."

"How did that possibly happen?"

"It happened because of who you are. Though you didn't know this at the time, your whole life you've made brave, difficult decisions, chosen your own special, unique direction."

"I'm still deathly afraid that some or all of the three of you will be badly hurt, or even killed. I'm especially worried about losing you, my dad."

"I don't think you're going to lose me. We'll all work hard to keep that from happening. But as hard as we try, there will be some risk. I agree with Itzac though. I think you can live with that risk, learn to tolerate it."

"I'm not sure if I can do that. I certainly don't know how to do it."

Callie jumped in. "Do it day by day, one step at a time. When I first knew your dad, I rarely came out of my restaurant. Truthfully, it scared me. Now, I'm ready to go to Haiti, masquerade as a Bahamian military officer and hijack a yacht to Cuba."

Itzac added, "One of the things I learned over the years is that you can change your direction almost anytime. To do that, though, you have to be discerning, insightful, as much as possible, you're trying to capture, actually figure out, the entire big picture. It helps to let all of your feelings in, the good and the bad, and then reassess as the situation changes. Keeping the frightening stuff out will make that much harder. Let it in, assess and measure it as best you can, and rethink your plans as needed."

"Try it Sara," Callie suggested. "Talk with any of us if it gets too hard...I know that you can do this."

Cash took her hand. "We have a long difficult task ahead of us, and there are many things that can, and likely will, go wrong. Don't deny that, but at the same time, let's also dwell on what we can all give each other—that includes Callie, Lew, Itzac, and Andre—in our little family. I think finally having that is worth taking these considerable risks."

"You are all so far ahead of me. And truthfully, as much as I love what all of you have said, as much as I believe you understand things that I still have to learn, I'm sure I can't do what you're asking easily, or soon. Please bear with me, as this is going to be long and difficult for me. Suppressing the fear, the frightening news, has become a way of life."

"Fair enough. I'll do what I can to help you. What I know we can do is talk about what you're afraid of. You'll be surprised how this will become easier for you."

"I hope that's true, and I'll do my best. But there is one promise I can make to you right now, it's one that I can make confidently... You see, what I do know, absolutely, is that I will do everything in my power to keep you safe. You can rely on that."

"I already do."

♦♦♦

Rosie and Yu were in their kitchen, listening to Lennie, who was on the speakerphone, "I just got off the phone with Sergeant Lincoln. All is well. They're going to send a picture of her in Havana, the day after they arrive. They should be there early tomorrow morning. I suggested she stand in front of La Plaza de la Revolución, with the image of Che Guevara behind her. They were fine with that. I told them to email the photo to me. They agreed. He inspected the documents, particularly the passport, for Ellen Laslow. They were satisfied. Is there anything further you'd like me to do?"

"No, nothing further now. That was well done. I don't want to even put a tail on her in Havana. Let her feel safe while we begin our cruise. We leave for Miami to meet Johnny tonight. Why don't you come back to LA, and—as they say in your colorful American idiom—'hold down the fort' while we're gone."

"Will do, I'll call you in Miami, when I'm back in LA."

Yu turned off the phone and turned to Rosie. "What are you thinking dear?"

"I'm getting concerned, nothing specific, but you know me—how I get—just a tiny little vibe that this is going too smoothly."

"How so?"

"Nothing I can put my finger on. She'll be out of the picture, unable to come back, and God knows Jose can take care of her easily once we're gone. We'll be out of the country, and there will be no way to connect us to whatever we do. But these people have somehow been a step ahead of us from the start, the get-go. I'd feel better if we had yet another layer of certainty, insurance if you will."

"My dear, as always, I trust your instincts. There is no harm in insuring our plan. I have a suggestion. What if I ask Eddie to go to Cuba, to back up Jose? He's very able. I'll tell him Jose isn't to know that he's there, and that there's nothing for him to do unless Jose doesn't complete his assignment timely, that is to say the precise agreed upon time. Once we set it, he will have, as always, a fixed, unchangeable deadline. If, for any reason, he doesn't meet it, if he even tries to delay it, we'll have Eddie step in and complete the job. What do you think?"

"Perfect. He's discreet, he'll report to us regularly, and in all likelihood, he'll have nothing to do except enjoy a little holiday in Cuba. I feel better. You never disappoint me, babe."

"Thank you. I'll set it up with Eddie today. No one else needs to know that he's in play, not even Johnny."

"Let's take our long, overdue vacation. I booked the Dorado Beach in Puerto Rico—for my money, the best resort in the Caribbean—for two nights off the boat, their best room, right on the beach. I want to go to the casino, kick back, gamble wildly like a girlish fool. You know how I can lose myself at the tables."

"Live it up, my dear. Play at the high-stake tables. We can afford it."

CHAPTER NINE

They were at the Macher's having breakfast, Sara, Callie, and Cash had all stayed the night. Later today, Cash and Sara were flying to Miami to meet the captain of the boat who was taking them to Cuba later that night. Callie was flying to Port-au-Prince, Haiti, to meet Andre, who had managed to get their forty-eight-foot (actually forty-seven-foot-eleven-inch) Cape Light boat to Port-au-Prince, where he and his team were already working to discreetly bring it up to acceptable condition.

The Macher, who'd gone into his private office to make some calls, came out and joined them. After taking some fresh coffee, he explained, "I located the man who's taken the job to kill Sara. His name is Jose Martinez. He's very capable. He's in fact the best of the four men that I thought they might choose. The good news is that I've crossed paths with him. I once did him a favor, and he's inclined to do me a favor in return. I asked him to do two things. First, slow down Yu's timing. Give us a chance to take them out of the picture. Second, walk away, let her live if we are able to remove Rosie and Yu. But he's smart, and careful. He wants assurances that Yu and Rosie will be out of the picture indefinitely. Absolutely unable to punish him. He also wants our assurances that he'll still be fully paid, if he walks away without fulfilling his job. I agreed to all of this. He already knew that Sara would be in Cuba tomorrow. Rosie and Yu wanted him to wait one more day, then they gave him thirty-six hours max, to take her out. I said we may need a few more days depending on their itinerary. Jose thought he could manage that. He'll stay at the location until I let him know that we've accomplished our mission."

"Are you absolutely sure you can rely on him?" Callie asked.

"Yes, for those few days. Years ago, I learned that a Russian arms dealer, who had used my diamond business, had sold out Jose's nephew on a job that I knew about. It's complicated, but I gave Jose a head's-up, well in time for his nephew to get away. That still counts for something."

"So this could work if we know exactly when they'll be cruising within twelve miles of Haiti."

"The question is *if* and when."

"Put your tech guy in high gear. Tell him to focus on their man Lennie's phone. He'll be the first to get the itinerary. I want it ASAP."

◆◆◆

Eddie didn't look at all like his brother-in-law, Johnny. Eddie was five feet six inches tall, well-muscled, cut and toned, with unusually strong grip strength. He had developed his body until it was well-suited for his hobby and favorite pastime—rock climbing. He was an avid, accomplished competitive rock climber, a bouldering champion, when he had time to do it. His climbing had further sculpted his torso and added powerful sinewy muscles in his arms and legs. When he wasn't climbing, Eddie was a truly frightening enforcer at three of the most prominent hotels in Las Vegas.

He'd gotten a text from Yu, and he was calling him back from his hotel, the Four Seasons in Seattle. He was using a new Android phone he'd just bought that day. He called a number Yu had sent, one that he didn't recognized. He admired Yu, and he was sure that he was being careful, directing him to call on an untraceable line. "Hello, sir, Eddie calling," he said when Yu answered. "Eddie, thank you for calling me promptly. Is your line secure?"

"Just bought it today. Hasn't been used, sir."

"Excellent. I want to ask a favor of you. And incidentally, please call me Yu. You're a trusted friend, and there's no reason to be formal."

"Thank you, I appreciate that. I'd be honored to help you however I can."

"I'll be in Miami tonight. I'd like you to meet me on Johnny's boat. When I see you in person, I'll explain what I need from you. You will be traveling for me, so please bring your passport. I'll look forward to seeing you on the boat tonight, say 9:00 p.m. Eastern. We leave for our cruise the following day."

"I'll look forward to it." Eddie hung up.

Yu was on the veranda of their Malibu house. He turned to Rosie, "Your idea to back up Jose was a good one, and Eddie is the perfect man to do it. He's polite, reliable, and quite capable."

"Thank you for taking care of that. I feel better, and I agree with your assessment of Eddie. People are genuinely afraid of him, and you don't get that rep without earning it. I'm told he enjoys his work and executes it both ruthlessly and mercilessly."

"All of that is true. Adding to his enviable reputation, he is said to have the highest percentage of successful debt collection in Las Vegas."

"I'm not surprised…Now, shifting gears. How about a special send-off treat, babe?" Rosie stood, kissing Yu on the ear, then whispering, "Why don't you please me, forcefully, right here on the veranda, a taste of what's to come, if you will, before we fly to Miami and begin our pleasure cruise."

Yu already had his hand under her dress, taking off her Intimissimi lace Brazilian-cut panties.

◆◆◆

Itzac, the Macher, came out of his office with an email he'd printed. "They leave on their cruise tomorrow, ten thirty a.m. Here's the itinerary they sent to Lennie. My guy just got it off Lennie's phone. I'm going to put Andre on the speaker—We'll need him for this." Itzac dialed Andre, using Cash's new phone, then put out a map, he'd also printed, on the coffee table. "Andre, we're all here. Can you hear me?"

"Loud and clear."

"Okay. Long story short, they're cruising down through the Bahamas, a stop at Nassau, then Andros Island, then another night at

Turks and Caicos Island." He showed them the places on the map as he described Rosie and Yu's itinerary. "As luck would have it, they're going past Haiti to Kingston, Jamaica, then from there to Puerto Rico, where they're getting off the boat to stay at the Dorado Beach, a very plush hotel for two nights. Our best opportunity is on day five, when they go right past Haiti to Jamaica. Can we be ready for that?"

"That puts us on the water in six days. Yes, we can do that." Andre announced. "But we'll have to work overtime. Callie, when do you get here?"

"Tonight…I'll be cooking for the entire crew, so get whatever you want to eat and find a stove I can use in the boathouse. I'll pick up whatever paraphernalia I'll need to do this properly…I'll also expect to go over the specifics of the plan with you. I'll want to sign off on each and every detail, including approving the crew, before Cash arrives."

"Good. I'd like your approval of the plan and the crew. Incidentally, if you hadn't agreed to cook, I was going to call the whole thing off. See you tonight." Andre hung up.

"Thanks for that," Cash told Callie.

She nodded. "I am not leaving the important details to two old pirates."

Cash smiled, then stood and turned to Sara. "We better pack for Cuba. We leave for the airport to fly to Miami in an hour."

"This is hard for me to imagine, to even think about. I mean I know it's hot, and I remember from *Godfather II* that they have wonderful old cars. Beyond that, I don't know anything about Cuba."

"I'll fill you in on our flight. Once we get there, you'll have some time to look around, maybe even learn some Cuban salsa dancing."

"Yes. Okay. I love to dance."

Itzac announced. "I'll count on going with you to the 1830 club at the end of the Malecon, a seawall and roadway along the coast, a taxi ride from your villa in Havana. We'll show off your new salsa moves the night I arrive. I'll arrive on day three or four."

"That's a date."

"Good. But I have another suggestion for you. I've rented a quiet comfortable villa for both of you in El Vedado in Havana. You've been going nonstop, on a whirlwind roller coaster. Why don't you take at least some of those days to relax. Lie in a hammock and get to know your dad. Walk with him, cook with him, talk about anything and everything. You have years to catch up on. You'll be surprised how much you'll enjoy that time, and how good some time off will be for you."

"I like that idea."

"As do I," Cash added.

"Your dad will be leaving for the boat on day four, and I'll take over keeping an eye on you for the next two days. I'll tell you stories, make you laugh, and if all goes as planned, on day six, I'll go to watch Rosie and Yu, in handcuffs, being interrogated by the Cubans with my help. During that time, you'll likely be out to dinner with your dad, Callie, and Andre."

"I'd like that."

"Okay then. Count on that," Cash said.

They left an hour later. Separate taxis, Callie to do her errands, Cash and Sara to the airport. It was the first time the two of them were going to be together for a long time without familiar company.

Unexpectedly, Sara started to cry, quietly, in the backseat of the taxi. What's wrong?" Cash asked.

"I think I've been taking too much of all of your advice, letting myself be afraid." She turned to him. "I don't like it at all."

"It'll get easier. Specifically, what are you afraid of?"

Sara tried to pull herself together. Cash gave her a handkerchief, and she dried her tears. "Okay, when I let myself feel it, it's a groundswell, a tidal wave. Truthfully, it's an overwhelming list. In no specific order, I'm afraid of being captured in our midnight boat ride. I'm afraid that the Cubans won't want me there. How about Yu and Rosie still trying to kill me, and what if the killer also goes after you? How about not getting my name and identity back, being stuck forever in Cuba? What if Andre, you, Callie, and the whole crew get arrested pretending to be the Haitian coast guard? What if Rosie and Yu have also put assassins after Samter and Lincoln?"

Cash took her hand, struck again by her quickness. "I see that you've got a flare for this."

"You just heard the tip of the iceberg."

"Let's start with that. First, Andre picked the captain who's taking us on our boat ride to Cuba. He knows him personally. You can rely one hundred percent on his judgement. Second, the Macher said you'd be welcome in Cuba, you can also rely one hundred percent on his judgement."

"I haven't known any people in my whole life, ever, that I could rely on one hundred percent. It's hard for me to believe that."

"Well get used to it. You now have at least four, including me and Callie. Furthermore, we know Rosie and Yu are trying to kill you, and we've slowed down their person. It's also why I'm here, and then the Macher, to make sure you're okay."

"Still, I'm very nervous. I think your psycho word is *anxious*. Why is that suddenly happening?"

"You're changing, and it's making you tuned in, rightly alert. Cuba is new, dangerous, and there's reason to be afraid. It's better for you to worry than to act like it isn't affecting you. It means that you'll be ahead of it, at least anticipating, if something goes wrong."

"Is that likely, with you and the Macher looking out for me?"

"I hope not. But we're taking on formidable, ferocious adversaries. I, for one, am relieved that you're alert."

Sara took his arm, leaned her head on his shoulder.

◆◆◆

Cash and Sara landed in Miami at six thirty p.m. They found a taxi with a thick plastic pane that the driver could close, giving them privacy in the back. Cash explained that it was a long ride, and he wanted to be able to talk privately about whatever she wanted. Sara appreciated that, and the driver understood. Cash directed the driver to take them to the

Impala Hotel in South Beach where Andre's friend, Alvaro, was waiting for them.

Sara enthusiastically took in the variety of colorful, lively things to see while driving through South Beach. She commented on the pastel-colored art deco buildings, the fancy shops, the trashier tasteless T-shirt vendors, the varieties of hotels, the palatial waterfront homes, the oh-so-hot South Beach nightlife spots, the sex shops, the roller bladders, the elderly—Cash explained that they were often part of Miami's large Jewish community—the gay community, the diverse less affluent community, and the wealthier people in expensive designer clothes.

She remarked, plainly interested, "There are so many bare legs, so many exposed bellies and barely covered breasts among the young women, cruising the streets and beaches, right beside fancy dressed celebrities. I think I saw Kim Kardashian on the street, and it looked like another star, drawing a crowd, as he went into Liv at the Fontainebleau. And what about the people working out at that beach we passed?"

"It's called Muscle Beach. It's an outdoor gym."

"And why are all of these old buildings we've seen so colorful—pastel red, yellow, light green, even purple?"

"We passed through the Art Deco historic district, the nation's largest concentration of Art Deco architecture, over hundreds of buildings. Built in the 1930s and 1940s."

"How do you know all of this?"

"I spent time here, years ago, working on a complicated project, a four-way trade, and this interested me."

"Okay. Now, can you help me understand why these big American cities are so different? This is nothing like Seattle or New York. I mean don't they speak the same language in all of these places, watch the same TV shows, read the same national news?"

"They do. Part of the differences are weather related, but they're also impacted by racial make-up and other factors. For example, these three specific places have significantly different patterns of immigration." Cash thought this over. "Tell you what, when this is over, I'll take you to

LA—we'll check out Hollywood, Malibu, Venice Beach, Bel Air, Topanga Canyon, even the San Fernando Valley. Different neighborhoods in the same city, each one a distinct culture. It makes your point."

"You're on for LA."

Cash smiled at her, feeling lucky.

They arrived at the Impala Hotel, a 1920s Spanish Mediterranean revival, well located on Collins Ave., a simple, smaller, yellow hotel, squeezed between two larger white apartment buildings. The quiet, lovely design of the little hotel was apparent from the street. The taxi driver, happy with his generous tip, left them in front, where Alvaro, who'd sent Cash a text, was waiting beside a new blue Mustang. It was 7:00. He was Cuban, dressed in jeans and a colorful shirt, friendly and likable, casually attractive. Andre had said he was thirty-four years old, though Cash would have guessed he was younger. Cash shook his hand, introduced Sara, who also shook his hand, saying, "Hola, y gracias."

"Mucho gusto."

Cash then said, "My name is Cash. Andre is one of my best, most trusted friends. He speaks very highly of you."

Alvaro nodded, "Andre's told me so many stories about you that I feel like I already know you. Most importantly, he said you're like his older brother. He said I should take especially good care of you both. You can rely on that. I've worked with Andre. I'll tell you some of our colorful history as we drive. We're going to Key Largo, where the boat is waiting—"

"Key Largo?" Sara interrupted, excited, "Oh my God, is that the same Key Largo where Bogart and Bacall made the movie of the same name?"

"It is."

"Is the bar in the movie still there?"

"Absolutely. The Caribbean Club."

"Can we stop?"

"Yes, of course. And I'm betting you'll also want to see the original century-old steam-powered boat from the 1951 movie, *The African Queen*."

"Yes! Yes! I'm so excited I can hardly breathe."

"She's an avid film buff," Cash explained. "She learned English working at a movie theater at nineteen. Since then, she lives and breathes movies."

"Yes, I can see that," Alvaro said. "I'm a serious movie fan too, so we'll have a lot to talk about. Let's see just how good you are, pretty lady. Here's one of my favorite films—*Streets of Fire*. Who's the director and who are the stars?"

Sara laughed. "Director, Walter Hill. Stars—Michael Paré, Diane Lane, Willem Dafoe. And an extra, it was made in 1984. You'll have to do better, Señor, and please don't call me 'pretty lady.' I had a dog named Lady—We called her pretty Lady…Sara is fine."

"Point taken, Sara. It won't happen again…As to the movies, you're the real deal. We'll have some fun with that later. For now, please make yourself comfortable in the car."

Cash and Sara both got in the back seat. Alvaro made sure that their seat belts were on, then they were off. Once underway he explained, "The drive is maybe an hour and forty-five minutes, which should put us there between eight forty-five and nine. Around ten, we'll take my boat to Cuba. Unless we run into trouble, we'll easily land in Cuba before three a.m. Ready?"

Cash nodded and before long they were on the Florida Keys.

Sara looked out the window, fascinated. The spectacular ocean views, the never-ending long bridges, the natural wonders, the rain forest area, the Straits of Florida and the Gulf of Mexico, the kayakers, the snorkelers, the variety of boaters and sailors, the beautiful endless beaches, the mangroves, and the abundant terrestrial and marine wildlife, were often unexpected and yet another mesmerizing piece of the spectacular make-up of this varied country. Sara had to ask about the first underwater hotel, the famous adults-only Bungalows Key Largo, and she insisted that they stop later to try Key Lime pie.

At a quiet moment, Cash asked Alvaro to tell his story about Andre.

Alvaro explained, "I was younger, barely twenty-seven, smuggling Cubans to Miami for good money. I knew Andre because he'd known my mother before she died, and later, from time to time, he used me to bring precious stones from complicated trades he was doing in the Yucatán."

"I knew about those," Cash said. "But I stayed away. They were too dangerous for me."

"Then you know more about it than I did. I'd pick up the stones and deliver them to Andre in Miami. It was a straight run, doable in my high-speed custom boat and excepting the one time I'm going to tell you about, pretty straightforward. This time, however, maybe an hour from Cancún, one of the Mexican renegade drug cartels, in three go-fast boats, fired shots over my speeding cruiser, stopping me forcibly. They boarded, took the jewels, destroyed my motor, tied me up, and left me to die in the middle of the Gulf of Mexico. After about an hour, I was able to free one hand, reach a phone I had hidden nearby on the boat, and get a text to Andre. He found me maybe eleven hours later. I have no idea how. He was in a helicopter. I was almost dead. He brought me to the hospital just in time."

"That sounds like Andre. He could do that. Did you keep smuggling?"

"No. I did a few more runs from Cuba, still do occasionally, for special friends, but I'd saved up enough money to buy my bar in South Beach, get some other work, and before long, I had a couple of night clubs. Now, I'm a successful, respected businessman, the owner of several hot spot night clubs in South Beach. The only reason I'm bringing you to Cuba is because Andre asked me to."

"Thank you again for that." Sara turned to Cash, "I don't mean to be harsh or nosey, but how do your friends stay out of jail?"

"They have very strict rules. They don't deal drugs. They don't kill people unless it's to save a life or in defending their own life. They don't deal weapons, nor any stolen goods, and so on. Mostly, they distance themselves, at least one step away, from the buyer and the seller who are likely not declaring the transaction and therefore breaking the law."

"How do you know so much about this?"

He thought about how much to tell her. He wanted her to know, he knew that much. "Okay, I'm going to make an exception and answer your question. Truthfully, end of the day, I'd like you to know about me... Alvaro, I'm trusting Andre's word that I can rely on your discretion."

"Of course. Absolutely."

"Thank you. Okay. I spent a fair amount of time trafficking goods internationally and into the US. Mostly it was legal. Occasionally, it wasn't. We moved carpets from Morocco, medical supplies, electronics, Japanese high-tech items, art, jewels, often diamonds from Africa and Europe, and so on. Basically, anything I could get cheaply in one country and sell more expensively in another was fair game. What got me in trouble was bringing Japanese ivory netsuke from Vancouver to Seattle. Callie had me arrested for smuggling them into her restaurant almost four years ago. Since then, I've had to step back, stay in the background. Neither Andre nor Itzac have ever been arrested."

"I'm not sure I understand the fine points of that, nor do I have to know right now. But later, I'd like to understand why Callie arrested you, and how now you stay safe...and please know that I appreciate your willingness to tell me about you."

"We can talk about this more in Cuba. You, of all people, should hear the whole story."

"I'll look forward to that. From arresting you to living with you. The incompatible, mismatched couple fall in love. Sounds like a cheesy movie."

"My guess, it's the kind of movie you'll especially like."

"Okay then...Speaking of that, Alvaro, I'm happy that you found safer work. So, let's go back to your game. I think we should only raise little known movies that we love. Here's one for you, *Nobody's Fool.*"

"I do love that movie—director, Robert Benton. Stars—Paul Newman, Jessica Tandy, Bruce Willis, Melanie Griffin, 1994."

"Well done. So how, Alvaro, did you learn so much about movies?"

"In Cuba, my father was a cinephile who worked as one of the directors at ICAIC—that's the *Instituto Cubano del Arte e Industria*

Cinematograficos. As such, he produced, distributed, and exhibited films. He was especially active in the office of exhibition and associated activities for educating people. He taught me his love for movies, and somehow, he managed to regularly bring home many fine films and TV series—how he got them I was never certain. At fourteen, in 2001, I started watching *The Sopranos*. I saw any episode my dad could get until 2007. I remember seeing *Avatar, Walk the Line, V for Vendetta*, and so many more. I watched all of them with him. My father died, a heart attack, when I was nineteen. My mother was an accomplished singer and through a Cuban friend, she had a chance to sing at a club in Miami. At that time, I was selling black market films on the street in Havana, and she was worried I'd end up in jail. So she decided that the move made sense for both of us. I was twenty when we left for Miami. At twenty-one, I began working on TV shows and films in Miami—*Burn Notice, Chef, Dexter, Marley & Me, Charlie's Angels* (the 2011 reboot), among others—When I started, I was mostly a goffer, but I watched tons of movies, and took movie courses, to learn as much as I could to be conversant in that world. I even joined an online film club that I still watch. Without intending to, I became knowledgeable, and finally expert at it. Before I left, I had some real responsibilities."

"It sneaks up on you, doesn't it? Like an addiction."

"Exactly. I still see as many, as often, as I can…"

"Hit me again."

Okay, here's another hard one for you—*The Clockmaker of Saint Paul*."

"Now you're talking, Alvaro! Director—Bertrand Tavernier. Stars—Phillipe Noiret, one of my favorite actors, and Jean Rochefort. This French movie was nominated for Best Foreign Language Film, 1974. Brilliant movie, yet another outstanding choice."

"I can't help myself—you're so smart. And you have impeccable taste. Also, you're sure of yourself, confident in what you know. Sara, truthfully, I think I'm falling in love."

"Don't be silly."

"How about at least a date?"

"Let's talk about that when I'm back from Cuba…You are a charmer, though, Señor Alvaro."

"I meant every word I said. Honestly. For now, all I ask is that you give me some hope."

"Okay. You remember *Jerry Maguire*?"

"Of course."

"…you had me at *Streets of Fire*."

Alvaro blew her a kiss.

Cash laughed out loud, surprised, but liking how his daughter moved so fast, so confidently. He turned to Alvaro. "She's my daughter. You'll need to get my approval."

"Fair enough. When this is done, I'll ask your permission. Now Sara, how did you learn so much about movies, and how did you develop such exquisite taste?"

"Short version. At nineteen, I worked for almost no money in a well-known French movie theater, cleaning up. They showed all of the American classics on multiple screens. I'd watch everything after work. It's, in fact, how I learned English. I did this for years. It's a long story, but during and after those years, I spent most of my spare time by myself. Mostly I watched movies on TV, on my phone, any way I could download them. I had no family that I knew of. As a half Algerian woman in Paris, raised in a harsh French orphanage, I had no French friends, in part by choice. I did have my movies, though, and I infused those movies with great meaning. They literally became my life. Truthfully, with hindsight, you could say that the movies saved my life."

Cash took her hand.

Sara shifted gears, turned toward Alvaro, "Enough movie talk. Tell me about your boat, then about Havana."

"Perfect timing," Alvaro said, as he turned into a closed boathouse parking area. He unlocked the door to show his specially-designed boat. "It's the Midnight Express forty-three-foot open. It's been a great boat— in English, suffice it to say it's fast as the wind, able to go more than sixty knots, that's over seventy miles per hour, relatively stable at choppy seas, plenty of space to carry both of you comfortably. I repainted it, blue and black, and named it *The Rum Runner*."

"Looks good."

Alvaro smiled at her. "In response to the second part of your question—though you won't see much of Havana tonight, I think you'll find it captivating. It's a world unto itself—painted in bright colors, beautiful old architecture, wonderful vintage classic cars, the rich Spanish heritage touching everything from art to music to architecture to the cuisine. I've found that the people are lovely, in the face of considerable hardship. You'll want to see old Havana, where most of the buildings are over one hundred years old, and many date from the eighteenth century. You should walk the colorful, lively old narrow streets, look up to see the overhanging balconies. Vedado, with its mansions, where you'll find your villa, is a different kind of treat. And there's so much more—the bay, the port, the mesmerizing music, singing, dancing, the street life. I fell in love with it long ago, and I think you will too."

"Who would have thought that my solitary, suddenly dangerous world would become so animated, even magical."

Cash whispered. "Sara, you deserve a little magic..."

Alvaro looked at the two of them, enjoying each other so much. "Okay you two. We'll leave in a little over an hour. Let's get some Key lime pie, see the Caribbean Club, visit *The African Queen*, then take a fast boat ride to Cuba."

Chapter Ten

About the same time Sara tasted Key lime pie for the first time, Rosie and Yu sat down for a drink on Johnny's boat, the *LIAN—Daughter of the Sun*. It was sixty-five feet long, with four cabins, additional crew quarters and able to comfortably carry eight guests. Eddie was already there, sitting up front with Johnny.

Yu said to Eddie, "Thank you for coming so quickly. Let's get our business taken care of, then we can enjoy Johnny and Rosie."

Eddie followed Yu to the aft deck to two chairs situated where they could talk privately.

Yu began, "This is a sensitive matter. No one, including your brother-in-law, is to know about it."

Eddie nodded. "I understand."

"I've hired Jose Martinez to eliminate Sara Cambert. Do you know him?"

"I know of him, but I've never met him."

"This is his photo." Yu took out a picture of Jose. "We're thinking that Sara arrives in Cuba early tomorrow morning. It's probable that the man, Cash Logan, will be with her. I will send Jose there tomorrow night. He will have exactly thirty-six hours to eliminate both of them without a trace. You should go to Havana tonight. If for any reason Jose doesn't eliminate them within thirty-six hours after he arrives, I want you to kill both of them and dispose of the bodies where they won't be found. Have I been clear?"

"Absolutely. You can rely on me."

"If, in fact, you do this job, I'll also want you to eliminate Callie James, Cash's partner, right away. She shouldn't ever suspect that Cash and Sara are missing."

"If you ask me to do the first assignment, I'll execute the second promptly thereafter."

That's good to know. In all likelihood Jose will fulfill his contract and you will have a pleasant few days off in Cuba. Either way keep me posted."

Eddie followed Yu back to the front where Johnny was ready to serve drinks.

◆◆◆

Sara was talking about taking a ride on *The African Queen*. "It was such a thrill for me. I was picturing Bogart watching Katherine Hepburn tossing his whiskey overboard." Before she could say another word, Alvaro's boat was at sea, making fifty knots, almost sixty miles per hour. It was 9:45 p.m. and the moon and a distant splash of stars were the only light reflecting on the black ocean. Cash and Sara sat behind Alvaro on a relatively comfortable cushioned bench. They both wore warm jackets and were covered in one of Alvaro's spare blankets. Still, Cash had his arm around Sara, who was leaning against him to stay warm. Fortunately, it was not a cold night, and everyone settled in for the long ride. Alvaro clearly had experience with this, and he turned off the lights whenever he saw a boat far in the distance.

At 12:30, Alvaro called the number that Cash had given him. It was the number that the Macher had given Cash to contact his prominent Cuban friend, who had a powerful position at MINREX, (The Ministry of Foreign Affairs). His name was Nestor, and he would be welcoming them later tonight, after clearing their arrival with the necessary Cuban authorities, including customs. The conversation was in Spanish, which Sara understood, and after, Alvaro simply said, "All good. He'll be waiting for us at the dock he suggested. It's owned by his friend in Cojímar, a sleepy fishing village, a quiet neighborhood less than an hour outside Havana. It's said that a local fisherman, Santiago, was Ernest Hemingway's fisherman in *The Old Man and the Sea*. It's an auspicious place to enter Cuba. Nestor will drive you from there to your villa."

◆◆◆

At 2:30 a.m., *The Rum Runner* tied up to a remote fishing dock in Cojímar. Nestor Mirabal, a senior official in MINREX was waiting for them. Nestor was almost six feet tall, had black hair, and was slightly overweight. He had a friendly, satisfied countenance, and looked you in the eye when he talked with you. He waited until they were out of the boat then Nestor said, "Welcome to Cuba," as he extended his hand.

Cash shook his hand. "I have warm greetings from our mutual friend Itzac. He will be here in two or three days."

Nestor nodded. "He's a dear friend," he explained, in usable English.

"Let me introduce Ellen Larson." Sara shook his hand. "And our excellent captain, Alvaro."

Alvaro responded in Spanish and shook hands with Nestor. "Once my friends are settled in your car, I have to go back. I'll stop at Key West to get some sleep and fill up the gas. Still, I have a long ride ahead of me."

"I brought some coffee for you to take with you," Nestor said, handing him a thermos.

"Gracias," Alvaro took the thermos into the boat, then came out with Sara's bag.

Cash brought his bag out of the boat. Back on the dock, he set it down and said, "Thank you, Alvaro. This was well done." He shook his hand warmly as he used his other hand to squeeze his shoulder. Without another word, Cash picked up his bag and asked Nestor to go with him to the car.

Sara took her bag from Alvaro, set it on the dock, then looked up and said, "You're a pleasant surprise."

Alvaro took Sara's hand. "You're a revelation." Then without warning, he put his hands on her waist and gently kissed her lips.

Though Sara didn't turn away, her kiss was more passive then passionate. Still, it was a kiss, and after, she looked at him carefully.

"I wish you the very best with whatever you are doing in Cuba. Please stay safe. I'll keep in touch with Andre, to get news of you. When you're back, I'll find you."

This time, Sara kissed him for real. She picked up her bag, smiled, then she turned to follow Cash to the car.

◆◆◆

Nestor drove a refurbished classic American car. When Sara asked about it, he explained, "This car was a gift from my wife's father that I intend to pass on to my own daughter. She already takes care of it and drives it often for tourists at $200 per day, which is, incidentally, a lot of money in a country where many people make $20 a month."

"Thanks for explaining that," Sara said. "And just tell me if I ask too many questions. I'm so excited to be here that I'm capable of it."

"You can't ask me too many questions about old, restored American cars. This 1951 Chevy is a hobby of mine."

When they were comfortably in the back seat, Nestor turned to face them. "There's one piece of business we should take care of right away. Your phones won't work here. I can explain all of this later, but basically your phones are 'locked.'" He handed them each another cell phone. "These are temporary cell phones, that you can use in Cuba. These phones are already unlocked and have a Cuban SIM card inside. With these phones, you can easily dial or text anyone inside or outside the country. I've also taken the liberty of passing your numbers on to Itzac."

"Itzac said you'd be taking care of us. I had no idea that it included this level of care. Having a phone that works is essential for us. Is it traceable?"

"Our expert made it very hard to trace."

"Thank you very much."

"My pleasure. You'll be safe using these phones. Now, let's go to Havana." With that, Nestor drove his old classic car on the rural road toward Havana. He was a good driver and managed the rural road comfortably. It was a dark night so they couldn't see very much except trees and occasional views through the trees of the dark waters beyond. "We will be going through towns on our way," he explained, as he drove through the darkness. "But you'll be able to get a larger, better feel for Cuba when we reach Havana."

"How far?"

"Less than an hour." Nestor nodded. "It won't disappoint, even on a dark night."

It was quiet then, as they drove, but Sara was excited by this new place and wanted to talk more with Nestor. She asked, "Your Chevy, what's the model, the year?"

Nestor turned to her briefly, showing a hint of pride. "The 1951 Chevrolet Styleline Deluxe Bel-Air."

She nodded. "It's a beautiful car, and I love the midnight blue color."

"Just repainted last year and please look at the detail inside. We recreated and refurnished the original interior at the same time. We also redid the engine. We can't import the mechanical parts, so we have to take them from other cars or recreate them. There's lots of improvisation."

Cash leaned forward, interested. "Just how many classic American cars are there in Cuba?"

"About sixty thousand. Seriously…Would you like to hear the story? I can talk endlessly about my old car, so please say no if I'm likely to bore you."

"Not to worry. We'd love to hear the story." Sara poked Cash's ribs in the back seat.

He took the hint. "You bet."

"Sixty thousand? Wow!" she added.

"Okay. In 1959, after the revolution, Fidel banned the importation of American cars and mechanical parts. In October 1960, the US declared an embargo. The embargo was extended in February 1962, to include almost all exports. The old American autos have been kept running with parts and pieces that were not intended for them. Locals have become very imaginative at preserving and maintaining the old cars. It's estimated that half of those sixty thousand are from the fifties, twenty-five percent from the forties, and another twenty-five percent from the 1930s. The cars have become family heirlooms, often passed down from one generation to the next. Cuban ingenuity has kept these old American cars on the roads. Today it's fair to say that Cuba is a living museum of classic American cars."

Nestor paused, raised his palm, pleased that they appreciated his car, then he turned back to Ellen. "Can I change the subject, fill you in on the set up here, Ellen?"

"Of course, and I don't know the protocol, but is it all right to still call me Sara?"

Cash responded. "I think with Nestor and people who know you well, it's okay for now, in private."

Sara nodded. "Good. Nestor, what do I need to know?"

"Itzac told me some of your situation, your overall objectives. He specifically asked me to help you with security. The villa I found for you is isolated, and I have two men watching it. As I'm sure you know, Itzac is well connected here. He's already spoken with my superior, in absolute confidence. I don't know how much he said, but he touched a nerve. I can assure you that the Cuban government will help you however we can. We're here to assist your entire group in succeeding with your mission. That's vitally important for us. As their representative, and as Itzac's friend, I'm going to want you to let me know as things unfold, as they develop. Please tell me if you need anything or if your plans change."

"Thank you, Cash and I will keep you informed. He, particularly, will know timing, and anything you can do to help. For now, mostly I'm looking forward to spending some relaxed time in the villa with my dad."

"Itzac told me about that." He nodded, then smiled warmly. "There's more to tell you, but the rest should be fun."

Sara liked him already. "Okay, then."

"Itzac must especially like you. He made a special personal request on your behalf, young lady." He paused, a twinkle in his eyes. "He said you'd like to learn Cuban salsa and asked me if I could recommend a teacher for lessons. My daughter, Alicia is a splendid dancer. For several years, she had a wonderful teacher, Maceo. If you agree, he'll be at your villa at two, the day after tomorrow. He'll happily get you started and come back if you want more."

"Thank you...Thank you. That would be wonderful."

"His English is not so good. Do you speak Spanish?"

"Si, and please tell Maceo that I'd like to speak Spanish with him."

"Perfect."

Sara turned to Cash. "You and your friends, and their friends, know how to make a girl feel welcome." She turned to Nestor. "Nestor. Muchas gracias."

Before reaching Havana, both Sara and Cash were sound asleep in the back seat. When they reached the lovely villa in El Vedado, Nestor woke Cash and together they managed to get Sara into an upstairs bedroom where, at 5:00 a.m., she was able to get some of her clothes off and fall asleep in the comfortable bed.

❖❖❖

It was 11:30 a.m. when Sara came down the sweeping staircase, walked through the charming downstairs rooms, then found Cash and Nestor outside in the patio having coffee. She helped herself to the coffee and sat down in a comfortable chair beside them. She looked around, admiring the carefully manicured greenery and the lovely garden. It was a handsome home, with multiple bedrooms, ample space, gracious living and dining rooms, high ceilings. Outside, it was possible to meander through the large, spacious property. "Charming...This is clearly the Macher's kind of place," Sara observed.

"The Macher?" Nestor asked.

"It's your friend Itzac's nickname. It's a Yiddish word that I just learned. It means—and I quote—'a powerful person, a person of influence who gets things done. Put simply, a Macher is a big shot.'"

Nestor smiled. "Itzac is certainly all of that."

Cash raised a thumbs-up to Sara, then changed the subject. "Sara, eat some breakfast, finish your coffee, then let's go see Havana. We can start at The Plaza de la Revolución, where we need to take your picture in front of the large Che Guevara mural."

Nestor stood up. "I think you're well situated here. The Plaza, for example, also called Revolution Square, is a municipality. It stretches from the square down to the sea at the Malecon and includes the Vedado district, where we are...I'm going to take you to the Plaza."

"Thank you," Cash said.

"Same for me," Sara added. She looked around the spacious grounds. "You chose a beautiful place for us."

Nestor shook his hand, then hers, then he said, "I have several errands to run, I'll be back at one or one thirty." then he was off in his 1951 classic Chevrolet Styleline Deluxe Bel-Air.

◆◆◆

Johnny's yacht, *LIAN—Daughter of the Sun*, was approaching Andros Island. It was a warm, beautiful day and the sea was calm. Rosie and Yu were wearing bathing suits, sipping cocktails. The text came on Yu's phone, it was from Jose. They'd set up a system where Jose would text him if he wanted to talk. Yu took another new phone and called Jose back.

"Hello, I'm responding to your text. You're on the speaker."

"With your permission, I'd like two more days to fulfill my contract. I will, of course, stay on schedule if you need me to, but let me explain why it would be useful to extend."

"Please do."

"I located Sara and the man who's traveling with her. They're in a well-appointed villa in El Vedado. The new relevant information is that there are two armed guards patrolling the villa. The target was to be two, maximum. Now, I think it may rightly increase to four. To do this properly, I'd like to bring in my best man. He can't arrive until the day after tomorrow. We would be able to execute the contract the following day. In other words, two days after you requested. But I can guarantee a successful outcome. I can do it as scheduled myself, but it could become messy, and it will be more complicated to make four bodies, rather than two, disappear inexplicably."

"What's the additional charge?"

"Travel expenses, and an increase of fifteen percent for the fee."

"Let me consult my associate, and I'll call you back." Yu hung up.

He turned to Rosie. "What do you think?"

"It sounds reasonable, but this kind of change is a potential sign of trouble. Let's ask Eddie to do this, right away. Let's step it up. He can execute the day after tomorrow."

"I agree. This is a bad development. Possibly—no, likely—what you were worried about. I'll call Eddie now."

"What are you thinking about the other two guards?"

"I'm going to suggest he knock them out, one at a time, with a non-lethal semi-automatic tactical combat pistol. It's a high-powered tranquillizer. I don't think we want to start eliminating Cuban policemen or even security guards. Then he can take out Cash and Sara and dispose of those bodies. I'll have Eddie lock the guards up in a safe place. We'll keep them quiet there for a day, then, once Eddie's long gone, call it in anonymously. At that same moment, I'll put Eddie on eliminating Callie James right away. We'll assign Samter and Lincoln right after. I could send Jose, but I'd rather wait for Eddie."

"That's all good, and I like getting it done sooner. What are you going to tell Jose?"

"For now, I'll text him, give him a tentative yes to his proposal but suggest we talk in two days. If in fact he's betrayed us, we don't want his new people to think we know that, or even suspect it."

"Your mind, not to mention the fabulous sex, is why I married you. No regrets babe."

"No regrets," he replied, nodding. Yu gently touched Rosie's cheek, then he composed a text. "Yes, to your new proposal, timing, and terms, request another call in two days." He sent it, then he called Eddie.

◆◆◆

Cash was on the phone with Callie, while Sara walked through the garden. "The boat looks as it should," Callie explained. "Andre, as usual, has done an excellent job. From what I understand, Haitian coast guard boats are not kept in perfect shape. This one will fit right in. The crew we've chosen are fit, reliable, hardworking, and very capable. Andre and two crew members walked me through the plan. It's detailed, carefully constructed, and they're ready to execute. Everything else is on schedule."

"Excellent."

"And your trip?"

"Long, but so far uneventful. The Macher found us an attractive villa with sizable grounds, in an upscale neighborhood. We haven't had time to explore Havana, but we'll see some of it this afternoon. The Cuban gentleman that the Macher set up to look after us is smart and knowledgeable. We're in good hands. He drives a souped-up classic 1951 Chevy."

"How cool is that? How's Sara holding up?"

"Glad you asked. The trip wasn't completely uneventful. Andre's friend, Alvaro, the talented, good-looking Cuban guy who took us to Cuba, has fallen head over heels for her. My never-a-dull-moment daughter is interested."

"Are you kidding, after one boat trip?"

"They're both maniacal film buffs. It's amazing to listen to them go through old movies."

"Doesn't she have enough on her plate?"

"I'd say so. He's gone, so it's not a current issue. But I have to say, they're just great together. He's a thoughtful, reliable, successful man.

And truthfully, Sara deserves a guy like that. I'm guessing that she's never been with a grown-up, interesting man like Alvaro. Ask Andre about his friend, I'm sure he's already heard from him."

"Babe, you're never boring. And you're certainly an unconventional dad…And I love you."

"Likewise, sweetheart." He saw Nestor's car pulling up. "Got to go. I'll talk with you tonight."

"Love to Sara."

"And she sends hers to you." He hung up, waved to Sara, who'd also seen the car and gestured that he'd meet her in the garden.

♦♦♦

Once they were in the Chevy, Nestor took over. He pointed out some of the better-known mansions as they drove through Vedado.

"Amongst all of these magnificent mansions, I'm seeing some old poorly maintained, deteriorated buildings," Sara mentioned.

"Yes, Vedado is actually quite old. Most of the buildings were constructed before 1960. Many of them have been poorly maintained, and they look like Old Havana or Central Havana."

"Why this discrepancy?"

"Vedado benefitted from the American invested sugar boom. It's also where the mafia invested heavily in the 1940s and 1950s, building many hotels and casinos, including the Hotel Riviera, on the ocean, the recently renovated Hotel Capri. I'd say starting in that time, Vedado began reminding visitors of the wealthy areas of the US in the 1950s. You know about the classic American cars, but there were 1950s–era cinemas, theaters, cabarets, and bars. And in the residential areas, people were building these incredible mansions with front and back gardens and large verandas, and extravagant grand hotels. I'll take you by the Hotel Nacional, now. It's on our way. By way of background, the palatial Hotel Nacional was opened in 1930, built by US owners as a hotel for US tourists. At that time, Cubans were not allowed to stay there. The hotel was also segregated. In 1956, singer Nat King Cole was not allowed to stay there. There is now a tribute to him in the form of a statue and a jukebox in the Hotel Nacional.

Fifteen minutes later, they were sipping mojitos in the Nacional's garden bar.

Sara looked at the palatial hotel. Nestor, anticipating her questions, explained, "On the seafront of Vedado, the hotel is on Taganana Hill. The rooms offer splendid views of the sea and the city. The structure is a mix of styles—Sevillian, Moorish, Roman, and Art Deco. The layout is based on two Greek crosses, allowing most of the rooms to have a view of the ocean. It was taller than most of the surrounding buildings with two towers overseeing the area. It's unmistakable with its grand design and conspicuous yellow color."

Inside, she could see the wide corridors, mahogany panels, high ceilings. "I've never, ever, stayed in such a fancy hotel."

"Nor I," Cash added.

"It's been the host to many famous movie people including Marlon Brando, Gary Cooper, Rita Hayworth, Fred Astaire, and more recently Steven Spielberg, Leonardo DiCaprio, and Francis Ford Coppola, to name a few. Most notably, in 1946 the hotel's casino was the setting for the Havana Conference, a meeting between the US and Sicilian Mafia. Meyer Lansky, one of the organizers of the meeting, was an owner of the hotel."

"That meeting was in *The Godfather Part II*," Sara said.

"Yes, but it wasn't shot in the actual hotel, they filmed it in the Dominican Republic."

"Good to know. And knowing something more about this great movie than I do is just so excellent."

Cash added, "That, sénior, is a great compliment."

"Thank you," Nestor smiled, then he went on, "The Nacional, renamed Hotel Nacional de Cuba in 1939, sits on a high point at the end of Vedado's main street, Calle 21. From here, you can see the city of Havana." He pointed. "You can follow the Malecon, nicknamed 'the longest sofa in the world,' an esplanade and roadway that stretches along the coast for eight kilometers from the mouth of Havana harbor in Old Havana along the north side of Central Havana and into the Vedado neighborhood. The outline of La Habana Vieja, the city's historic center, is there—" Nestor pointed again. "In the distance, you can see across the harbor to the fortresses across the bay of Havana then out to sea, the Gulf of Mexico. Florida is ninety miles away."

"The hotel, the view, the history…" Sara raised a glass. "You're a good guide."

When they finished their drinks, he suggested moving on. Just minutes later Cash pointed ahead, "Is that The Revolution Square? It's huge."

Nestor nodded. "You're seeing part of it. The Plaza de la Revolución is one of the largest city squares in the world, measuring 780,000 square feet. Fidel Castro addressed more than a million Cubans there, often. Pope John Paul in 1998, and Pope Francis in 2015 held masses there during papal visits to Cuba." He slowed. "There's the José Martí Memorial featuring a 358 foot tall tower and a fifty-nine foot statue. It dominates the square."

"Who was he?"

"José Martí, called the Apostle of the Cuban Revolution, was a poet, a journalist, a philosopher, and more. He was the driving force behind the final Cuban insurrection against Spanish rule in the late nineteenth century. Among many other things, he wrote the poem that was later turned into the song, 'Guantanamera.'"

"The Pete Seger song?"

"Pete Seger sang it in the sixties, and then it became an international hit after it was recorded by the Sandpipers in 1966, but the song was written long before by Joseíto Fernández. The song was popularized when he sang it, and it appeared on the radio, as early as 1929. José Martí, who wrote the original poem, died, killed in battle against Spanish troops in 1895."

"Sorry, I don't mean to be disrespectful."

"Not a problem, I've never seen you be disrespectful."

"Thank you, what else am I seeing around me here?"

"Many government ministries and the National Library are located around the Plaza. Behind the memorial sits the Palace of the Revolution, the headquarters of the Cuban Government and the Communist Party. Opposite the memorial, façades feature matching steel memorials of Che Guevara and Camilo Cienfuegos. Che Guevara's giant mural is on the eastern façade of the Ministerio del Interior, a gray concrete monolith on the northern side of the Plaza. That's where we'll stop."

Nestor parked the car in a street cutting through a wide plaza opposite the huge mural. Sara was, characteristically, naming all of the old cars. "A Cadillac Eldorado, a Chevy, a Buick Super, a Ford Edsel, even a Mercury Monterey. Are they on display?"

"In a manner of speaking. They're for rent, as taxis," Nestor explained, and then he led them toward the memorial.

Cash placed her in front of the huge memorial setting her far enough away to see Che Guevara's face in the picture. When he was satisfied, Cash took several photos. Looking through them, he chose one to send to Lennie. Cash didn't notice the man sitting on the low distant wall talking on the phone.

CHAPTER ELEVEN

Rosie and Yu were sunbathing lying on comfortable chaise lounges in the front deck of Johnny's boat. They were drinking their preferred cocktails, a mojito for Rosie, a Cuba Libre for Yu. He wasn't sure why he favored this drink, but since starting the cruise, it was his only cocktail. He liked it with extra fresh lime. At the moment, they were rounding Great Exuma Island in route to Turks and Caicos. The email came from Lennie, and Yu nodded, satisfied with the picture of Sara in front of the Che Guevara steel Memorial.

He showed it to Rosie, who smiled, then said, "He'll need a day to plan it all. He can execute tomorrow night, latest."

"I'll call Eddie again, confirm the details." Yu got his new phone, sent a text, then waited for Eddie to call.

The phone call came in less than two minutes.

"You're where?"

"At the Che Guevara memorial…You saw them take the picture?… You'll be ready to go tomorrow night?…Perfect…Please confirm via text to Lennie…Please also set in motion the follow-up assignment we discussed for Callie James…The day after tomorrow for execution would be excellent…Thank you." Yu hung up, turned to Rosie.

Rosie said, "We'll be in the harbor at Turks and Caicos tomorrow. Let's go out to eat on the island. Celebrate."

"I'll ask Johnny to recommend a restaurant."

"Just the two of us for dinner?"

"Yes, absolutely. As we finish this unexpected chapter, I feel like we're at a crossroad. It's a good time to reinvent ourselves, consider some new directions, explore some exciting new possibilities."

"You're reading my mind, sweetheart. First Sara Cambert and Cash Logan. Then Callie James. Next, the policemen, Lincoln and Samter. A clean sweep. By then we'll have left the Dorado Beach, on our way back to Miami, my copious gambling winnings in tow. During that trip, we'll finish reinventing our new lives. Babe, there's nothing we can't do."

Yu raised his Cuba Libre. "To my one and only."

"Ditto, baby." She clicked his glass with her mojito. "Skies the limit!"

◆◆◆

Andre had found and rented a large, remote boathouse at the edge of the harbor in Port-au-Prince, Haiti. Inside, he and his team of five Haitians were hard at work transforming the old Cape Light boat into a credible Haitian coast guard ship. The boat he'd found had been like an old Canadian coast guard boat. In fact, the Canadian coast guard had, in the past, gifted several boats to the Haitians, including several like these. The team had already put on red and blue stripes on both sides, Haitian colors, making sure to include signs of wear and tear. They were working now on aging the paint throughout.

Callie had asked Andre to set up a stove in one corner, then to move a long table beside the stove, which now held everything that she needed for the chili she was making for dinner. She waved at Andre who came over. He looked good, she thought. This kind of work agreed with him. "Andre, a question for you."

"I already know. Yes, I heard from my friend Alvaro, and yes, he's taken—no, I think the correct word is *smitten*—with Sara."

"Is that like him, falling so quickly?"

"Absolutely not. I've never heard him talk like this. This is a smart, charming, attractive man. As long as I've known him, at least ten years, he's had women chasing after him. He's always gently held them off and stayed single. This is different."

"Tell me about that, about him."

"He's always kept to himself. He lost his mom when he was twenty-five, and his dad died just before he left Cuba. He lives by himself. He's very capable, self-sufficient, and I trust him completely."

"That's high praise coming from you. Please tell me more."

"His mom was a wonderful Cuban singer. I used to spend time with her. I first met her son when he was maybe twenty-three. He was doing odd jobs for local TV and film crews. He was resourceful and able to get work, but it wasn't moving fast or far enough for him. After his mother died, he wanted to make more money. I watched him get a go-fast boat that he used to smuggle Cubans to Florida. Maybe two years later, I had him do some diamond exporting for me. He was cautious, honest, and reliable. We were both smart outsiders, and unexpectedly, we began talking to each other regularly. Without intending it, over time, he became a very close friend. Truthfully, he's like a son to me."

"So, you're telling me you turned this resourceful TV and movie person, a young man you cared for like a son, into a smuggler—of people and diamonds."

"Callie, sometimes you can be too judgmental and very irritating."

She made a face, pouting. "Okay. Maybe that's true. Andre, you know I love you, and if you tell me this young man is like a son to you, I know you did right by him. I'm sorry. As you know, I can be too quick to judge. Forgive me. Please go ahead and explain."

"In fact, when he had enough money, I encouraged him to give up smuggling Cubans to Florida. Then I helped him buy a night club in South Beach. Today, he's a well-respected businessman who runs two truly fantastic nightspots. He only took Sara and Cash to Cuba because I asked him to."

"Why do you think he's fallen for Sara?"

"He said that she's a breath of fresh air, that she somehow brings out his very best. He actually told me that she makes his heart soar. He's thirty-four, and I've never heard him talk like that before."

"Is the age difference an issue?"

"On the contrary, I think he's old enough to genuinely understand and trust his feelings."

"What do you think?"

"Sugar, I'm no damn good at predicting things like this. I would never have bet on you and Cash. But I can tell you this—Alvaro will never lie to her, and he'll work very hard to make her happy. If she cares for him, he's worth a chance."

"That's a damn good start. And don't call me Sugar."

♦♦♦

Nestor had dropped them in Old Havana to walk, after making them a dinner reservation at one of his favorite restaurants. He also gave them the names and directions to two classic bars. As he explained it, "Floridita, open in 1817, where Hemingway went to drink the best daquiris in Cuba, and Bodeguita del Medio, said to make the best mojitos. He also gave them a map where he'd marked the Museo de la Revolución, where Fidel's boat, the Granma, was on display and then in Vedado, the John Lennon park, a place he recommended seeing."

Sara and Cash meandered through streets with colorful three-and-four story buildings—vivid pink, blue, yellow, green, and more in long blocks. In unexpected spots on some of those long streets you might find French colonial architecture, old Spanish style homes, or old apartments in good, and not so good, condition. They walked through a lovely old city square, lots of inviting restaurants, and stopped into a very old convent. There were, of course, the classic old American cars riding by beside more modern foreign cars, and a variety of people, a sampling of the many socioeconomic walks of life in Cuba today, a melting pot of young and old, skateboarders, rockers, older people sitting on balconies, looking down on the street life, young adults moving more quickly.

After a while, Sara led them into a large open market. There were many long carefully arranged stalls of fresh vegetables and fruits, including giant watermelons and ripe pineapples. In one corner, Sara pointed out bottles of picante Afrodisíaco, loosely translated as very spicy hot pepper aphrodisiacs. Cash bought a bottle to harass Andre.

Outside the market they caught a cab. Sara found a red and white '58 Ford Edsel convertible, and she was thrilled. She asked the driver, a woman her age named Paz, in Spanish, to take them to the Museo de la Revolución. It was a clear warm day and a wonderful ride, often along the water, in the convertible. Paz wore jeans and a blue Cuban T-shirt that was printed in English, in white, "actually, I'm in Havana." She had dark curly hair and a warm expressive face. Her dark eyes seemed to get wider when she flashed her appealing smile. Paz answered Sara's nonstop questions in Spanish, including telling her that her T-shirt was designed by two gifted women designers who had created Cuba's first independent sustainable fashion brand, Clandestina. It took just a few minutes for them to have a relaxed, friendly rapport. Sara learned that Paz was at the University of Havana, and was particularly interested in hearing how positively Paz felt about her studies—she wanted to be a college professor, and she was studying comparative literature, contemporary Spanish, and English.

Before long, they could see the large glass structure that housed Fidel's boat. When they left the taxi, Sara asked Paz to wait, then they made the short walk to see the glass enclosed Granma, the yacht Fidel Castro boarded on November 25, 1956, with eighty-two fighters of the Cuban Revolution, to make the voyage from Mexico to Cuba. It was a difficult, perilous journey, and they disembarked on December 2 on the Playas Las Coloradas. The location was chosen to follow the voyage of José Martí, who sixty-one years earlier had landed in the same region during the war of independence from Spanish colonial rule. They were forced to land in a swampy area, fifteen miles south of the designated spot. Still the revolution was underway. The revolutionary forces triumphed on January 1, 1959.

Enjoying the taxi ride, Cash and Sara decided to ask Paz to take them next to John Lennon Park. It was about a fifteen-minute ride and both Cash and Sara enjoyed the street life. On the way, they stopped to listen to three talented street musicians, drums, a clarinet, and a saxophone, playing pleasant, lyrical Cuban music. Eventually, Sara and Paz continued their conversation in Spanish, while Cash happily watched the city go by out the window.

Paz somehow got Sara to admit that she'd met an interesting Cuban man, and Paz had lots of practical advice on that subject. When asked, Paz told Sara that her boyfriend was an American, a university student from Miami, writing his thesis about health care in Cuba. This, in turn, caused Sara to counsel her, until Paz stopped not far from the park, to let them walk in. Again, Sara asked her to wait. As they walked, Cash asked what they were talking about, Sara simply said, "girl stuff about our boyfriends." Cash tactfully refrained from asking when Alvaro had become her boyfriend.

In the park there were lots of people walking or sitting on benches, kids skateboarding or playing games with coins on the ground. Sara and Cash stopped and sat on a bench not far from the brass statue of John Lennon, wearing his glasses, happily seated on a bench. Sara was intrigued and, in Spanish, she asked a young woman coming by to tell her the story of the John Lennon statue. The woman liked Sara's smile and smiled back warmly, then told her, "The Beatles were banned from Cuba in the sixties and seventies. They were considered decadent influences during a time of revolution. Twenty years after Lennon's death, Fidel changed his mind, dramatically. He created the John Lennon Park, unveiled the bronze statue you're looking at. Fidel said, and I still remember his quote, 'I share his dreams completely. I too am a dreamer who has seen his dreams turn into reality.'"

Sara took her hand, then, in Spanish, "Thank you for sharing this wonderful story. I am new to Cuba, and your generosity speaks well of this country."

The young woman said, "Thank you," and then she was off on her way.

Sara went back and sat on the bench beside Cash, taking a minute to think about this place. Eventually she turned, "I like Cuba, very much... why do you think I feel that way so quickly, so easily?"

"How about that they really don't care that you're half Algerian? Or that it's pretty, with lots of vivid colors. How about that there's great music and fine dancing, and you love to sing and dance? And there are beautiful old classic American cars everywhere. Or that the people can be warm and generous—think about Nestor, and lest we forget, Alvaro."

"All true. But there's something else. It's way too early to know, but I feel oddly, just a hope actually, that I could relax, be comfortable here in a way I never expected. I feel like I fit in. I never felt that in France. I liked Seattle and New York City, but they didn't look or feel like my place. There are so many different looking people here. People look accessible, like this girl I just talked to, or Paz, our taxi driver. That would never happen for me in France. I could walk down the street here and no one would know I'm not Cuban."

"This is interesting. You have this fast, insightful mind, and as you become more self-aware, it goes nonstop…Take your time. Let this percolate, settle in. Why don't we move on to one of the bars Nestor recommended, have a Cuban drink, and carry on our conversation."

"Okay, but Dad, I'm sensing that something new is happening to me here. I think I like it, but it's still way ahead of me. And some of it is hard to understand."

"When you're ready, I'd like to hear more about that."

"Soon. Give me a little more time to think about it, then we'll talk."

They walked back to the Edsel, quiet, just looking around, each of them lost in their own thoughts. Sara asked Paz in Spanish if she knew El Floridita, the bar. Paz nodded, told Sara in Spanish, "Oh yes. It's very popular."

"Do you go there?"

"Occasionally, my boyfriend and I go there, for nostalgia. We both love Hemingway."

"Nice…So that makes me think about another question. Are you and your boyfriend movie watchers?"

At the word movie, Cash sat down on a bench to wait this out.

Paz thought about this, then volunteered, "Yes, we watch lots of movies, however we can get them, mostly he brings them, and we watch them on his computer. But we have very different tastes. We never like the same things."

"Such as?"

"I love period romances—like *Sense and Sensibility*. Great love stories. He likes off-center action—fighting movies—*Kill Bill*. We take turns choosing, and we watch each other's selections, but it's hard for us to find a movie that we both love."

"Humor me, a few more questions…Do you like *Shakespeare in Love, A Room with a View*?"

"Yes, I love those movies."

"And I'm guessing he favors *The Warriors* or *The Deer Hunter*?"

"Yes, he had me watch both of those with him."

"Paz, I have an idea for you. I think I know a movie you'll both love."

"That would be very hard, likely impossible."

"Bear with me…I'm going to suggest *Last of the Mohicans* with Daniel Day-Lewis and Madeleine Stowe. I'm guessing you know the novel."

"I do know the James Fenimore Cooper novel. It's assigned in my American literature course this semester though I haven't read it yet. I don't know the movie."

"It's a 1992 movie…It's both a period romance and an epic drama set in 1757 during the French and Indian war. For your boyfriend, it has breath-taking, very exciting action, intense fighting. For you it has a heart-stirring period romance. Best, for both of you, it's totally unexpected, off-center, especially the people, the relationship. And if he's the man I think he is, he'll love you forever for suggesting it."

"How can you know that?"

"Trust me on this, Paz."

"Well, okay." She smiled. "If this works, I'll treat you to my private bar tour."

Sara touched Paz's shoulder. "Please call me after you watch it together."

"Deal, absolutely."

And shifting gears, "Perfect…Okay…Back to the moment, how far is Floridita?" Sara asked.

At the word Floridita, Cash stood up, opened the car for Sara.

"Maybe fifteen minutes, it's not far from where we were earlier, at the Granma. I'll take a different way back." Paz sat behind the wheel, and then they were off. After neither of them knew how many blocks, Cash pointed out the Hemingway bar, El Floridita. At the corner, it was an unpretentious pink building with a colorful blue and green sign above it. Opened in 1817, it was over two hundred years old. As Nestor put it, "This bar is 'the cradle of the daiquiri' in Cuba." It was busy with yellow taxis nearby, and visitors coming in and out. Outside, Sara said goodbye to Paz, and said they'd walk from there. Paz gave her a hug, which Sara responded to warmly, though it took her by surprise. Paz gave her a card saying, "Call anytime if you need a driver."

"I will. You were great." Sara nodded. "Thank you."

"My pleasure." Paz gave Sara a second card, saying, "For your phone number."

Sara wrote it down, handed it to her, adding, "Please call after you see the movie."

"I will."

"I'll look forward to that." Sara turned to Cash, who, she knew, would leave this friendly woman a generous tip.

Cash opened the door for Sara into El Floridita. Inside, it was crowded. There was a long black bar with bartenders pouring daiquiris in cocktail glasses. Behind the bar were handsome, long, red-colored cabinets with black trim. The room was full, with red tables to sit around. There was another room with tablecloths on the tables where people were eating. They took a moment to look at a statue, a giant Martini glass with a white painted glass perched on top of a long bright red stem. From there, they stopped to admire the bronze statue of Hemingway, seated at his favorite spot at the far corner of the bar. Memorable photos, including one in which he was with Fidel Castro, sat on the corner wall behind him.

A moment later, Cash and Sara found two stools side by side at the bar. Sara ordered daiquiris for each of them. Their cocktails came quickly, and they raised their glasses in a silent toast before tasting this famous drink.

Sara smiled, looked around, unexpectedly feeling vaguely apprehensive, not sure about what. After a beat, "Lots of tourists here."

"Too crowded, too loud." He tasted more of his drink. "But the drinks are fantastic. Once I finish one, I'm ready to move on." He checked his watch. "To use your word, 'Wow!' It's already five thirty. Our dinner reservation is at six. Let's walk over there, have a memorable dinner."

"Yeah. I peeked at the menu when Nestor proposed it. It's real Cuban food. I'm dying for suckling pig."

"Perfect. Let's go."

♦♦♦

The restaurant Nestor had chosen was called Al Carbon. Ivan, the chef, was especially known for his charcoal roasted Cuban classics, specialties he prepared on his unique indoor wood-fired barbeque. Sara explained that Al Carbon means "charcoal" in Spanish.

It was a short pleasant walk, less than ten minutes. Along the way, Cash led her into the Hotel Kempinski, originally Cuba's first European-style shopping arcade. It was gutted and converted into a 246 room hotel in 2017. The hotel now features a ground floor shopping mall. Inside, Cash found a cigar bar. He couldn't resist stepping inside, checking out the walls full of Cuban cigars stacked in neat piles. Sara had to pull him out, saying "Dad," almost a whine, "I'm way too hungry to watch you smell cigars. Can we do that another time?" A warm, Sara kind of smile, then, "Please."

Maybe five minutes later, Cash and Sara easily found the unassuming yellow building and walked into the lively, welcoming Al Carbon space. The walls and open spaces were completely covered with all different kinds of artwork, decorative plates, assorted antiques and vintage objects from various periods, favorite photos, varied posters, drawings, an unexpected playful mounted statuette, festive chandeliers, flowers, potted plants, colorful table cloths, and a dark wood counter sat on a red brick base with the busy open kitchen dramatically visible beyond. It was cozy, lots to see but never intrusive, thoughtfully, carefully presented, but not self-conscious. Cash and Sara took it all in, then they were seated at a quiet table against the wall. There was no air conditioning inside, and they were glad that the big doors stayed wide open on the street.

Cash kept looking around, then offered, "This is a special place. Without a word, it somehow welcomes you, pulls you in, and invites you to enjoy the treat that is unquestionably soon to come."

Sara laughed, "All true and very fancy. How about I already love this place?"

"Not so fancy, but pretty damn good."

Before she could respond, the waiter brought a large portable written menu. Cash looked at the big menu, then handed it to her. "I don't do too well reading Spanish. I know I'll have Cuban beer and the suckling pig. If you're agreeable, why don't you pick out appetizers and a dessert that we can share."

"Happy to do that."

A few minutes later Sara signaled the waiter that they were ready. When he arrived, she ordered in Spanish, "We'll have two Cuban beers, Cristal. For appetizers, please bring us the Crab with Avocado, one ceviche, and one vegetable skewers, then your Suckling Pig for both of us. For dessert, could you please describe the Four Milks (Cuatro Leches)?"

The waiter responded in Spanish, "Tres Leches is a famous Latin desert. It's sponge cake, or butter cake, soaked in three kinds of milk—evaporated milk, condensed milk, and heavy crème. Chef Ivan's desert is called 'Four Milks,' his personal spin on Tres Leches."

"Perfect. Muchas Gracias."

The waiter nodded. "Thank you. Excellent choices," then he left.

"Well done. Please explain it as it comes," Cash asked.

"Can do."

It was quiet then, as they took a thoughtful moment, each of them in their own worlds. It was a long comfortable silence, but after several minutes, Sara seemed concerned about something.

The waiter came back with two Cristal beers in their colorful green bottles with the name written in white on a red banner.

Before Cash could propose a toast, Sara, suddenly anxious, whispered, "Am I doing all right with you? I hope I'm not disappointing you."

"Why would you ever worry about that?"

"Here's the thing, lately, I've been worrying unexpectedly, about unexpected things."

"Do you know why?"

"I've thought about it when I can. It's like worries pop into my mind when I'm not actively shutting them out."

"That's unusual for you isn't it?"

"Absolutely. I've never been like this."

"Why do you think it's happening?"

"Part of it has to be that I'm overwhelmed. I think it's likely that this wild rollercoaster ride has finally caught up with me."

"I'm sure that's true. Can you be more specific?"

"Sort of…" She took a beat, thoughtful. "Think about what it's been like for me…One minute, I'm on a boat in the San Juan Islands and someone tries to kill me, then I meet my dad for the very first time. Right away, there are several violent conflicts. Soon after, I get some high-powered advice about being more aware of my feelings. Several days later, I'm on a fast boat, sneaking into Cuba where I'm staying in a fancy mansion in Havana. The first day there, we're sending pictures to the people who tried to kill me. That same day, I'm sending my first whole day alone with my dad. Soon, you're getting on a boat to kidnap those same people, and that's worrying me. But there's something else, something new, that keeps taking over—I have to say this—in between all of this, I met the first man I've ever known that actually might interest me romantically, seriously interest me—"

"Whoa, that last piece is news to me. And that's a big deal. Please tell me more."

"In less than one night, Alvaro touched a part of me that no man has ever reached. I'm not sure how to describe it—"

"Was it the movies?"

"No. Lots of people know movies. But in that there's an example of what I mean. Think about the movies he chose to ask me about. I guarantee you, no one would ask me about *Streets of Fire* or *The Clockmaker of Saint Paul*...He got me—my quirky, eccentric taste... my carefully worked out, uncommon sensibility—not because he figured it out intellectually, but because he recognized it—*it was somehow like his own*. We're both interested in unconventional people, in outsiders, who try to understand what's going on around them. It's like what Itzac said to me about being self-aware. I do so want to be that, and so does Alvaro. I'm sure of that. I could talk with him for hours, about anything, and it would never be boring. I've never, ever had anything like that. I'm sorry to keep going on about him."

"You're sure about this?"

"Yes. Yes, I think so."

"I think you've opened Pandora's box."

"What? Who's Pandora. What's Pandora's box?"

Give me a second, I'll read it from Merriam-Webster. Cash looked it up on his phone. "Okay...'The god Prometheus stole fire from heaven to give to the human race, which originally consisted only of men. To punish humanity, the other gods created the first woman, the beautiful Pandora. As a gift, Zeus gave her a box, which she was told never to open. However, as soon as he was out of sight she took off the lid, and out swarmed all the troubles of the world, never to be recaptured. Only Hope was left in the box, stuck under the lid. Anything that looks ordinary but may produce unpredictable harmful results can thus be called a Pandora's box.'"

"I love that story...So falling in love may produce unpredictable harmful results."

"May, but not necessarily. I think falling in love has, for you, raised all kinds of worrisome possibilities. But if you know what's causing you to worry, let's open the box again, reach under the lid and take out hope. Go slowly, spend some time with him. I think your worries will become more manageable. Here's what I'd suggest: Let's finish what we set out to do here, then why don't you invite him to Seattle? No one can host a celebratory dinner like Callie."

"I'm sure that's true. And seeing him would be really good, wonderful for me."

They paused as the waiter brought their appetizers. Sara asked for two extra plates.

"Three appetizers?" Cash asked.

"I couldn't resist."

"I'll try them all."

Sara gave each of them an extra plate, then passed all three appetizers to the middle of the table. They helped themselves to portions of each. After they tried each, and expressed how good they all were, she asked him, "You have any fatherly advice for your overwhelmed daughter?"

He looked up from eating, thinking about her question.

She took another bite, swallowed, then went on, "I mean what you've said is helpful, but honestly, this really caring for someone is so new for me. It's—I dunno—both exciting and unsettling."

Cash took another helping. "My suggestion—go slow. Take your time. Baby steps are fine. If it's what you hope it is, it will only get better, get easier."

"I'm not sure that slow is in my repertoire."

"Then it's about time you tried it. This man has become very important for you, and you've only met him once. Make him confirm those feelings you have, when it isn't easy, under pressure...over and over, again and again. When you know that you can rely on him, thick or thin, period, you can go as fast as you'd like."

"I'm guessing that should take me about ten minutes, max."

"Yes, who am I with?...okay then...understanding that, it's all the more reason to slow it down, make an exception on this. Especially now, when you're already overwhelmed. Time is your ally. You won't lose anything by slowing down. In fact, if what you hope is right, your feelings will only deepen as you go slowly. If you pay attention, you'll see that, feel it happening."

She finished her plate. "Huh, you really think that?"

"I do."

"Maybe, but before I try that, I gotta ask this…Are you mostly talking about sex?"

"My plain-spoken daughter. I do love that you're not timid with your dad. The answer is no. Sex is only a piece of it, and you can try that whenever you're ready. It's mostly deep feelings, commitment, that I'm talking about."

"The sex part is good news…" She smiled. "The rest feels forced… unnatural…not like me."

They paused as the suckling pig arrived and the waiter sliced it beside the table. He added new plates, then helped prep each person's plate.

They began eating, raving about the pig, then Cash asked, "Have you ever been in love?"

"I loved my mother, but I never really loved a man, a partner…"

"That makes what I'm saying even more important."

"How long before you knew and trusted your feelings for Callie?"

"More than three years."

"Wow, when you say go slow, you mean like glacier speed, maybe taking steroids then inching like a tortoise…what happened?"

Cash laughed, swallowed another bite. "Truthfully, until just before we got together, it never occurred to me that she might be a romantic interest."

She cut another piece of pig. "That's different from me… What happened to wake you up?"

"She kept surprising me."

"Like what?" She leaned closer, liking talking about this.

"Well she demanded more from me than any woman I'd ever known. At first that irritated me, but I found myself rising to the occasion, and by the end, we both started liking those conversations."

Another swallow, a pleased sigh, then, "I'm not sure I understand."

"Fair enough. It took me a long while to understand it myself. I'll try to explain…Here's what I was eventually able to figure out. Okay…I was always pretty good at pleasing women, but there was some part of myself I always held back. Over time, I realized that it wasn't a part—like a piece—but rather a portion of my unusual intensity. In other words, I only offered as much as a woman looked for—some essential emotional minimum—to sustain the relationship. I came to understand that it wasn't something I did consciously, but rather it was a strong, keenly sensitive person's way of unnecessarily protecting a partner from unwanted, possibly unsettling intensity. It's who I was—everything I did, I did well, but sparingly. So in some way I didn't understand, before Callie, I was choosing women who were less intense than I was." He took another sip of his beer.

Sara watched him, waiting.

Cash went on, vibrant, he understood this. "Callie was the first woman I'd ever been around—and this was even before we were together—who demanded one hundred percent from me at all times. At first, it wasn't often, and it was simply annoying. Over time, I tried not to hold anything back from her—still, she always wanted an explanation, an elaboration, an argument, or an answer to a difficult question. She was relentless and even when she wasn't aware of it, every bit as intense as I was. The out-of-the-blue way that this steadily progressed between us, the strength of it as we finally got together, was something entirely new and constantly surprising for me. Along with this, almost unnoticed, she kept stepping up, unexpectedly, under pressure. Between both of those things, I came to think about her differently. It took me a long time to understand that this careful, often anxious, occasionally inflexible woman, when faced with new, difficult things, was working very hard to respond thoughtfully, helpfully, while being true to herself. And as I got that, I realized that, especially when it got too hard, and it did, she had an exceptional, strong, fine heart." He nodded, done, then went back to eating.

Sara finished, set down her fork and knife. "At every turn, you're this unexpected thinker, and that's quite an unusual, lovely story you just told. Still, you have to admit, I think I'm way ahead of where you were when you started."

"Maybe, certainly in some ways, but I stand by my advice."

"I'll think about what you said…Talk with Alvaro about it."

"That's a good start."

"So that's a deal. Can I change the subject?"

"Of course."

They watched the waiter clear the remains of the pig, mostly the head.

"Another question, something I've never asked about…" She paused, nervous about how to ask, deciding not to overthink it. "Did you love my mother?"

"That's a good question. I've been thinking about your mother, too…" Cash took her hand across the table. "I was younger, and it was different, but seeing you, knowing you, I understand now that I loved her. Yes, I still love her."

"I'm so glad. I love her even more, if that's possible, since I met you."

"She'd have loved to see us together, be with us."

"For me, she's here, especially today."

They let that sink in as the waiter brought and served dessert and the creamy sweet, brown-sprinkled coffee.

❖❖❖

The Macher had arrived in Haiti on a helicopter. He wore a handsome Brunello Cucinelli black Cashmere coat and a white Borsalino fedora with a black hatband. He set his coat and hat on a chair at the head of the table, then he had Andre walk him through the work-in-progress Haitian coast guard vessel. He approved of the boat wholeheartedly, especially liking how it was convincingly scuffed throughout. Andre nodded, pleased, then invited him to join Callie and the crew for dinner. Callie had prepared a delicious large chili with lots of condiments—onions, various cheeses, scallions, mushrooms, even sausages—and a colorful rainbow Orzo salad. She served it with her own zesty vinaigrette, a favorite she'd invented at her restaurant.

The crew were well-built, strong Haitians. Though they'd already met Itzac before on the phone, Andre introduced each of them, again, by name. Itzac expressed his pleasure with the team, specifying that they were well suited for this job.

After, the Haitians returned to eating their chili hungrily. The Macher sat at the end of the long table with Andre and Callie, asking them about their plan.

Andre detailed their strategy—from boarding the LIAN as it came through the Windward Passage between Cuba and Haiti, then specifying the kidnapping, and finally delivering Rosie, Yu, and Johnny in their boat to Punta de Maisí, the easternmost edge of Cuba. There, they'd be driven to the airport then put on a plane to Havana. At the end, Andre said that he presumed the Macher would be there to consult with the senior Cuban negotiators in Havana."

The Macher nodded.

"Cash, Callie, and I will also fly to Havana on that very day."

"Yes, this all sounds good. I'll helicopter to Cuba tomorrow, to take over from Cash with Sara. What do you hear from them?"

Callie replied, "The usual—never a dull moment. Sara and Andre's friend, Alvaro, who took them to Cuba, are at the earliest stage of a romance. If you want to learn more, talk with Andre."

Itzac looked at Andre, who nodded. "He's a fine young man. In another time, when this is over, they could be very good together."

"Callie, what does Cash have to say about this?"

"He's all for it. You'd think he'd be more protective of his newfound daughter, but you know him. He just really wants her to be happy. Truthfully, I kind of like how he is. He should be calling soon, if you'd like to talk with him."

"Please…Actually, I've been thinking about your unusual partner, and I'm very interested to hear more about how he's doing with fatherhood. He's what, forty-seven, and he's just started with a twenty-five-year-old daughter."

"He's working hard at it. It's like he got this remarkable, unexpected gift. He's making a genuine effort to talk with her, listen to her, get to know her. I can tell you he spends a lot of time thinking about her.

I'm guessing that she's met a profound need he never allowed himself to have. Truthfully, he smiles more often. I genuinely love watching the two of them, they're so alike in some ways—you've seen them sing "Crazy." They enjoy each other enough, that I often expect them to pinch themselves—to confirm it's not a dream."

"I'm not surprised, and how is it for you?"

"It was complicated at first—I wasn't sure how I fit, and I was worried, maybe even a little jealous. But it's actually become a treat for me, and unexpectedly, it's good for Cash and I together. Although she's not my daughter, she's part of our family, and I love the way I have a new role—she treats me like a valued advisor, a wise, elder statesperson."

"Interesting. How did that happen?"

"In part it's because I'm Lew's mom, but it starts with Cash. In his way, without drawing attention to it, he includes me. Because of that, Sara knows he talks to me and that he listens to me, really pays attention to what I think."

"Yes, of course he does."

"She's interested in that, and she's come to respect me…Mostly, she wants to figure out her dad, even though she doesn't always understand him. She hopes that I can help her with that."

"She's smart. Say more."

"You know how he thinks about, tries to understand, new things. This is an entirely new, very important event for him to figure out. You can see him working on it. He doesn't quite have it yet, but you and I know he'll get there. She's hoping so, but she's not sure. She listens when I try to answer her questions."

"Good. I'm sure you're helping her."

"She knows he's working hard at learning about being a father. She can already tell how important it is to him. I mostly watch, marveling at his intensity, the energy and caring he brings to it. Sara can't quite allow herself to trust that this is working out as well as it is. But Itzac, here's the thing—In the midst of all of this, of reassuring her—I'm seeing how I'm so very lucky myself. This is the unexpected thing for me. With

Sara in the picture, being with Cash just keeps getting richer, more complex. I've never understood that more than I do now."

"That's perfect. Most partners would be envious, resent Sara's time and attention with him."

Andre stood, put his hand on Callie's shoulder, squeezing gently. "You're too judgmental, quick to criticize, and capable of being impossibly irritating. That said, you're not selfish, you're unusually insightful, and you're capable of real change." He leaned in, gently squeezed both of her shoulders.

Itzac added, "It's a pleasure to watch you navigate through something like this." He put on his fedora, then tipped it high. "Chapeau."

CHAPTER TWELVE

It was 10:30 p.m. when the taxi dropped them at the Villa. It was a warm, dark night and a sliver moon was the only light in the cloudy sky. Sara and Cash sat outside on the patio on lounge chairs, with comfortable cushions and ottomans. They'd had a wonderful dinner and were still savoring their lovely conversation. Cash was raising up to make more coffee when he felt the gun pressed against the back of his head.

Eddie simply said, "don't move." With his other hand, he injected the syringe into Cash's neck. The syringe contained a synthetic narcotic analgesic. Cash was just about out on the chair when Sara turned and saw their predicament. Eddie turned the gun to her head, then deftly injected the syringe into her neck, putting her out on the other chair. When Cash feebly tried to move his head, Eddie smashed the gun down on his face, breaking his nose, causing blood to drip down his mouth. In another moment, he was out. After confirming, again, that they were both unconscious, Eddie tied their hands behind their backs, covered their mouths with duct tape, then left both of them there as he hurried down the road to retrieve his car.

A moment later, Eddie returned driving a Volkswagen Passat rental. He backed the car against the chairs, opened the trunk, then, using his strong muscular upper body, lifted first Cash, then Sara into the uncomfortable trunk. Next, he locked the trunk and drove off. He'd done his homework, then sent one of his best men with a Cuban contact person, one that he'd hired through a well-placed, Miami friend, to find a suitable place. This afternoon he'd gone himself almost to Soroa to scout it out. He liked what he saw.

Now, he turned the car off the road. It was almost an hour since they'd left the villa. He drove ahead on a dirt road winding through a wooded area not too far from Soroa, stopping fifteen minutes later at a decrepit, abandoned cabin near a long, useless old stone well. He got out of the car, opened the trunk, checked that they were both still out, then he texted Yu and waited for a call back.

"I have both of them," Eddie explained, on his new phone, an amenity from his Cuban contact. "They're tied up, unconscious in my trunk, at the location I found."

"Isn't this earlier than you anticipated?"

"Yes, one day ahead of schedule. The opportunity presented itself." He added, "The security guards are tied and locked down in the basement of the villa shed."

"Excellent." Yu replied, clearly pleased.

"As you asked, I'm asking for your permission to complete the task, as we agreed."

"Yes, text to confirm completion. Send it to Lennie, in LA. He will securely send it on to me. I'll let him know to expect your text."

"Will do. I'll send 'mission accomplished' with the initial EX to Lennie in LA."

"He'll look forward to your text."

"Good."

"Also, send an email to Callie James. Send it from Cash's phone. Tell her 'All is well. I'll call in two days.' Confirm this email as well in your text to Lennie."

"No problem. I'll add 'email sent' to my text." Eddie broke the connection.

He returned to the crowded trunk and lifted Sara out. Eddie dropped her on the ground. He returned to the trunk, checking Cash. Once he confirmed that Cash's hands were tied, his mouth gagged, and he was still out, Eddie used his powerful upper body to pull him out of the trunk. Rather than leaving Cash on the ground, Eddie carried him several yards before placing him over the top of the well, his upper body facing down the deep, open hole. Cash had blood around his broken nose, his mouth, and dripping down his chin. Eddie confirmed again that Cash was unconscious, then returned to the car, checking on his way that Sara, on the ground, was unmoving, her body twisted in an odd position.

In the car, he retrieved his gun on the front seat and took a flashlight from the glove compartment. Eddie went back to the well. He set down the flashlight and the gun while he carefully positioned Cash, still lifeless, adjusting him well over the edge. When he was satisfied, he took the flashlight, turned it on, then looked down the light into the well. Carefully, he confirmed that there was nothing protruding into the well that Cash's body could get snagged on. When he was satisfied, Eddie brought Cash's head up by his hair, adjusting him again just so, then he raised the gun to the back of his head.

Eddie turned, off guard, as Sara screamed. He barely saw her then, a mirage, a flash, hurtling through the air, still howling her rage, arms extended, legs poised, just before she fiercely kicked his nose with her heel, destroying his face. He got off one shot, a micro-second before he fell to the ground crying out incoherent sounds, his ravaged face, oozing blood, semi-unconscious. Sara was on him, a sharp knife in her right hand, grabbing his hair from behind with her left hand, her knees behind his head. With her right hand, she deftly slit his throat, blood surging into the air. She held his head back until he died.

Cash had barely managed to wake up and lift his head when she screamed. He saw her flying through the air, like a trapeze artist, just before she twisted as her right heel decisively struck Eddie's nose. He watched her cut his throat from behind, blood gushing, even after he died.

With a tremendous effort, Cash pulled himself off the well and onto the ground, convinced he was in a dream. His face was still covered with blood.

Sara sat on the ground against the well, near Cash. She was heaving, great breaths, crying, calming herself. Blood was spilling from a hole in her left upper thigh, where she'd been shot. There was blood on her sleeves, her pants. She turned, leaning into Cash's ear. "You're safe. It's over." She gently pulled the tape off his mouth.

He pressed his cheek against hers. "Oh my God, Sara, you're hurt, bleeding...There's a lot of blood."

"The bullet is still in my thigh. Luckily, I twisted into my kick as he shot. It hurts like hell, but I'll live. Most of the blood on my clothes, it's his."

"Thank God." He spoke slowly, carefully.

"Help me untie your hands, then patch me up, and I'll tell you exactly what happened, how it happened."

Cash turned his back to her, so she could reach the ropes around his hands. It took several minutes to free him. After he turned on his knees to face her. Sara put her hands around her father's neck. Cash wrapped his arms behind her back. Sara was the first to cry, then Cash's tears flowed freely.

Cash eventually asked, "Did you actually do this?...kill this assassin...smash his face with your foot, then slit his throat?"

"Yes, I did."

"Sorry. I'm still in a dream...Let me fix you up as best I can, then I'll ask my questions."

Sara nodded, plainly in pain. Cash teared his shirt sleeve off and had her put it over the hole in her thigh, hoping to slow the bleeding.

When she had it in place, Cash applied considerable pressure over it, to reduce the bleeding even further. When she stopped screaming, he went to the car. In the front seat, he took the roll of tape the assassin had used on the security guards and on them. Next, he pulled off a headrest he could use to prop up her leg and left it on the floor of the back seat. In the glove compartment, he found a flask. He opened it, smelled it. Okay, it was rum. He took the tape and the flask back to the well where Sara was still sitting, holding the sleeve over the still bleeding bullet hole. She was crying, softly. Cash unbuttoned her pants, pulled down her jeans, then he tore his other shirt sleeve. He covered the new rag with rum, then he said, "This is going to hurt," and he washed away the blood, cleansing the wound as best he could. Sara cried out several times.

He took out his clean handkerchief, folding it in four layers, then used it as a bandage to cover the hole. With the tape, he tied the make-shift handkerchief bandage over the inexpertly cleaned wound. He helped her apply pressure over the bandage. It was still bleeding, though not as much.

When he was done, she added, "It did hurt."

"Better now?"

"Just barely."

"We'll get it properly taken care of right away. But first, please, can you tell me what happened?...How did you do that?"

She took a careful breath, then spoke painstakingly, "For many years, I trained in martial arts...combat...from my shady boyfriend in Paris...He was a black belt specializing, off-the-record, in real combat." She paused, took another difficult breath. "But I never did anything as deadly as this."

"Are you okay to talk, or should we wait?"

"It's painful, but not as bad as it looks. I'd like to try...Okay. I woke up slowly in the trunk...After working hard, I was able to loosen one hand. Untying knots from behind was part of my training...I also learned to carry a small hidden knife, a two-inch expandable steel blade in a light soft handle I could easily clip inside the back of my pants..."

"How long have you been carrying a hidden knife?"

"Since I promised to do whatever I could to keep you safe. At Itzac's in New York City."

"I remember that, though I never would have guessed a hidden knife...Go on."

Another slow breath. "...I knew that I would have only one shot, and it would have to hurt him, somehow put him out...I planned exactly what I'd do, how I'd do it..." She paused, pacing herself. "Specifically, how I'd get up on the front of the car softly...On the ground, I could see how the killer was facing the well, and the front door was open...

so it made an easy step up." Another careful breath. "I freed my mouth. Then, I focused on one thing, one thing only, I had to save my father's life…I had to save my dad…Once I was in the air, the rest was years of practice. Once he was out on the ground, killing him scared me…I couldn't breathe…my heart was pounding like crazy…but I knew I had to do it…"

Eventually he said, "You did save my life."

Sara took his hand. "Since finding my mother in the hospital at fourteen years old…saving your life is the finest thing your daughter has ever done." She smiled, just barely.

"Sara, you've given me, and the two women I love most—you and Callie— a second chance together." He hugged her again, closely, then checked her bandaged wound. "There's more to say. But now, we need to get you to a doctor."

"That would be good…I'm feeling some pain, and I'm getting very tired…What about you?"

"Still waking up, covered with blood from my broken nose, but so far, no lasting injuries. Let's figure out what to do and make some calls to get help. I'll send a text to Callie, to have her standby."

Cash wrote, "Not to worry, we're okay, but lots to report. Please be ready for my call soon. Have Andre and Itzac there if possible."

She responded quickly, "Relieved to get your text. We'll await your call."

Cash pointed to the killer on the ground. "Do we need to confirm that he's dead?"

Sara looked at her dad. "Are you kidding?"

"Okay, your sense of humor is still intact."

Cash took out his phone, called Nestor, who answered right away. "Cash?" he asked.

"Yes. I don't know where we are. Please listen carefully. They tried to kill both of us. Sara saved our lives, but she has a gunshot wound in her upper thigh. The bullet needs to be taken out right away. She needs a doctor and medication. I don't think we should go to a hospital. We're in a wooded area more than an hour outside of Havana. I'll drive us out of the woods and call you when I find a landmark. In the meantime, can you trace a location from this phone?"

"I have access to someone who can. I'll get on it right away. Find a doctor and find you as soon as possible."

"I'll call you right back when I know more. I'll leave the phone on for your phone tracer."

"Sara, I'm going to carry you to the car. We can talk as we go."

"I heard one thing from the trunk...when I was waking up, that you should know...He was on his cell phone..." She caught her breath. "He said he'd send a text...'Mission Accomplished'...to confirm successful completion...signed with the initials EX." Another pause. "...I presume that means we're dead at the bottom of the well..."

"I think so too. Let's find his phone and send that text."

"He said he'd send it to a man named Lennie."

"Lincoln or the Macher will know that email address."

"The assassin also agreed to email Callie from your phone... tell her that you're fine...that you'll call soon, day after tomorrow..." She regrouped, speaking more slowly now. "He wanted Lennie to know when that was done...The assassin agreed to add 'email sent' to his text..." then softly, "Why did he want that?"

"It's to keep Callie from worrying about me. Remember I'm supposed to be dead. I'm betting that he also wanted the same guy to kill Callie right away—he'd want him to have time to get to her, before she knew she was in danger and took extra precautions."

"Man oh man...happily, I couldn't hear that...The guy also said that the security guards from the villa were tied in the basement of the shed."

"At least they're alive. I'll tell Nestor right away."

Cash stood, searched the dead man. He took his phone, his wallet—his name was Eddie King—and his keys and a little notebook. He also picked up Sara's knife, which was on the ground beside him. Then, without a word, Cash picked him up and dropped him into the well. When he looked down, Cash couldn't see the body.

Sara murmured, "Good fucking riddance…"

Cash raised the small black expandable knife, wiped it clean with his handkerchief, looked at Sara. She nodded, then took the small knife casing off the back of her pants, handed it to Cash. He dropped the knife and the case into the well.

"What happened to his gun?" Cash asked, looking around.

"It went into the well as he went down. Otherwise, I would have shot that asshole with it."

Cash just looked at her, then came over, put a hand on her neck, massaging it gently. He took his cell, called Nestor again. "The security guards from the villa are still alive, tied in the basement of the shed."

"Good to hear. I'll have someone free them. I'm in the car, on my way to you. My man found a rough location. You're near Soroa. Please let me know when you can identify anything specific. Be careful."

Cash turned off his phone, opened the back door of the car, and then went over to the well to tend to Sara. First, he pulled up her jeans, then he lifted her gently in his arms under both legs and carried her to the back seat of the car. He carefully lay her on the back seat. He raised her left thigh over the head rest he'd pulled off from the front seat, then he closed the door and went into the driver's seat. He could hear that Sara was crying again, softly. He started the Passat and drove down the dirt road toward the highway.

◆◆◆

Callie picked up the phone right away. It was after 1:30 a.m., and she and Andre and Itzac were still in the boathouse.

"We're all here," She began.

Before she could say more, Cash began talking, "Please listen carefully. We're okay, driving in the car toward Nestor and a doctor. Eddie King, one of Rosie and Yu's hit men, kidnapped us from the villa and tried to kill us. They obviously had another professional in place behind Jose, the man we slowed down. We missed it. In spite of our mistake, under pressure, Sara killed him, more on that later. She saved our lives, but she's been shot in the thigh, and it needs attention. While we wait for a doctor, the immediate thing is that I dropped Eddie down a well, and we need to send a text right away to their man Lennie that Eddie's mission is accomplished. Also, that the email he sent from my phone, to keep Callie unaware that I'm dead, has been sent. This will put us in the clear until we take them on their boat. I have the exact wording and Eddie's phone, but I need to confirm the email—"

The Macher interrupted. "I have it from Lincoln. I'll give it to you now." He did. "I'll also track down Eddie King and his connection to Yu and Rosie."

"Good. You can stay on the line while I send the text. It won't take long." Cash used the phone he took from Eddie. He sent: 'Mission Accomplished. Email sent. EX.'

"Done," Cash announced, then he continued, "Eddie also captured the guards, tied them up, locked them in the basement of the shed. Nestor is releasing them. I'd put Sara on, but she's in the back seat lying down in considerable pain. We are on speaker so she hears you."

"Okay. What can we do?" Callie asked.

"Everything should go as scheduled. Itzac can you be here tomorrow morning?"

"Yes, I have a helicopter, which I can give to you for your trip back here tomorrow."

"Excellent. There is some possibility that you'll have to capture their boat without me, depending on Sara's progress. I'll let you know later tonight, after we've seen the doctor."

"That's plenty of time," Andre reassured. "We hope it goes well, and that you can join us."

"Your call," the Macher added.

"Yes, but fingers crossed," Callie said, then she shifted gears, asking, "I can't wait another second. How did Sara kill this low-life, son-of-a-bitch assassin?"

Cash answered, "Okay, here's what I saw, no kidding...Eddie had me over this old, deep well, he was raising his gun, intending to shoot me in the back of the head, when I heard Sara howling like a savage predator. I looked up, barely in time, to see her flying through the air like a trapeze artist, just before she twisted and her right heel decisively struck Eddie's nose, smashing his face and knocking him down, semi-unconscious. Sara was on him like a wildcat, pulling his hair back and slitting his neck from behind with a knife she'd hidden at the small of her back."

"Oh my God, your daughter did that?" Callie asked, unsure.

"Yes, absolutely."

"She did that after she was shot?"

"Yes…He shot her as she twisted in the air, right before she killed him."

"Oh my God, Sara, you are, without a doubt, your father's daughter… Bravo!" Callie said again, before she started to cry. "Thank you, Sara… Truthfully, you saved my life, too!"

Andre added. "How long have you had a knife?"

"It's a small expandable blade, two inches of stainless steel. Legal, easy to hide. My American martial arts boyfriend in Paris bought it for me and taught me how to hide it, how to use it."

"I see…I never would have guessed that…Thank you Sara, I'm impressed. You did difficult, frightening work. You've helped us all in this little family, helped us immeasurably."

Cash slowed as he approached a town. He pulled off the road beside a sign. "I'm going to sign off. I need to call Nestor to give him our location. I'll keep you all posted. In the meantime, Itzac, can you arrange another place for us to stay tonight? I didn't ask Nestor, he has too much on his plate."

"You're more sensitive than I am. I'll call him right now in the car, work out a place."

"Thank you. I want Rosie and Yu to believe that Sara and I are dead, that Eddie accomplished his mission. I'll keep Eddie's phone in case Yu tries to contact him. I'll figure out how to respond if that happens."

"Understood," Callie said. "I'll write that email, send it back to you, if you don't have time. Call me anytime if I can help or just to talk. Most importantly, take exquisite care of your daughter, she's my heroine. Period."

The Macher added, "Sara, we didn't see this coming. I apologize for all of us, particularly for myself. It won't happen again. For now, we're going to make sure you're well and safe. You're a gift, young lady. As compelling, as unlikely, as magical as the miracle of Hanukkah."

From the backseat Sara feebly cried out, "What's the miracle of Hanukkah?"

"I'll explain it tomorrow."

Sara replied, softly, almost a whisper, "We'll have time...I'm going to have to cancel my salsa lesson."

◆◆◆

Cash talked with Nestor, who gave him directions to a quiet place, a turnoff for Mariel, where they could wait safely. It was a small open area between a group of trees, easy to find on the right side off the road, about half of the distance between them. It was deserted at 2:15 a.m., and Cash pulled off into a secluded area. Sara was dozing, fitfully. He looked at her, worrying. There was sweat on her face, and when he lightly touched her brow, she was feverish.

He watched her carefully. He realized that this young woman had guilelessly captured his heart. It wasn't like romantic love, what he felt so intensely for Callie. It was a new feeling for him, a prodigious sense of well-being, a visceral connection—pride to know her, to be her father. He wasn't sure how that had happened so quickly, so easily. He knew that when she saved his life it was a definitive moment, a punctuation mark. Cash said a silent prayer, a thing he never did, so thankful that both of them were still alive. He knew that they had years of unexpected experiences to share, and he was very grateful for that.

He was lost in thought when Nestor arrived. Nestor hurried over with another person, a woman, who went straight to look at Sara in the back seat. Nestor explained to Cash, "She's an excellent doctor and a friend that I trust. She'll examine Sara right now. Her name," Nestor added, "is Dr. Eva Montero. She doesn't speak much English, but I'll translate."

Dr. Montero had a large black bag and a bottle of water with her. She removed the headrest, then she washed her hands with soap and water. Next, she lowered Sara's wounded leg, took down her jeans, and took off their make-shift bandage. After examining the wound, she checked Sara's breathing, took her temperature, looked at her face and throat, then confirmed with Cash, through Nestor, that there were no other injuries. Then, she cleaned the area around the wound. Dr. Montero turned to Nestor, speaking Spanish. Nestor translated that the reddish medicine was Betadine, an iodine-based antiseptic, used for first aid and wound care. He continued, "The bullet has to be taken out right away. It's too early to know about infection, but she'll still need to give her antibiotics. Time is of the essence, so she'd like to do all of this right here, right now. She'll need your help to hold her down. This will not take long. She'll give her a shot but taking out the bullet will still hurt."

Cash held Sara's shoulders from behind. Next, Eva gave Sara a pain shot. She also gave her some sort of soft cloth to squeeze between her teeth, before she quickly opened up the wound. Next, she inserted her forceps, probing for the bullet. Sara screamed. Cash held her down. The bullet was reachable, and Eva was expert, able to remove it quickly. She dropped it in a small container that she'd taken out for this purpose. Sara closed her eyes, moaning, as Eva covered the wound. First, she applied more Betadine, then she covered it with gauze and bandaged it properly. After she closed it and bandaged it, she gave Sara another shot, an antibiotic.

When Sara was resting, Eva turned to Cash and Nestor. Nestor translated, "We got to her in time. The bullet was fairly deep but accessible. She'll be fine. She'll explain to you how to treat the wound going forward. She'll come see her again tomorrow afternoon." Eva turned to face Cash as Nestor said, "She thinks she should tend now to your nose and face."

"Thank you, Nestor," Cash replied.

Eva cleaned his face. After, she set his nose carefully, then bandaged it capably. When she was satisfied, she said to Nestor, who translated for Cash, "You'll be okay, too…not so good looking for a while, but fine… If anyone ever asks about Sara, this didn't happen here, in a car."

"Understood," Cash said. "And thank you so very much for coming all of this way and helping her and me."

Nestor translated.

"Nestor is like family," she managed to say in English. "He said he likes you, 'Yuma.'"

"Yuma?" Cash asked.

Nestor smiled. "It's Cuban slang for Americans or, occasionally, for other non-Spanish speaking foreigners. It's not offensive. People who care about the origins, trace the term to *3:10 to Yuma*, the cowboy movie."

"A classic," Sara managed to whisper. "Remade in 2007 with Russell Crowe and Christian Bale."

"Thank you, Sara. Now please take it easy." And to the doctor. "Nestor's a fine man." And to him, "Thank you, Nestor, for all of your help."

"I'm just getting started. Itzac called me, and you'll be staying tonight at my house."

Cash frowned, started to speak.

"Not a word. This is done, finished. We have a guest room for Sara, and you can sleep in our son's room. He's away in college. Even if you argue, it's too late to find anyplace else."

CHAPTER THIRTEEN

Sara woke up in Nestor's apartment at 10:30 a.m. Her upper left thigh ached, and she couldn't stand up easily, so she called Cash, who came right in. "How's your nose?" she asked, first thing.

He touched the bandage that covered it and spread to his cheeks. "It's growing on me. I like the little twist to the right." He pointed at her left leg, which was raised and covered.

"Hurts. I can't move it easily, and it's swollen." She made a pouty face. "Enough complaining. The doctor will check me later, and truthfully, I woke up feeling very lucky."

"That makes two of us, Sara. Itzac is here. Can I get you some coffee and invite him in?"

"Absolutely. Yes, it would be a treat." She adjusted her blanket. When Cash left the room, Sara straightened her hair as best she could.

The door opened and the Macher came in with a beautiful bouquet of flowers. He handed them to her. "This is from all of us—Callie, Lew, Andre, and me. It's a token of our profound admiration and appreciation."

She held the flowers to her chest. A single tear flowed down her cheek as Itzac continued, "I've thought about what you did for us. Though he'd never say it, Cash is the center, the unspoken leader, the heart if you will, of our carefully crafted family. We all rely on him in ways we're not even aware of. We talked about you and Cash late into the night. You kept our hard-earned family intact, and we'll never forget that."

The Macher took out his handkerchief, dried her tear, took the flowers and gave them to Cash, who set them in a vase. "You're part of that family. We're all profoundly aware that you've protected it, and you've enriched it."

She took Itzac's hand, aware how important this older man had become to her. "I had only five years with my mother. Until now, I never even knew my father. I was never part of a family. So you can't know how much this means to me. And I can't imagine a family I'd rather be a part of. Truthfully, Itzac, you're becoming like a grandfather to me, something I've never had."

"I'll be pleased and proud to be your grandfather. Now, we'll have more time to talk about this after Cash is gone to Haiti. Before he leaves though, I'd like to hear more about your new boyfriend."

"Boyfriend? I just met him. How do you even know about him?"

"Get used to your new family—news, especially good news, travels fast. I heard about him from Callie, from Andre, and from your dad this morning. What I hear about him is very positive. What do you say?"

"My dad, the Yuma—"

Itzac interrupted, smiling, "Yes, I know what that means. It suits him, and you're sounding more like a young Cuban woman every day."

"I like that movie, and I love how they've taken the name. And as soon as I heard it, I knew that it fit him. Anyway, when I tell you how I feel, he's going to get mad at me for going so fast." She looked at him, mouthed "Right?…Sorry," then turned back to Itzac, "But I think I'm in love, no kidding, and I hardly know him."

"This Alvaro is a very lucky man."

Cash stepped forward. "I tried to slow her down, every reasonable way I knew. I carefully, gently, argued for baby steps. She heard me out, nicely, politely, and even made an effort, but clearly it didn't convince her. And I've learned something important already about my daughter— when she sets her mind to something, she's unstoppable."

"I've seen that too. Are you going where I think you are?"

"Yes, absolutely…So now, my friend, since I'm in her debt, I'm going to suggest another way. And I'll need your help."

"You can rely on it."

Sara was looking at one of them then the other, confused, even a little exasperated. She finally interrupted, "I don't have any idea what you two men are talking about. How about explaining this to me, even use a topic sentence?"

Cash nodded. "We're way ahead of ourselves, but I'll put my idea out there. Allow me to build up to it, present it in the proper sequence. First, we have to hijack Rosie, Yu, and Johnny's yacht, get them to Havana. They'll have to return Javi's stolen money. Next, they need to restore your identity to you. All of this should be set in motion in three or four days. This will give you, Sara, time to heal. And that's a good time to execute my idea."

Cash looked around. The Macher was nodding, he knew where Cash was going. Sara was getting antsy again. Cash took her hand, looked her in the eye. "Rather than waiting to get your identity back and regrouping everyone in Seattle after we turn Rosie and Yu over to the Cubans, I propose we throw a remarkable party for you, Sara, right here in Havana. I'm sure the Cubans will help make it an unforgettable event, and most importantly, the guest of honor will be your friend, Alvaro."

Sara clapped out loud, adding, "Yes, yeah!"

Itzac added, "I'm guessing that you'll need me to make sure it's safe for Alvaro to come back to Cuba."

"Yes, exactly. It's the least we can do for Sara."

"Okay then." Sara hesitated before asking, "But I have to ask this— how can you guys even think about a party with so much dangerous work ahead?"

Itzac smiled. "It's the ideal time for it—something really extravagant, even wild, a thing we can genuinely look forward to. Truthfully, it relieves some of the tension, the apprehensiveness, about what still has to be done. And incidentally, you always end up spending more money than you intended to because you're operating on adrenalin, reminding yourself, 'a life like ours is often too short.'"

Sara was laughing. "You guys are nuts—great, but really nuts. And this family is even crazy by my quirky standards. But don't worry, I'm catching on, and I'm in. Dad, will you ask Andre to get the ball rolling?"

"I'll tell him when I see him today, have him give Alvaro a heads-up. Andre loves a great party. It's a good time for him to show you his tattoo.

That could be a special event. And yes, I'll even have him ask Alvaro to call his wounded sweetheart."

"Sooner the better."

♦♦♦

Rosie and Yu were having a late breakfast on deck, when the email came in from Lennie. It was to the point, "Mission accomplished. Email sent. EX." Yu handed it to Rosie, saying simply, "Exactly as we agreed. Phase one is complete."

"Perfect." Rosie smiled. "Let's celebrate tonight. Turks and Caicos' best restaurant."

"Done. Johnny made the reservation."

"What is the timing for Callie James?"

"Eddie is on it. He's targeted Callie James for the day after tomorrow."

"Good. Now, what are you going to say to Jose?"

"Listen to me and you'll see." Yu sent a text to Jose, who knew the secret number to call.

Not five minutes later, Yu's new phone rang. He picked it up. "Hello Jose. Please don't take this personally, but when you requested a delay, out of perhaps excessive prudence, we went ahead with this job without you…No, we won't need further work from you now…Of course, I'll pay the cancellation fee…You're a valued associate, and we'll call on you again." Yu hung up and turned to Rosie.

"You're a wily one, my darling. Well done. Pay the cancellation, no reason to alienate such a man. Having said that, it's likely he betrayed us, and we should find out what happened, respond appropriately when we get back."

"Yes, we will do that."

She smiled. "Let's celebrate our good fortune."

♦♦♦

Cash arrived in Port-au-Prince, Haiti, at 4:00 p.m. The Macher had arranged for a local official to walk him through customs. Once he cleared customs, Cash went fiercely into Callie's embrace. It was, he knew, the longest time they'd been apart since he'd been kidnapped over a year ago. As soon as that happened, Callie, in turn, had skillfully kidnapped the only person his captors couldn't possibly allow to lose, then successfully negotiated his release. Their kiss was intense, even spectacular.

She stepped back. "I missed you like crazy. Hard to bear crazy."

"Yeah, same here. I kept turning to say something to you, only you weren't there."

She looked him over. "Your face is not as bad as I feared. Truthfully though, I'm so glad that you're alive, that nothing else matters." She held him again, tightly around his neck and back, then she began to cry, long, loud tears. It was a flood, a torrent of tears, and she couldn't stop.

After a while, he stepped back and used his handkerchief to dry her wet face.

"I love you," he softly said. "Sara made it possible for us to continue our life together."

"I know. It's still unbelievable. It's like a dream for me."

"You should have seen her flying through the air, risking a bullet, relentlessly intent on saving her dad's life."

"I've never used this word, but she's a badass heroine, the real deal."

"Yes. The image of Sara flying through the air, unstoppable, has been branded, imprinted forever in my brain."

"Is she okay?"

"She's fine. She's better than fine, she's madly in love."

"I want to do something for her, something unforgettable."

"I have just the thing."

"I want to hear all about it. Let's go to the car. We can talk on the way. For the record, I love you more than I ever imagined I could love anyone. It's almost as much as I love Lew."

Cash smiled. "That's a lot."

◆◆◆

Sara and the Macher were sitting in Nestor's lovely veranda looking out to the garden. Sara was propped against a pillow on a comfortable chair. Her leg was extended on an ottoman. Eva, the doctor, was there, finishing her exam. She spoke to Nestor who translated for Itzac, "Good progress. There's no infection, and you'll be up and around in a few days."

Eva smiled, then spoke in Spanish to Sara, "I'd say salsa dancing is maybe a week later."

Sara gave her a thumbs-up, then replied in Spanish, "Your care and concern for me has been exceptional. I don't know what I would have done without you."

Eva took her hand. Sara took Eva's hand with both of hers, then she drew her toward her face. Effortlessly, naturally, she kissed Eva's cheek. Eva kissed Sara's other cheek then rose to leave.

When Nestor and Eva were gone, Itzac sat down next to Sara. "You have a lovely, authentic way of making others feel appreciated. It's a gift."

"She's an easy person to appreciate."

The Macher nodded. "We have the evening together. Nestor is going out with his wife, and he's kindly volunteered to pick up some dinner for us before they leave. Nestor proposed smoked grilled pork loin, rice with corn, and a side of Cuban-style paella. He'll provide his own fine wines to accompany our meal. How does that sound?"

"That sounds wonderful."

"I propose that we eat here on the veranda. I make an excellent mojito. While we wait for dinner, let's drink, and I will answer any questions you might have about your unusual, understated dad."

"Wonderful just became perfect…I'm ready for my first mojito, prepared by my own, adopted grandfather, who will tell me little-known, marvelous stories about my dad."

Itzac went inside to make the mojitos. Sara closed her eyes, picturing Alvaro in her mind. Just thinking about him got her excited. This was new for her, unexpected, and she took a moment to enjoy it. She turned it off just in time, as Itzac came in. She had a wet towel on her bedside table that Eva had brought in for her. She used it to rinse her flushed face before the Macher arrived. He carried a tray with two beautifully made mojitos. He had his own favorite recipe, which included his secret, a touch of Worcester sauce, a dash. He'd learned his secret from a bartender at Ambos Mundo, the hotel in Havana where Hemingway lived, wrote, and drank mojitos among other things, for seven years, 1932–1939. Itzac placed the tray on a table that he'd set beside her bed, then he moved another chair where he could sit on the other side of the table.

After she raised her cocktail, he raised his own and touched it to her glass. "Let's toast to your father, Cash Logan, as fine a friend as I've ever had."

She clicked his glass, then said, "To my dad, Cash, the Yuma." They clicked glasses again, then tasted their cocktails. "Yummy," she exclaimed. "Absolutely addictive." Another sip. "So please tell me more about him. How about things he'd be too modest to tell."

"Okay, here's an early story about your dad and I, one of my favorites…" The Macher paused, dramatic, like an actor getting ready, then took a dramatic sip, set down his drink, and began, "Soon after I met him, your dad was buying rugs in Morocco and selling them to me for three times what he paid. I, in turn, inflated the prices, a useful money laundering technique. It was a good deal for both of us. Diamonds were the method of payment. For the transaction I'm describing, my diamond broker in Amsterdam paid him half a million dollars of three, three-and-a-half millimeter round brilliant-cut melee diamonds in parcels."

"Melee?"

"Melee diamonds are small diamonds. They're sometimes called diamond chips, though jewelers don't like that term. Most of the diamonds mined, cut, and produced in the world are melee. A single parcel of melee diamonds can be sold and resold three to four times a day. Here's where it gets interesting. On a hunch, your dad had the diamonds inspected. He learned that a quarter to a third of the diamonds were synthetic."

"What does that mean?"

"Produced in an artificial process, lab grown. In other words, forgeries. Worth twenty to thirty percent less."

"Uh-oh…Was he angry?"

"Well, this is the point of the story. Your dad had only begun to know me, it was—what?—twelve years ago, but he instinctively judged that I wasn't responsible, and he never wavered, he absolutely trusted his judgement. A smart man, he also guessed I didn't know what my broker was doing. Finally, and most importantly, he suspected that I was doing much bigger deals than his with people who wouldn't be so forgiving about what would, at that level, be more than a thirty percent loss."

"What did he do?"

"He called me up, explained the situation. I was just beginning to know him, and he surprised me with his candor. He told me that he didn't care that I was marking up his rugs to launder money, that he didn't even care that I had shortchanged him, though he did expect me to pay him what he was owed. What impressed me most was what he said next. He explained that he'd come to like and trust me while doing business together, and he was worried if my broker was cutting his stones with synthetics, some of my larger customers would have me hurt, or even killed, if they ever learned about it—which sooner or later they would, perhaps getting punished themselves, after using the stones for another transaction. He said that time was of the essence, and he simply volunteered to help. We made a list of four deals that this broker had paid with his processed diamonds. Your dad got on the phone with me as we called them all. Three didn't know and were happy that we were fixing it. However, the fourth was more complicated. I'd owed money to a powerful Eastern European warlord. I'd brokered an arms deal with him, and diamonds—thirty million dollars in diamonds— were the method of payment. Diamonds provided by my Amsterdam broker. The warlord had discovered the synthetic diamonds and put out a hit on me. I made him whole and the hit was called off at the eleventh hour, but only because your dad had his close friend "Doc," a well-known diamond trader who'd done business with the warlord's regional military commander, intervene on my behalf. Your dad and I have been fast friends since then."

"I'm not sure why he came to you and volunteered to help."

They took another sip of their drinks as Itzac considered the question, then replied, "I've thought about that. Over time, I came to understand that his decision was carefully thought through. It grew from an aspect of his character that makes him distinctive, uniquely who he is. He's very able to work on the edge, or just outside the law, but he has rules and values. One of those rules is to help his very few, true real friends, when they're in trouble. He taught me about what that actually means, and how rare it is. Rare, not only because it's dangerous, but because real friends are so very hard to find. They have to be identified, then trusted, unconditionally. Early on, way before I was even aware of it, he chose me as a real friend. Once chosen, he never hesitated. His ability to do that is one of the things that make him so unique. It's become part of the glue that holds our little family together. He has many friends that he enjoys, but his real friends only include Doc, me, Andre, Callie, Lew, and now you."

"Thank you for explaining that. It makes perfect sense, but I'd never have put it together without you. It also explains why he wants me to go slow with Alvaro."

"Yes. A great boyfriend is also rare."

"No one knows that more than I. I've never had a great one...It is rare, but, at the same time, I'm sure that the way you find it—if you do— is by trusting your instincts, like my dad did with you..."

"Yes, relatively early on he did that."

"Even more than my dad, I trust my instincts completely, unconditionally. It's what I relied on for so many years to stay alive, on my own. It's—I dunno—like a lonely, unhappy, frightened young girl's secret weapon. And like that girl, I'll never, ever, not listen to that. It doesn't matter, not at all, how fast I get there."

"I think your dad is starting to understand that. But like a new dad, he's a little overprotective of his lovely young daughter. Don't worry, between us, we'll teach him to trust *your* instincts. And incidentally, you're an articulate, persuasive young woman."

"Thank you, truthfully, you're teaching me why I need a grandpa…" Sara took his out-stretched hand, squeezed it, and then released it. She shifted gears, took another drink, set it down. "Okay, good, that's settled…" A warm smile and another question. "So now, who's Doc? I never even heard about him."

"Doc was perhaps your dad's closest friend. He was a Marine corps captain. They served together in Afghanistan. Doc received the silver star in 2002 for saving three wounded soldiers after he'd been wounded twice in an ambush. He was going back for a fourth man when two more bullets brought him down. Cash carried him out. In 2003, Doc left the corps and went to work with Cash. He and Andre worked on "projects," mostly import/export deals, with your dad off and on, until Doc was killed in an attack on Callie's restaurant about a year ago."

"Oh my God…" She thought about this, sad faced. "Was he the one that put game sausages in the cassoulet?"

"Yes, how did you know that?"

"Something about how they talked about it, almost reverently."

"He inspired that kind of feeling. At times, you'll see Cash and Callie raise a glass to someone who isn't there, or even mentioned. That's Doc. He's unforgettable, irreplaceable, never too far from us."

They were quiet, pensive. Sara knew she loved learning these things about her father. He was, she decided, one of the most conscious, thoughtful men she'd ever known. Her thoughts were interrupted when Nestor arrived with their food. He spread it out on the table. She recognized the smoked grilled pork loin and the rice with corn, but though she'd eaten paella in France, she'd never actually eaten fine Cuban-style paella. It looked and smelled delicious. Before she could ask, Nestor explained, "Spanish paella is traditionally made with Valencia rice. Cuban paella uses standard parboiled rice. Cuban-style paella is served in a cazuela, a round ceramic dish, cooked in a covered pot, then finished in the oven, which makes it different from what you know—also different, we often add lobsters, smoked oysters, and more."

She nodded.

Nestor advised, "Start with the paella. I'll serve a fine Spanish white wine with that, then go on to the smoked pork, and I'll open an exceptional red wine you can enjoy with that."

"Thank you, Nestor," Sara said.

Itzac helped Nestor set the table and then helped Nestor pour the wine.

◆◆◆

Andre carefully walked Cash in and around the reconstructed Cape Light Haitian coast guard boat once, then again. Cash said simply, "Well done, Andre, you never disappoint."

After carefully examining the restored coast guard boat yet another time, even testing out Andre's new radar, able to pick up incoming craft easily ten to twenty nautical miles away, they went to the long table. On the table, Callie had attractively laid out a festive dinner for them and the Haitian coast guard crew. She'd served barbequed ribs, corn on the cob, fresh French bread, and coleslaw with her special dressing, including apple cider vinegar and her own homemade mayonnaise. It was a hearty American-style BBQ, and there was more than enough food for seven very hungry men.

After they began eating, Andre took over saying, "I want to walk through the sequence tomorrow one more time for Cash. To begin, I want to reintroduce and describe our crew." To the Haitian crew, he said, "Please repeat your names to Cash, who will need to know them soon enough."

They stood, one at a time.

"Samuel," he said, then nodded.

"Junior," and a wave.

"Evens," he raised a hand.

"Stevenson," he announced, then nodded.

"Emmanuel," he told them, smiling.

Andre went on, "Ironically, Junior is the oldest at forty-two. All five of them are strong and very fit." He further explained, "Emmanuel is a weightlifter. Samuel is intimidating, with his fierce scar from the side of his right eye snaking down along his neck. He's also an experienced medical assistant, expert at treating wounds. Stevenson, who can't see without his glasses, holds the highest rank of all as a Haitian coast guard captain. Evens is the youngest, at thirty-five, and he retired from the coast guard to become a weapons instructor, training people on rifles and pistols. Evens has supplied the appropriate guns for the crew and additional guns and rifles to have on the boat. It's an exceptional team, and I feel fortunate to work with them."

Callie added, "They're fine, very hardworking men, and they've done an exceptional job on this. I've watched them rehearse the take over and kidnapping. They execute confidently, excellently. Furthermore, they can eat more food than any five men I've ever met."

"That's because you're such a fine cook," Junior explained. The other four joined in clapping for Callie.

"Thank you all," she said, plainly pleased.

Andre went on, "I'd like to detail our plan one last time for Cash."

When he finished, walking through the specifics, Cash repeated some details, nodded, then gave him a thumbs-up. "Excellent." He added, "Callie told me that you've practiced hailing the yacht, the boarding, the capture, and the plan to restrain them on the yacht?"

Stevenson replied, "More times than you can imagine."

"Good. I'm reassured by all of you crew members. Thank you for your help and commitment."

"We are honored to work for Andre on something so important," Stevenson explained.

The other four crew members all nodded or added, "Absolutely," or "Thank you for asking us."

"We meet here tomorrow at five a.m. Everyone sleep well, we will have a long day." Andre turned to Cash and Callie, "After thoughts? Concerns?"

"I think we're ready," Cash said, nodding again.

Callie smiled, adding, "I'm pretty sure that you boys actually like hijacking a yacht and kidnapping the principal passengers."

Andre nodded. "You bet, sugar."

"Agh, don't call—"

"Just sayin' you're sweet..." He smiled added his unmistakable wink. "I didn't call you Butterface or Scuffin' Muffin. You do remember Butterface?"

"How could I forget? A woman with a fine body...*but her face?* And I repeat—that's disgusting." Callie made a face. "Scuffin' Muffin? What—"

Cash interrupted, "Don't ask...just let it go."

♦♦♦

They'd finished a delicious meal along with two mojitos each. Sara especially liked the paella, and, of course, she confessed a fondness for Itzac's mojitos. She was listening now as Itzac told how he and Cash had gone with Doc to Saville. Apparently, Doc loved flamenco dancing. He'd organized an overnight stop on Cash and the Macher's "so-called business trip" to Amsterdam to watch his favorite flamenco dancer, Isabel. She was Doc's long-time lover, so he was staying on. Itzac was describing Cash trying his hand at flamenco dancing with Isabel. Sara was laughing out loud, when Nestor came back in carrying his phone. He handed it to Sara, "For you, Sara."

"Who's calling me? Is my dad okay?"

"Everything is fine. This is a special caller, and I think you'll want privacy." He handed his phone to Sara and led Itzac out of the bedroom.

Sara took the phone, heard Alvaro's voice and loudly said, "Thank you, Alvaro." Then louder, "Thank you, thank you!...I think of you every day."

Alvaro replied, "I think of you every minute of every day. Are you okay?"

"I'm going to be fine. Truthfully, I'm already way better just hearing your voice."

"I have something to tell you. When I learned that you'd been shot, my heart stopped. I couldn't breathe. I couldn't bear that I might lose you. I decided then and there, that I had to see you as soon as possible."

"I'd love that. When I got—"

Alvaro interrupted, "When can I see you, Sara?"

"Here's my hope. Tomorrow, Tuesday, is a very big, tense day. If all goes well, my dad will be back tomorrow night. I'll call you after I talk with him, Wednesday, Thursday latest."

"Of course. I'll wait by the phone."

"There's something I want to tell you…but, oh my God. My dad is going to be very unhappy if I tell you now. He thinks I go too fast, so I'm going to wait. I'm going to wait until I see you again."

"Soon, very soon, I hope…In the meantime, here's a little-known film that grabbed my heart when I learned you'd been hurt. It wouldn't let go. And I couldn't stop replaying this movie in my head. This is more than our guessing game. I actually sensed, somehow knew, that you'd know and love it, too, that you'd know everything about this beautiful, unconventional movie, and that you'd instantly understand why it came over me. The movie is *Don't Look Now*."

"Oh, Alvaro…Alvaro…How could you know me so well?…I adore this movie. It's a stunning, haunting classic…1973…Director, Nicolas Roeg. Starring Julie Christie and Donald Sutherland. It's an uncanny psychological thriller. Rather than big scares and terror, it creates unrelenting dread, grief, and apprehension. It also has, in my view, one of the most passionate, intimate, truthful love scenes ever filmed. I hope that's why you thought of it. Don't tell my dad I said that."

"When I thought you might die, I did feel the dread, the angst that this film so expertly creates. I was this man, this couple in Venice, after they lose their daughter in a tragic accident. Of course, I lingered over their compelling love scene, so deeply felt. It made me think of you, long for you."

"I'm so glad…" Sara sighed softly, listening to her own pulsing heartbeat.

"I'll call you as soon as I have a plan for us to be together. Good night, Alvaro."

"Good night, Sara."

After he hung up, Sara realized that she was flushed again. She reached for the wet towel, took a moment to savor the feeling, then she put down the phone and called Itzac, who came in. "That was Alvaro. This is going really fast, which feels awfully good to me. When can we get him here?"

"They'll be taking the boat tomorrow, Tuesday, then negotiating for another few days. I'm guessing we'll make the deal by Friday or Saturday, latest."

"I told him I'd call him Thursday."

"At the very least, you can give him an update. I'd guess you can propose a plan to him by then."

"Can you get him in the country quickly, without too much bureaucracy."

"I'll talk with Nestor tonight. It shouldn't be a problem. I can also have my pilot pick him up in our helicopter, fly him here."

"Perfecto!...One more favor, dear Itzac?"

"Of course."

"I remember that you're quite good on the piano."

"Yes, as a young man, I was very good."

"If I gave you a song from one of my favorite movies, could you learn to play it?"

"Of course, why?"

"I'd like to learn to sing it to Alvaro."

"That's a lovely, classic Sara idea."

"Can we practice when you have time?"

"My pleasure."

"Am I going too fast, Itzac? This is all very new for me. But I am so excited."

"You're a sensitive young woman who's experiencing her first real love. It may or may not finally work out for you, but don't deprive yourself of the intensity you're experiencing. Trust your heart, it's a good one."

"Thank you Itzac, I will. Yes, I'm going to follow my heart and see where it takes me. My God, I can't wait."

CHAPTER FOURTEEN

Their camouflaged restored Haitian coast guard vessel left Port-au-Prince at 5:30 a.m. It was a calm, sunny day, good for following the irregular Haitian Western coastline, heading north, working their way toward Mole Saint-Nicolas. The camouflage technique was simple, but carefully conceived—nontransparent heavy white, water resistant oilcloth, neatly taped down over any identifying features such as printed words like GARDE CÔTE and numbers on the front and in the back and, most importantly, the diagonal red and blue slashes on either side were also covered by oilcloth. The slashes had been carefully scuffed or simply removed under the water so that they weren't visible to a passing boat. The heavy oilcloth pieces were wide enough, nicely scuffed, and so well matched to the scuffed white paint on the side of the boat that from a distant, they were unnoticeable. Antennas, visible onboard technical equipment, and the yellow metal rails were all stowed below. A light white rail was temporarily set up in the stern. They added several large, colorful flags flying high, and most importantly, deck chairs and a small portable bar were set up in the open stern deck. There, two crew members relaxed in bathing suits, shirtless. Cash and Callie leaned against the new white rail in bathing suits enjoying a drink. Everyone else stayed out of sight in the wheelhouse. To a distant watcher, it could have been a pleasure cruise.

By 11:30 a.m., Andre, who had the radar on, was able to identify and locate a large yacht, just entering the northern tip of Windward Passage heading south between Cuba and Haiti. He tracked its course, noting it stayed well outside Cuba's territorial water, picked up its AIS transponder that broadcast its name, course, and speed, confirming that this was, in fact, the LIAN. He gave the word, and their boat quickly put on the finishing touches of becoming a proper Haitian coast guard vessel. The camouflage had already been removed, the yellow metal rails restored, the flags were down, the deck chairs and portable bar stowed away. All of the crew members wore uniforms and carried guns. Now, two crew members took positions in front, in the bow, wearing life jackets. Three stood in the stern. Cash and Callie were out of sight, hidden in the wheelhouse. Stevenson drove the boat from inside the wheelhouse. Andre, dressed in his Royal Bahamian blue military uniform, stood beside Stevenson. He checked the radar, then marked on the map the LIAN's course. Their captain had clearly been directed to avoid Cuban's jurisdiction. Andre confirmed that the LIAN was well inside the legal jurisdiction of the Haitian coast guard, then he signaled Stevenson to point straight toward the yacht.

Several minutes later they could see the LIAN, steadily coming south less than half a mile ahead of their coast guard boat. From their angle, with binoculars, and tuning in once more to the AIS transponder, Andre reconfirmed that this was the LIAN. Stevenson turned slightly, so they were moving directly in front of the boat. When they got close, he picked up the radio and hailed, "LIAN, LIAN, LIAN…This is the Haitian coast guard. Please switch to channel 22."

Then, when that was done, he asked, "What is your last port of call, your next port of call, and how many people are on board?"

"Last port of call, Turks and Caicos Island. Next port of call, Kingston Jamaica, six people on board."

"Heave to."

When the LIAN stopped, Stevenson said, "Permission to board."

"Permission granted."

"Are there any weapons on board?"

"Yes, several rifles and two pistols."

"Where are they?"

"Secured down below."

"Our first man to board will isolate them for the duration of the boarding. Coming aboard."

Stevenson came right behind the stern where there was an entrance onto the LIAN at water level. Junior took over the wheel in their wheelhouse. Stevenson, Andre, Evens, Emmanuel, and Samuel prepared to board the LIAN. Evens went first to secure the weapons. When he signaled that that was done, Stevenson, Emmanuel, Andre, and Samuel boarded.

On board the LIAN, Johnny, Yu, and Rosie watched the boarding party. All five of these men looked and dressed like an experienced Haitian coast guard crew, except Andre, who was dressed in a Bahamian military uniform. Rosie, Yu, and Johnny were polite and cooperative with what seemed like a routine operation. Once onboard, Andre took charge, sent the others to search the boat and stepped forward to address Johnny, Rosie, and Yu, who gathered around him.

"I am a commander in the Bahamian navy. The Haitian coast guard is helping our military to capture a fugitive who is trying to reach Haiti. We appreciate your cooperation. This shouldn't take long—"

As they focused on Andre's explanation, the Haitian crew quietly got into position—Emmanuel and Evens moved softly behind Johnny, Samuel behind Yu, Stevenson behind Rosie. This was happening, unnoticed, as Andre said, "We're almost finished and—"

That was the signal, and as Andre continued, each of the crew members put their guns abruptly to the back of Johnny, Yu, and Rosie's heads.

When Johnny took an abrupt step away, swinging his long right arm, Evens shot him deftly in his right upper chest, between his shoulder and his neck, as Emmanuel shot him in the left knee. He went down, where Emmanuel, using his considerable force, cracked a sap against the back of his head, knocking him out.

Andre went on, harshly now, "Put your hands behind your back, now, carefully. If—"

Rosie interrupted, loudly, "Are you fucking crazy? Do you know who we are? Do you have any idea how easily we can hurt you?"

"We know exactly who you are, and what you actually do. We are aware of your power and are taking steps to render you helpless…Now, I'm going to cover your foul mouth…And, if anyone else protests, he or she will be instantly shot."

As Rosie and Yu complied, speechless, they were both handcuffed behind their backs, then cuffed again to a railing on an interior wall along a stair going down. Andre covered their mouths with duct tape. Emmanuel cuffed Johnny, who was still unconscious, bleeding, then cuffed him again, still on the floor, to a lower railing behind a cushion on the deck.

As that was going on Evens eased onto the upper deck, where the captain was very accommodating as soon as Evens showed his gun. "Turn around and put your hands behind your back. We don't want to hurt you." Evens cuffed his hands behind him, then cuffed him to an interior rail. Evens left him there, after turning off the engine, then went below where Andre and the others had gathered the cook and the remaining crew member. They, too, had been cuffed to an interior railing. Stevenson went up to the upper deck to take over piloting the yacht.

Down below, Samuel asked where he could find a first aid kit. When Johnny, barely conscious now, managed to tell him, he found it, and went to work treating Johnny's wounds. He had a bullet lodged in his left knee. Fortunately for him, the bullet in his upper right chest had passed through.

Andre called Cash, "All is well. They're secure, immobile, and only one casualty. Johnny was shot in the shoulder and knee before he was subdued. Come aboard and see for yourself."

As soon as Cash and Callie boarded the LIAN, Emmanuel took the cook, the crew member, and the captain back to the coast guard boat, then turned toward Haiti. Once they were aboard and off, Stevenson turned the LIAN toward Cuba. In the distance, the *Tropas Guardafronteras*—the Cuban Coast Guard—waited to escort them in.

Cash and Callie looked at their prisoners, who were uneasy now. Rosie was confused, uncertain who they were. Yu's face was stone cold, unaware of who these white Bahamians could be.

Cash took off Yu's duct tape, then Rosie's before he said, "Your lives have just changed forever."

"Who are you?" Rosie asked, prickly.

He leaned in. "My name is Cash Logan, and this," He pointed, "This is Callie James."

They watched their stunned reactions. Yu and Rosie had never seen a picture of Cash, and Callie didn't look at all like the old photo they'd seen of her.

"Why are you doing this?" Yu finally asked, ice cold. "Why are you taking this risk?"

Cash's face turned hard, foreboding. "You tried to kill my daughter, Sara Cambert."

Yu's face shriveled.

Rosie's face flushed red.

The Cuban coast guard boat came alongside, sounded their horn. It was gray, with three stripes: red, white, and blue. It was slightly longer than the Haitian coast guard boat had been. The crew wore life vests over blue uniforms. When he had their attention, the Cuban captain on deck gave a salute. Andre, and the Haitian crew, saluted in return. When the Cuban captain signaled, Stevenson put the LIAN smartly right behind them as he began to follow them in.

Rosie, who'd been watching this, yelled, "What the hell is this about? What are you crazy bastards doing?"

Cash replied, "We're taking you to face charges in Cuba..."

Callie stepped closer. "We call this—Rough Justice."

Rosie screamed expletives, furious. Callie slapped her face, then covered her mouth again with duct tape. When she turned to tape Yu, he was pale, unsteady, spittle dripping down his chin.

◆◆◆

Sara and Itzac were outside on the veranda, overlooking Nestor's artfully conceived and carefully maintained flower gardens. She was admiring an orchid, and before she could ask, Itzac explained, "It's the white ginger or the white Mariposa, also called the Butterfly Jasmine. It's Cuba's national flower."

"Why did I know you'd know that?"

"Because I'm eighty-one years old, and if my math is right, that has given me fifty-six years more than you to learn the names of flowers. Furthermore, most of the interest in learning that, at least in my case, comes later in life, which you haven't even started."

"I get it...that makes sense."

"Sara, can I change the subject? Can I ask you a personal question? You can feel free not to answer it."

"Of course."

"Things have gone very fast for you, and you've covered complex terrain successfully. You've done that quickly, and everyone admires you. Still, it's too much for anyone to possibly absorb, or to integrate all of those new things. So here's my question: I'm starting to know you, and you think about everything—I'd like to hear about what's concerning you, what's bothering you...what's worrying you about your dad and Callie, about being in a new family?"

"You don't waste much time on foreplay..."

Itzac laughed. "And you don't miss a trick or mince words. As I said, you don't have to answer."

"No, I'd like to try and answer. I'm glad you asked about that. It's been on my mind, more and more. The simple answer is that I love both of them. They're thoughtful, perceptive adults that truthfully, are such a pleasure that it's way outside of my experience. Having said that, I'm finding that the better it gets, the more I worry. I'm a coiled spring, poised to make an unintentional, harmful mistake." She paused, thoughtful.

"Can you say more about that."

"I'll try. I'm living with two competing realities—how could I possibly have all of this good fortune, and how, at the same time, could I be in the midst of such terrible danger? Both are true, but how long can they coexist? And in that uncertainty, that tension, I'm afraid I'll make a mistake, and then one, or more, of my worries could come true."

Itzac nodded. "Okay, I get that. But can you be more specific about those worries?"

"Here's my short list…Will I make Callie feel like I'm taking too much of my dad's time, pulling him away from her?…Will Lew resent me taking up too much space in his family?…Am I too confident?…Am I going too fast with Alvaro? If I don't overthink things, if I trust my instincts and allow myself to take a risk with him, will my dad be disappointed?"

"Good questions, especially hard to sort out when you're also coping with real danger…What would you say is the big picture worry, the one that comes over you when you can't sleep at night?"

Sara thought about that. "I think it's this…Can I ever actually be part of this family if I'm starting twenty-five years late?…It's just too much, too fast, and the thrill of meeting my dad has been taken over by a host of newly perceived, unlikely but possible problems and worries. That's what I think about more and more. And I don't know the answer… Does that make any sense?"

"Yes, of course it does. One of the things I admire about you is that you're constantly raising, and actually engaging, hard questions. Every one of your questions is important to ask and unfortunately, it's way too early to know the answers. But ask them all to your dad, to Callie, and to Lew. Ask each of them separately and ask them together. It's exactly what you need to work out as a family. I'm sure that every one of them has similar questions and worries themselves. They all want to make you comfortable, part of this family, but this is new territory for them, too. If you raise your questions truthfully, it will make it easier for all of you. I don't think you know this, but you're a leader, Sara. Though you may not yet see it clearly, or understand it, you're showing intimations of being a gifted leader—you're already a diamond in the rough. You lead people to go faster, more deeply than they would or could without you. Don't be apologetic or bashful about that. It's a gift."

"How can you know that?"

"I absolutely know that. It's something I've come to rely on. I know it instinctively, as reliably as the way a salmon knows to swim upstream returning to spawn at their birthplace."

"You do make me feel better, though I don't have a clue what you mean about the fish knowing where to spawn."

"Not my best metaphor, but it's true. Don't overthink things, trust your instincts, you have good ones, and above all, write this down and post it where you can see it every day—it's okay to make a mistake."

"'Okay to make a mistake?' I've never felt like that. That doesn't come naturally to me, at all."

"Write it down, work on it. You're not the first leader to have this problem, and you can overcome it."

"Jesus, grandpa. You're so intense, I need a nap."

"Takes one to know one." His phone rang, and Itzac answered, put it on speaker. He mouthed to Sara, "Your dad." Then to the phone, "So?"

"All good."

"Excellent. Sara is here with me, listening in."

"Good. Sara, are you okay?"

"I'm better, dad. I'll fill you in later."

"Okay…Here are the specifics—we've arrived at Punta de Maisí." Cash explained. "We've just watched Rosie and Yu, handcuffed, being escorted by Cuban police to a waiting van. Johnny was carried off on a stretcher. He's getting medical attention. We called ahead, and our escorts had a doctor here waiting. There were a group of Policía Nacional Revolucionaria who met the boat as well as several military personal. Nestor is here and several others from the Ministry of Interior, what they call MININT. Rosie, Yu, and Johnny are being driven to Gustavo Rizo Airport. We'll follow with Nestor and catch another plane. Everything is on schedule."

"Bravo…I'll meet them at the minister of Interior at the Plaza de la Revolución where the negotiations will begin after they arrive."

"That should be helpful…Sara, tell me more about how you're feeling?"

"Better now. I was worried about you. My leg is better, though I'm not ready to dance. Grandpa Macher is giving me all kinds of advice, some of it hard to understand, and even harder to believe, but if this is possible, he's both exciting me with his ideas, and, at the same time, actually calming me down."

"He does that to people, especially his friends."

"I can't wait to see you."

"How's dinner tonight with Callie, Andre, and me?"

"I'd love that."

"Can I suggest a restaurant?" Itzac asked.

"We're counting on it," Cash replied.

Sara asked, pointedly, "Can we talk at dinner about when Alvaro can come to see me?"

Cash laughed. "I just hijacked a yacht, had your would-be killers arrested, hopefully recovered $75,000,000 for the Cubans, and got your identity back. Can I have the night off? Can we sort out your love life tomorrow?"

"Absolutely not!"

"What was I thinking? Sorry…Uh, why don't we work that out tonight too?"

The Macher gave Sara a thumbs-up.

"Thank you, dad. If it makes you feel better, I took your advice. I've been waiting, going slow. I haven't told Alvaro how I feel yet. I told him I had to wait to really talk with him because my dad thinks I go too fast. So I've been waiting, and it's been almost two days."

"Let's talk tonight, and you can call him tomorrow. I should have trusted your instincts, Sara. My mistake."

"Wow, Itzac said you would get that. How did he know? How did you change so fast?"

"Itzac was right. I'll try to explain tonight."

Sara gave Itzac a thumbs-up. "Uh, dad, can we make a plan tonight, so I can call Alvaro after dinner?"

"You've waited almost two days!...My God!...I think you should definitely call Alvaro tonight...See you soon."

◆◆◆

Itzac walked past the huge Che Guevara portrait into the Ministry of the Interior building. Inside, a policeman led him to the meeting room where, for the first time, he actually saw Rosie and Yu in person. They were seated, still handcuffed, tired, disheveled, and visibly uneasy, but even so, something about them was formidable. Around the table, the Macher saw Nestor beside one of his superiors at the Ministry of Foreign Affairs, and around the table, there was a higher-up, an older senior government authority from The Ministry of Interior, a decorated PNR Colonel that the Macher guessed was both an observer and an ambassador from the government police, and a deputy Prime Minister that he recognized. There were two policemen standing behind Rosie and Yu. Nestor came over and told him that Johnny was locked in a room downstairs, handcuffed and sedated, under a doctor's care. The Macher understood instantly that the Cubans were not even remotely inclined to be merciful. They intended to recover their money, find Javi, and put Rosie, Yu, and Johnny in prison, indefinitely.

After he was introduced by Nestor, Itzac sat down. He waited until everyone introduced themselves and then the senior man from The Ministry of Interior, Osvaldo, stood. He was to be the chief negotiator.

He spoke in Spanish, but there was a translator beside him, speaking to Rosie and Yu, translating his words into English.

"I am going to make this brief. You are both wanted in Cuba for collaborating in laundering and stealing $75,000,000, and creating a new identity for General Javi Garcia and helping him disappear with that money. The penalty for this will be life in prison with no parole or perhaps death. We will enforce this unless you return the money and locate Javi. Furthermore, you are required to restore Sara Cambert's identity to her. This is not complicated—life in prison or death, unless, and this is nonnegotiable, you turn over Javi, return the money he stole, and restore Sara's identity. If you cooperate, we will negotiate—perhaps a nicer prison, even the possibility of parole after ten or fifteen years, if and only if, all of our conditions are met. You have an opportunity now to speak." Osvaldo sat down.

Yu stood. "Sir, we are the victims of inexplicable confusion. We don't know General Javi Garcia. We have been kidnapped because of some ill-advised misunderstanding—"

Osvaldo stood, interrupting, "You are wasting our time. We are extending a courtesy. If you can recover the money, give us Javi, and restore Sara Cambert's identity, we can discuss your punishment, perhaps make it less severe. This offer is only valid if you can accomplish all three of those things within seven days. I'll give you an hour to consider your predicament, then we'll regroup." Osvaldo signaled the policemen who took Rosie and Yu out of the room.

◆◆◆

Itzac had recommended the Paladar La Esperanza restaurant near the water in Miramar, adjacent to Vedado, near the end of the Malecon. Itzac had explained that a Paladar is a private home that operates as a restaurant downstairs mostly in someone's dining room and the food is prepared in their kitchen. Cash, Callie, Andre, and Sara were seated in one of four tables in the intimate, beautiful inside rooms. There were two additional tables outside on the patio. They'd ordered and been served cocktails. Sara drank a mojito. Callie tried a Cuban Ginger, a drink with apple liquor, alcoholic ginger ale, and a fine rum. Cash also had a mojito, and Andre was trying out the Havana Loco with rum and rich tropical fruit.

Cash proposed a toast, "To Sara, who's brought us all together in this very beautiful, full of life, exotic, and mysterious place."

They drank to that, then Callie added, "To Sara, we're so very lucky and grateful to have you in our family."

Andre simply said, "Sara, you may not know this, but you've made all of us stronger, more generous people. Bravo!"

They all joined in raising their glasses, adding, "Bravo!"

Sara cried, tears flowing softly, an unusually intense release she didn't even know she needed so much. She understood that somehow, whatever came next, the worst was over. "Thank you. Thank you all so much." She wiped her tears with her napkin. "Now before I fall apart completely, let's take a moment, in grateful silence, eyes closed." She held out her hands.

They held hands around the table, eyes closed. They all understood how lucky they were to be together.

It was quiet as they each held hands, then opened their eyes, happily. Andre offered, "I know this restaurant. Would you like me to tell you it's story?"

"Of course," Cash spoke for all of them.

"Okay. Years ago, Mrs. Esperanza took the current owner, Hubert Corrales, into her home when he first came to Havana at twenty-three years old. They became friends, eventually as close as family. When she died, she left the house to him, and that's when he had the idea to open a Paladar, named for her, Esperanza. The Paladar opened in 1995, at the height of the Cuban Special Period, a time of economic crisis primarily due to the dissolution of the Soviet Union. During this time, Castro made Paladars legal. The house is still adorned with Esperanza's beautiful memorabilia including her China collections, Chinese embroidery, lovely old plates on the walls, and her personal photo albums from the fifties. Hubert and his chef, Manolo, added warmth, classic old Cuban music, wonderful ambiance, and exquisite taste. The owners make the atmosphere even more inviting with their own sophisticated camp style."

"It feels like I imagine the fifties," Sara said.

"It does feel like the fifties," Callie agreed. She was looking at the kitchen. "And the food...Do they have menus?"

"No. He'll tell us what's available tonight."

"If others agree, why don't you talk with him then order a variety for all of us," Cash suggested.

Andre nodded, as did Sara, enthusiastically.

Callie turned to Sara, "Why don't you come with me, and we'll find the owner, Hubert."

"Done." They left, Sara moving ably with crutches, toward the kitchen.

"Your daughter looks very happy." Andre said to Cash.

"Yes, doesn't she. She goes so fast it's hard to keep up with her... Can you tell me a little more about Alvaro? He's a lot of what's making her feel so good."

"She has good taste. As I told Callie, he's like a son to me. I trust him, and I admire him, the way he thinks about things. I've seen him with a lot of women, but I've never heard him talk about any woman the way he talks about Sara."

"What do you think that's about? He's spent less than twenty-four hours with her."

"I don't know. I don't think I've ever had that kind of head over heels falling in love with a woman. You know more about this than I do. Don't put too much stock in my impressions. As I told Callie, I wouldn't have guessed that you and she would be together in the way you are. You may not like this, but truthfully, I'd try not to think too much about this. In fact, I think you should stay well out of it, Dad. I'd trust both of them to find their own ways."

Callie and Sara came back, smiling, in time to hear Andre's advice. Sara piped up, "Thank you, Andre. That's terrific, no, perfect advice."

"Good luck with that," Callie opined.

Cash smiled. "I'm going to surprise you all. I'm not only going to stay out of this...what I will do is to help them facilitate spending time together. It's Wednesday. If the Macher thinks it's not too early, why don't we invite Alvaro for dinner Friday or Saturday latest? Let's see how the negotiations have progressed. If it's as quick as I think it will be, we can have Alvaro come to our celebration dinner one of those nights."

"Yes! Great! When will we hear from Itzac?"

"He's coming here when his meeting is over."

They were distracted then, when another party, a family of eight, arrived, and were seated in a large table in the adjoining room. They were known here, warmly welcomed, with champagne already on the table. Two of the children were in their twenties or thirties, and as the champagne toasts began, Callie guessed that one of the couples, the youngest, were just married. The festivities made Sara happy.

They turned then as Hubert and a woman, Isabel, who was helping him, brought the first course to the table. He described, in capable English, "Appetizers include a mix of lobster and shrimp, green salad with smoked salmon, octopus carpaccio, tomatoes with Parmesan, and one you didn't order, but I've brought you a special soup to try, pumpkin cream with cheese. There's also Oshun's banana on the side."

They placed the food in the middle of the table, then asked if people were ready for more drinks. They were. Everyone was helping themselves to various appetizers when the Macher came to the table, all smiles. It was 9:15. There was already an empty chair for him, and Cash pulled it out. He ordered a mojito then sat down.

The Macher borrowed what was left in Cash's mojito, then raised his glass. "Mazel tov," he began.

"Toda" Andre replied.

Itzac nodded then added, "to you, my *Mishpocheh*."

"What?" Sara asked.

He turned to Sara "This is a special occasion, so I began in Yiddish. First, 'Mazel tov' congratulations or good luck, to which Andre replied, 'Toda' or thank you. Then I said 'Mishpocheh' to family, a word that doesn't refer to my blood relatives but to close friends who are like family, meaning to the four of you."

"Got it. Thank you."

New drinks arrived, including one for Itzac. He took his own, raised it. "So, as I said, this is a special occasion. I bring exceptional news from our negotiation. The Cubans were masterful. They made it unmistakably clear that their demands were nonnegotiable. Rosie and Yu are very smart, they understood that they were facing certain life in prison or even death if they didn't meet the Cubans' demands promptly. They also knew that these are harsh prisons, where an inmate could be killed unexpectedly. In their time alone, they shrewdly concluded that given that, their best chance was to make clear that they were not afraid to die, that if the Cubans wouldn't give them something to live for, they'd rather die now, giving the Cubans nothing. Then they wisely suggested an alternative. Yu explained very articulately that they could meet all of the Cuban demands within five days. All of them including at least 98 percent or $73,500,000, of the stolen money. But in return, they wanted the opportunity to earn a chance to live more comfortably together. They suggested that they make financial contributions to causes that were important to the Cubans, provide whatever community service they could do with the skills they have, from prison. Then after four years, they wanted the Cubans to review what they'd done, then give them a chance to live together in a more permissive prison, even a small prison house where they could continue their service. The Cubans said that they'd serve ten years each in separate prisons, such as La Condesa for Yu, a male prison where foreign criminals often go, and a woman's prison, Guatao, for Rosie. After that time, they'd review their accomplishments. There was back and forth, and they settled for a first review in five years, no guarantees about what the Cubans would do, but on the table will be other prisons, then in two more years, another review. If after that review, the Cubans are satisfied, they will move them to house arrest. They separated Johnny, a lesser offender, for his own hearing later.

"How did this all happen so fast?" Cash asked.

"Rosie and Yu understood right away that the Cubans were prepared to kill them, or even worse, imprison them ruthlessly, mercilessly, for the rest of their lives. I think they realized that their only chance for any kind of life, for the opportunity to fight another day, was to give them everything they wanted and more. To demonstrate their intentions, Rosie and Yu agreed to meet all of the Cuban demands, including recovering *all* of their $75,000,000, within five days. They even agreed to restore whatever monies Javi had spent, more than $1,000,000 from their own funds. I think that they're hoping that over time, if they can prove their value, other options will emerge. In fact, I think that they will have their right hand man, Lennie, immediately mobilize their considerable assets—prominent political figures and celebrities, athletes, business leaders, not to mention their vast financial resources—in hopes that their allies will intervene and then they will have the opportunity to revisit all of this again. They may even be hoping that their strong allies will explore a trade, offer something for their freedom that the Cubans want."

"I'm sure you're right, that this is far from over, but for at least the next few years, it is over for us." Cash took Sara's hand. "Specifically, Sara is safe, and it will take years for them to get the Cubans to reconsider, to budge another inch, on their punishment. Now, let's watch as they return the money, reveal Javi's whereabouts, and restore Sara's identity. Itzac, is there anything further that we can do now that will guarantee all of our safety forever?"

"Yes, I've been thinking about that, and I had one idea. It's counterintuitive, but it might work."

"Uh oh…" Callie muttered.

"We meet again tomorrow to finalize the deal, to specify the banking details and the exact timing. Suppose I build it into the deal, some kind of condition that any contact with any of us, under any circumstances, will postpone their review indefinitely. At the very least, that will give us six years."

"Will the Cubans agree to enforce that?" Cash asked.

"Right about now, the Cubans want to make us happy. They rightly believe that we delivered $75,000,000 to them, and they'd like to express their appreciation."

"You earned that, Itzac." Callie said.

"We all did that, everyone at this table." Itzac said, then went on, "I'm also thinking that we should have Lincoln sit down with Lennie.

We can even include Detective Samter as well. At this meeting, they can explain that Rosie and Yu are known criminals now, and that they intend to send them back to prison in the US if they ever do get out of prison in Cuba and come back home. Lincoln and Samter can present a list of further crimes—including, and especially, against Sara, attempted murder and identity theft—that they're prepared to prosecute them for if they return. If we do this properly, we can keep them out of the US indefinitely."

Andre looked around, then said, "I have one further idea, an aide-mémoire, so to speak. Let's meet with them directly. Let's tell them convincingly—I'll do this—that any attempt to even find one of us, and we'll have them both killed in prison. Or if they're under house arrest, we'll have our people kill them there."

Cash nodded. "Andre, you never disappoint. And your delivery will be priceless, unforgettable to watch, I'm sure. Yes, I think it's a good idea to sit down with them, present all of these possible consequences. We won't leave until we're one hundred percent satisfied that they're out of our lives, forever."

Sara simply said, "Thank you. All of you. I've never, ever, been so well taken care of."

Itzac added, "Sara, you've inspired this, as only you can do it."

Callie confirmed, "You bring out the very best in all of us, even Andre. Speaking of which, this is a good time to see his tattoo."

Others started clapping, only slowing down because the next course of their dinner had arrived. Andre buttoned up the top of his blousy black shirt as Hubert and Isabel presented: Pollo Luna de Miel (honeymoon chicken), Cordero Estofado (lamb stew), Langosta Grille (grilled lobster), Camarones al Ajillo (garlic shrimp), and Filete de Pargo (snapper filet).

They took turns taking portions of the impressive dinner offerings in front of them. It was quiet for a moment as they tasted the various dishes, complimenting everything that they tried, to whomever would listen. The lobster, the lamb stew, and the honeymoon chicken were all especially popular.

They ate slowly, savoring Manola's delicious cooking. They were listening to the Macher's description of Rosie and Yu when dinner was cleared and dessert was brought in. Tonight, they brought flan, Boniatillo Cubano (a sweet potato, wine, egg yolks, and cinnamon dessert), and Key lime pie. Sara loved Key lime pie and was delighted with her first taste of Boniatillo Cubana.

Heads turned when Nestor arrived, standing beside their table. He carried two packages. Hubert brought another chair that fit easily between Itzac and Cash. Nestor sat down. He waited until dessert was finished, then stood up and said, "I bring gifts from very appreciative Cubans, who are so very pleased with the work you've done in bringing Rosie, Yu, and Johnny to face Cuban justice." He opened the first package, which had a handsome brown wooden box inside.

He opened the box with considerable fanfare revealing a beautiful bottle of Havana Club Máximo Extra Añejo Rum. He explained, "This is the finest rum in Cuba, perhaps in the world. It is made from the oldest reserves on the island. Only 1000 bottles are created each year. It has flavors of oak, pear, other subtle fruit tones, and dark chocolate. It is a very special bottle meant to celebrate amongst close friends on special occasions, such as this.

Hubert recognized the rum, delighted, "Bravo! Bravo! This is the finest rum I've ever tasted, likely the finest rum known. I will bring the proper glasses to taste it."

Nestor smiled, opening the second package. Inside there was an identical wooden case, with a second bottle of the same stunning rum. He took it out of the box as well. "In case we need it," he announced.

Hubert returned with six four ounce whiskey tasting glasses. He set one in front of each of them at the table, as Nestor poured two ounce shots in each of the beautiful Tulip glasses. When everyone was served, Nestor raised a glass, "It has been my pleasure, indeed my honor, to meet and work with all of you. I bring this gift expressing the heartfelt appreciation of the Cuban people for what you've done for us." He touched Sara's glass, then each of the others. "You're always welcome here."

They drank to Nestor's toast, then Cash said, "Thank you, Nestor, for making us feel so welcome in Cuba. Before we continue, I'd like to introduce you to Callie James." Callie stood and shook Nestor's hand warmly. Cash said, to her surprise, "Callie has been our touchstone, central to all that has been accomplished since Sara arrived."

Andre and the Macher stood to second that.

Cash raised his glass, they all toasted.

Sara waited until the others had another sip, then she raised her own glass and turned toward Callie. "To Callie, the woman that inspires me. I salute her grace, her sensitivity, her generosity, her thoughtfulness, and her strength."

Callie came and embraced Sara. Sara held her, then sat.

Nestor poured another round of rum. He insisted on offering a shot to Hubert.

Andre proposed a toast, "To Hubert, for this remarkable restaurant in his home, and his lovely ability to make us all feel so welcome."

Everyone drank. Itzac picked up his phone, listened, then stood. "Sara, I want you to close your eyes."

She did.

Itzac blindfolded her with a dark cloth, then he said, "Please stand up."

She did.

Itzac signaled to Andre, Andre stepped out of the room to the patio, then outside. He returned with another man with him. Still in the shadow, in the entrance the man stepped behind Sara. Others could see him now. Cash whispered to Callie. They were both amazed, and somehow pleased, that this man was here. Cash raised his arm, a salute.

The man gently put his hands on Sara's shoulder.

"Who is that?" she asked.

He kissed the back of her neck, gently. "Alvaro," he whispered.

Sara turned, crying out her delight, as she took off the blindfold, then opened her eyes into Alvaro's warm, welcoming smile.

"Alvaro," she said lovingly, tearing now, so happy to see him, then she put her arms around him, kissing him, tenderly. Alvaro swept her up in his arms and there was pandemonium, a thunderous joyous uproar around the table.

Chapter Fifteen

Callie, Cash, and Andre were outside, having coffee and pastries on Nestor's patio. It was a beautiful morning, and Cash and Callie had slept until 10:00, which was rare for both of them. Andre had come by a few minutes ago, almost 11:00, and he sat down beside them after serving himself some coffee. The Macher had gone early this morning to the Ministry where the negotiations were finishing up. He'd be back soon. Callie turned to Andre, "Great night last night. I'm still smiling at some of the toasts, and the look on Sara's face when you showed her your tattoo. She actually screamed, didn't she, when you made the naked Vietnamese women dance on your chest."

"She did scream, like a banshee. She's the loudest yet," Andre nodded, knowingly.

"I'm not surprised," Callie said. "She was so excited seeing Alvaro, and all of the festivities, not to mention the excellent rum…Alvaro is really great. Your description didn't do him justice."

"I said he was like a son to me. Only you, Callie James, could find fault with that."

"Andre, you'd happily take a ne'er-do-well stealing bartender as your new son if he liked your tasteless stories."

"You mean like Cash?" Andre quipped.

"Let it go," Cash interrupted. "Alvaro is an exceptional young man, and I think he and Sara are a wonderful, unusually happy couple."

"I agree," Callie said. "They already finish each other's sentences."

"Okay then. What I said was absolutely right."

Callie laughed. "Absolutely, Andre, like I just said."

Cash shook his head, changed the subject. "We closed the restaurant, Paladar Esperanza, didn't we?" Cash asked.

"Yes, around three in the morning. He would have stayed open, but we were out of rum and everyone was pretty tipsy and very tired."

"Could you tell me again how Alvaro got to Cuba and how he was able to surprise all of us?" Callie asked. "I remember that it's a great story, but it's all a little bit hazy for me this morning."

"I'd like that too," Cash added. "Exactly how did Alvaro get here? And who gets the credit for that?"

"I can still tell that story." Andre nodded, then began, "Itzac is wholly responsible for this wondrous unexpected surprise. After talking with Sara about her feelings for Alvaro, he had his helicopter be ready to take Alvaro to Havana. He set it up late yesterday afternoon, on his way to the negotiation. He also called me and then Nestor. The Macher believed that a deal would be struck quickly with Rosie and Yu. He was confident enough that he called from the negotiation and had his helicopter bring Alvaro here. If the deal had fallen apart, if there were complicated problems, he could have sent him back any time. But the deal came together, and Alvaro arrived to surprise Sara at Esperanza. Nestor had someone at Terminal 5, a special terminal at the airport for private flights, to pick him up, move him easily through customs, then bring him there around ten, when we saw him."

"This has the Macher all over it. Everything from his boldness, his confidence, and the detailed arrangements. I'm sure you played a part."

"I called Alvaro and told him to be ready. You should have heard him when he learned that a helicopter was going to bring him to Sara, in Cuba."

Itzac came into the garden, thumbs-up. "Success, my friends..." He looked around, drawing this out. "Details? Oh, perhaps no, another time?"

"No, right away. As you, our wiseass, man of the hour, certainly know," Cash grinned.

"Moi?...Okay, they're wiring all of the money in three days, Friday, after all of the security sales settle. They're sending it from a Cayman Island bank account directly to the account in Cuba that Osvaldo specified. Osvaldo and I pressed them, convincingly, until Yu admitted that their investment company, which was managing the money, was a wholly owned subsidiary of an offshore shell corporation whose single corporate shareholder was an unidentifiable subsidiary of the bank. As such," Itzac explained, "the entity could do business worldwide and no one would ever know the true beneficiary of the transaction. What mattered for the Cubans' purposes was that the Cayman Island Bank could wire funds to a Cuban bank, no problem. Secondly, Rosie and Yu identified where Javi was living in Mexico City and gave Osvaldo his new identity. Finally, for our purposes, they're sending Sara's passport with her visa to Osvaldo today. He should have it in several days, Friday latest, and he'll turn it over to Nestor for Sara. They'll also give Nestor the real name and current location of the woman who used Sara's identity. We can pass that on to Lincoln and Samter to have the FBI arrest her. When Sara has her passport, she'll have no problem returning to the US."

"Well done," Callie said.

"There's more. In addition, I also discussed with Rosie and Yu the consequences to them, specifically to their review, if they have any contact with any of us, under any circumstances. Osvaldo was there, and he confirmed. They understood and accepted. I told them about what Lincoln and Samter would tell Lennie. They were very unhappy about it, but they understand that LA and Seattle authorities will prosecute them for other offenses, including the crimes against Sara, if they ever come back. I finally set up another time this afternoon for you, Andre, to present your message. I will be there with you, and I think Cash should be there as well. Osvaldo does not need to hear about that."

"Good," Cash said, pleased. "I think by Friday we will have accomplished our goals."

Callie added, "Okay then, it's time to plan a party for Sara. Are we ready to talk about that?"

Everyone nodded. "I'm always ready to hear about one of your parties," Itzac added.

"I'd like to do something unforgettable for Sara. A memorable celebration of who she is and a heartfelt sendoff to her new unrestrained life."

"Unforgettable is great, but hard," Cash noted. "What are you thinking?"

Before she could answer, Nestor came onto the patio, also coming back from the meeting, stopping by to check in on his guests. "Great dinner last night."

"The rum was remarkable, incomparable," Andre declared. "Can I buy a bottle?"

"Impossible to get, and outrageously expensive."

"Sorry, but I've got to ask?"

"$1500 a bottle. I shouldn't tell you this, but we drank a little more than $3000 worth of rum. I should have brought more. I'll try to get a bottle for all of you."

"Excellent," Andre said. "Speaking of which, Callie is planning a party for Sara. She set the bar pretty high with unforgettable."

"Yes. I'm glad you're here Nestor. Here's what I'm thinking. A celebration at my restaurant, Le Cochon Bronze, in Seattle, say twelve days from now, on a Monday night when the restaurant is closed, and we can have the party downstairs in our main dining room. This is not just a celebration, it's a special hat's off, a salute, to Sara, thanking her for saving Cash's life, letting her know how pleased we are to have her in our family, and welcoming her new boyfriend, Alvaro."

Nestor spoke up, "Please allow me to interrupt. One request. I'd like to host another party, this Saturday, in Havana, presented by your grateful Cuban admirers. Among others, I'll invite Cubans who have helped us accomplish our goals during this period, specifically those who helped us with Sara."

"Outstanding, I'd love that. Who and what are you thinking?"

"Please, leave this up to me, a surprise."

"Okay then…Do we know how to reach Sara? Do we even know where she is?"

"I talked with Alvaro," Andre said. "He's driving her to a remote favorite place, a beautiful large forest with preserved wetlands. I can reach him today, tell him that they have to be back by Saturday, nothing more."

"Perfect. Then we're set."

Cash turned to Nestor, "A few more things to do before we leave. Nestor, can you set it up for Andre, Itzac, and I to talk privately with Rosie and Yu this afternoon?"

"They're still in the Ministry. I'll set it up there for two. How much time will you need?"

"Half an hour, max," Andre said.

"Done." Nestor dialed a number on his phone.

Itzac took Cash aside. "One last thing. I just learned that Eddie King, the man who tried to kill you, he's Johnny's brother-in-law."

Cash put his arm on Itzac's shoulder. "Thanks. I'll tell Sara."

◆◆◆

At two p.m. Nestor led Cash, Andre, and Itzac to another room in the Ministry. Rosie and Yu were waiting for them, each of them had a wrist handcuffed to a rail along the wall behind their chairs. They were haggard, though still lucid, showing some resilience in their manner.

Cash made introductions as the three men pulled chairs in front of them. Rosie and Yu didn't respond. Cash went on, "We're here to insure, with absolute foolproof certainty, that you will never harm any of us, or our friends and colleagues, ever again."

"I think you've made that point, forcefully, already," Yu replied, ice cold. "No one has ever put us in this position. Or threatened us as effectively as you have. Ever."

Andre stepped up, looked down at both of them. "You can rely on our threats. Still, we're not satisfied. We don't trust you. So this is a final reminder, what we call in French, an aide-memoire—an aid to the memory. Listen carefully…If there is ever any attempt to find even one of us, we'll have both of you killed in prison, instantly. If you make a single inquiry when you're under house arrest, we'll have our people kill you there, instantly. This should be imprinted in your brains. Never forget it."

Yu responded quickly. "I have a long reach, even from prison, but you are formidable, frightening people, and you've made your point. You have my solemn word, we will never, ever, look for any of you or even ask about any of you."

Rosie looked at each of them. "Who are you? Where do you come from? Do you have secret, high-powered training from some malevolent country? I will never believe that mere untrained mortals could possibly do what you've done."

"You're wasting my time," Andre snapped, angrily. "I'm still not convinced that you will remember and respect my warning. Yu, if you don't convince me NOW, before I leave Cuba, I'm going to put out a contract on Rosie in Guatao, the woman's prison where she'll be living. She won't last a week." Andre took her uncuffed wrist, then pulled her head back by her hair. "Do you still believe you're untouchable, that you can order people around, hurt then, and kill them at will?" He pulled her hair back even further. She cried out, tearing.

"Stop. Please." Yu implored. "I will convince you, now. I will give you access and passwords to our private bank accounts and our investment accounts. I will never change that precious information. If I have to, I'll let you know. I'm trusting you with whatever future we might have left. I'm giving you access to know anything we might try to do from prison. Any day you can enter those accounts and take out whatever money is there in cash, usually tens of thousands of dollars. If I give you that information, will you believe that we took and respected your warning?"

"Yes. I will go into those accounts randomly and take out one hundred dollars. If ever I can't do that—"

Yu interrupted, "Yes, I understand. You'll have us both killed instantly."

"Yes." Andre released Rosie's hair, her wrist. She was visibly shaken.

"Agreed. I promise you that you will be able to do that for as long as we're alive."

Andre turned to Cash and Itzac, "Are you both convinced, absolutely satisfied?"

Itzac nodded. "Yes. This will convince me if the information is right. I'll want the information now, before we leave, and I'll want you to test it Andre, today."

Cash put a pen and paper in front of Yu.

Yu wrote all of the information down.

Cash took out his phone. "I'll want you to write a text that I can send to your man, Lennie, confirming this convincingly, believably, without a doubt, and giving Andre access to all accounts. Include some personal directions, code if you will, that will make this absolutely convincing. You can also tell him to expect my call soon to explain the situation and set up his meeting with Sergeant Lincoln and Detective Samter later this week. I must be pleased with what you write, satisfied, completely. Any hint of deception will be fatal. There will be no second chance."

When Yu began writing the text, there was a slight tremor in his hand. Before he was finished, Rosie began to cry, long, hopeless, piteous sobs.

Four Days Later

Cash, Callie, Sara, and Alvaro were outside on Nestor's patio. Sara had made mojitos for all of them, a drink that Alvaro had taught her to prepare with his preferred blend of extra lemon, just a touch of sugar, and a special, hard-to-find old dark rum. When she brought the drinks on a tray, Cash and Callie commented on how she was moving more easily now, without crutches.

They raised their glasses as Alvaro toasted, "To Sara, the woman who takes my breath away, every single day."

"Thank you, cariño." Sara smiled. "Life has certainly gotten very much sweeter in four heart-stirring days." She stood, walked around to Alvaro's chair, put her hand on his shoulder.

"Okay," Callie announced. "So I don't need to ask if you two had a good time...Tell me where you were."

Sara turned. "It was amazing. We went two hours south from Havana to Ciénaga de Zapata. It's one of the Caribbean's largest forests and one of the world's most preserved wetlands. Alvaro, please take over. You can do a much better job describing the specifics of this spectacular place."

"My pleasure. Ciénaga de Zapata is a haven for wondrous birds, rare species of fish and animals, including, for example, the West Indian Manatee, a huge rare sea cow, often weighing 1000 pounds."

"Alvaro rented us a private hut, over the water. It was unbelievable, very romantic."

"Sounds wonderful. Tell me more. Did you do any exploring?"

"We went diving in beautiful reefs, including an old shipwreck. I did a lot of diving with my mom, but this was my first time ever scuba diving."

Alvaro added. "This woman is like a fish under water."

"I loved scuba diving. To be able to breathe underwater is fantastic."

"We also went to Cueva de los Peces, the cave of fish," Alvaro said. "It's the deepest cenote or groundwater sinkhole in Cuba. It's seventy meters deep."

"It's very beautiful. We spent a long time there. On the way back, we stopped to pick up groceries, and Alvaro cooked for me. He's actually a good cook, Cuban seafood seems to be his specialty. Over several days, we had wonderful shrimp, creole with lobster, scallop and shrimp, and, of course, fish stew...It's pretty cool to find a guy who really knows movies...and is also a good cook."

Alvaro put his arm around her, then picked up his phone, listened then said, "Yes." He turned, "It's Andre. He's ready to meet us for dinner.

◆◆◆

Andre had told him where the restaurant was. Though he'd never been there, Alvaro knew the area, Miramar/Playa, very well. He drove them there easily. In the car, Cash said, "It will be great to have some time just the four of us and Andre. I for one, am eager to hear what you two are thinking about and planning."

"We've just started thinking about it, and all we have so far are preliminary, mostly fantasy, ideas," Sara replied. "Still, it would be fun to talk about."

Callie listened, pleased that these two young people seemed to do so well together. She was also pleased that they clearly had no idea of Nestor's surprise waiting for them at the restaurant.

"Okay." Cash pointed, "We're here."

La Cocina de Lilliam, the restaurant that Andre had given them, was not too far from Esperanza. It was also a Paladar, set in the gardens of a beautiful villa in Playa, adjacent to Miramar. It was considerably larger than Esperanza with lovely inside and outside spaces. Walking in, beyond a wooden gate, there was a romantic artfully lit garden with fine greenery and little sculpted blue fountains. As they moved toward the entrance to the restaurant, there was a Cigar Rolling Table. Two Master Cigar Rollers, in white shirts and elegant white fedora hats with black bands, sat at the table. One of them was rolling cigars that he placed on a wooden platform in front of him. On another table, three different older bottles of rum were on display.

Andre came out to greet them. Cash went ahead to find their table. Andre embraced Sara and Alvaro. "It makes me very happy to see you two young people looking so well," he explained, then added, "We'll try some of these fine cigars later, paired with proper rums."

To the side was another outside area, Andre pointed out two pigs roasting. Alvaro explained, "These pigs are each in La Caja China, a Chinese box, an outdoor cooker, where after the pigs are gutted and prepared, they're skewered in wide wire mesh then roasted over hot charcoal. Something delicious to look forward to."

Andre led them through the entrance to the dining room, which was oddly dark. On his cue, in the back of the room, a piano player in the dark broke into "Crazy," while Cash began singing the song to Sara. At exactly the same moment that the piano began, the lights came on revealing about twenty guests clapping. Sara and Alvaro raised clasped hands as they realized that all of this was for them.

Sara made her way to Cash at the piano. She comfortably, beautifully joined singing the song with him.

When they were finished, the room filled with joyous cheering for the father and daughter duo.

After the cheering subsided, everyone sat around two tables spread side by side in the wide room. Sara and Alvaro were seated at the head of the table.

As they sat down, servers from the restaurant put dinner on another two tables they'd set up in the back toward the kitchen. They placed elaborate dishes on large plates, buffet style. They included: Jamon serrano, assorted Spanish sausages, lamb stew, garlic shrimp, lobster with pineapple, and most importantly, four large displays of carved roast pig. Guests served themselves, then returned to sit and eat at the tables.

The piano player played classic Cuban songs—including "Lágrimas Negras" (Black Tears), "Como Fue" (The Way It Was), and "El Manisero" (Peanut Vendor)—as dinner was served and enjoyed.

Once everyone was eating comfortably, Nestor stood. He spoke in Spanish, then in English. "Thank you all for being here. First, thank you to my distinguished Cuban guests. You have been invaluable, instrumental, in accomplishing our remarkable success. Thank you also to our Haitian guests, who took dangerous risks to bring our enemies to justice." More applause. "Finally, please stand—Cash, Callie, Andre, Itzac, and of course, the guest of honor—Sara Cambert, and her partner, Alvaro. You've done every single impossible task you set out to accomplish. We're in awe, and we're in your debt." Another round of applause. "The cigars and the rum outside are gifts from the Cuban government, a sincere expression of our appreciation. Now, let's have a memorable party. First, with Andre's and Itzac's help, I'd like to introduce all of you to one another."

Nestor introduced all of the Cubans. Andre introduced the Haitian crew, all five of them had come, then Itzac mentioned his friend from FINIMEX, and his friend from the National Assembly, Maceo."

Next, Andre introduced Alvaro. He told a little bit of his history with Alvaro, then ended by saying, "I inadvertently introduced Sara to Alvaro. In my long exceptional life, I've never done anything finer."

Finally, Nestor asked Sara to stand up. She did, and Nestor continued, "All of this began when the people we've captured and imprisoned stole Sara's identity and tried to kill her." Nestor took out a large manila envelope, took several documents out of it. "Sara please come beside me." She came to stand beside Nestor. "I've learned a little bit about Sara this past week. Sara, I know you've faced unimaginable obstacles—being on your own, without an identity, in a country where you don't know a single person, coming into yet another unknown country, and in both places being attacked by professional assassins. Sara, I know that you persevered in the face of all of those frightening things. Tonight, I'm pleased and privileged to tell you that all of that is finally over. It is my great honor to give you back your identity—here's your own passport and your visa."

Sara looked at her passport from Nestor, then put her arms around him in a warm hug.

The people around both tables went from enthusiasm, to heartfelt congratulations, to wild celebration.

Cash came beside her, took her hand. Sara hugged her dad, then she turned to face the cheering people.

In the tumultuous applause, Alvaro joined Sara, his arm around her waist.

Callie, Andre, and Itzac joined the young lovers and Cash at the front of the room. They whispered, then the six of them joined hands. They raised their joined hands high, facing the Cubans and the Haitians sitting at the tables, and together they cried, in unison, chanting to all of the seated guests…"Bravo! Thank you…Bravo! Thank you all!…Bravo!"

The seated guests stood, joining hands, and chanted back in Spanish and English, "Enhorabuena!…Gracias!…Felicidades!…Thank you!"

When the cheering subsided, Nestor invited everyone to the Cigar Bar for fine rum and great cigars. As people happily made their way to the patio, all knew that a memorable party was well underway.

EPILOGUE

Seattle, ten days later

Le Cochon Bronze was ready for a party. Callie, Cash, Will, and Lew had spent most of the afternoon putting up festive decorations—ribbons, balloons, tear drop banners, twinkle stars, a multi-colored painted banner saying, "Hooray Sara, Welcome Home!" on a colorful background, crepe paper streamers, and so on. It wasn't a birthday party, not quite a celebration of a graduation, not really a recognition of an important award, nor even honoring the recipient of a new coveted job. It was hard to characterize, to capture, finding your dad, discovering a new family, getting your identity back, saving your dad's and your own life, and more, but they clearly wanted to let Sara know that she was loved, appreciated, and welcome in Cash, Callie, and Lew's unexpected extended family, which included Itzac and Andre. They were especially pleased with the portion of a wall they'd filled with photos of Sara from the past three weeks.

They'd organized one large table in the dining room that would hold twenty people and, in the corner, an attractive, temporarily created, well-stocked bar. Between the large table and the booths, tables had been removed to provide a comfortable area for dancing, and in that corner, a piano and a place with stools was ready for the salsa musicians. From the entry, Callie looked around the room—through the decorations, she could still recognize the familiar dark mahogany floors, the carefully chosen light wood for the tables and chairs, and oak-brown Italian leather for the booths along the back.

She turned to the far wall that attached to the cherry wood mullioned picture windows beside her. On the wall, they'd taken down several paintings. In their place, they'd put up the various pictures that they and others had taken of Sara. Sara in the restaurant with her dad, with her dad and Callie upstairs in the bar, with Lew and Callie in the kitchen. At the Macher's apartment, singing "Crazy" with Cash. One she'd taken herself with Sara, Cash, the Macher, and Andre at the Saloon in the Oyster bar in Grand Central Station. Sitting next to Hemingway's statue, drinking a daiquiri at the Floridita Bar. Sara beside the 1958 Edsel convertible taxi talking movies with Paz. Having a festive dinner at Esperanza, before Alvaro surprised her, flying through the air in his arms, after she was surprised. Finally, several with Alvaro, taken later on their first vacation, then after they were back, at the party at Cocina de Lilliam. A picture of all of them—Sara, Alvaro, Cash, Callie, Andre, and Itzac, thanking the Cubans and the Haitians for their help, then later Cash, Alvaro, Sara, Olvidado, and Nestor smoking cigars and sipping rum at the cigar bar outside on Lilliam's patio.

Cash came beside Callie, who was looking over the pictures. She turned to him, "She's like something in a fairy tale, or a European allegorical movie, the unknown young woman that comes out of nowhere, then, effortlessly, makes everyone around her better off, happier."

The Macher had come in, and he was listening. He added, "She's had that effect on me."

Callie took Cash's hand, "That's your daughter, babe."

They were interrupted as people started arriving. Andre came in with Sergeant Lincoln and his beautiful wife, Cherry. Cherry was younger than Lincoln, maybe thirty-eight. Her hair was short, her skin a deep black, and her very presence seemed to cause people to relax. Callie and Cash liked her instantly. Next was Nestor, who'd brought his wife, Lillana, his daughter, Alicia, and her husband, Camilo.

Others arrived shortly. Mary, Callie's old friend, the local doctor who'd tested Cash and Sara's blood to confirm that they were father and daughter. Lew's lovely girlfriend, Lisa, a sixteen-year-old girl. She was almost a year older than Lew, though that didn't seem to bother her. He came to find her, and she took his hand. Eva, Sara's Cuban doctor arrived next. She came on her own but quickly began talking, in broken

English, with Mary. Callie thought that there must be some kind of unspoken communication that allowed doctors to identify each other. Callie was surprised when Mary switched to Spanish. Next was Detective Ed Samter. He brought a new girlfriend, Kate. He introduced her right away to Cash and Callie, explaining that she, too, was a police officer. Unlike Samter, Kate was warm and communicative. Callie thought she was perfect for the soft-spoken, withdrawn, detective.

Everyone wandered around the dining and dancing room areas, introducing themselves to one another, usually stopping to see the collection of photos of Sara. Callie had created the attractive bar in a corner downstairs, and Jill was expertly serving drinks. Andre was helping her, especially encouraging the Cubans to try the Bronze Pig— "the pig"—his special cocktail.

In another corner, Sergeant Lincoln and Detective Sumter were telling, again, to Cash and Itzac, about their meeting with Lennie. They were all pleased that Lennie was so totally taken aback, blindsided, by Rosie and Yu's predicament. He definitely understood and was both mindful of and worried about their threats. Lennie had actually asked them for advice about whether he was in danger himself. They told him that they wouldn't prosecute him if he observed the rules that they had laid out. They'd prosecute all of them, including Lennie, if Rosie and Yu ever came back to the US.

About ten minutes later, at seven thirty, Callie asked everyone to take a seat at the table, which was beautifully decorated and tastefully enhanced with fresh flowers. People sat wherever they liked, leaving two places at the head of the table for Sara and Alvaro.

After everyone sat down, Callie explained that Cesaire, her chef, had prepared dinner, with several choices, and more detailed descriptions would follow after Sara and Alvaro arrived. People relaxed, more drinks were served, and conversation around the comfortable table, in this beautiful room, was lively.

No more than five minutes later, Sara and Alvaro, came in. When they removed their coats, everyone stood, applauding. They were beautifully dressed. He wore a long sleeve traditional Guayabera shirt of the finest blue linen over white dress pants. She wore a Catalina-embellished, long sleeve, black gown designed for salsa dancing. No one had ever seen Sara dressed like that, and she was stunning.

Cash and Callie embraced both of them, then led them to their places at the head of the table. After they sat, Callie said, "All of you know Sara and Alvaro. We are gathering here together tonight to welcome Sara to her new family, her new home. We'd especially like to thank her, and to celebrate, for all that she's given to us in so many ways. We'd also like to warmly welcome her friend, Alvaro, to our community."

Sara stood. "Thank you, Callie, for making me and Alvaro feel so welcome, in all of the ways that matter…" Sara bowed in Callie's direction.

Callie reciprocated, then stood, smiling.

Sara smiled back, then she turned toward Cash. "I'd also like to thank my dad, who has made possible all of the good things that have happened for me in the last few weeks. Every single one of them. He'll deny that, but it's absolutely true." She turned to Alvaro, lovingly. "Except one—Alvaro. My dad doesn't get the credit for that." She turned back, then Sara embraced her dad. "Thank you," she whispered.

He replied, "Thank you…I have one request. Before we eat, I'd love to watch you and Alvaro dance."

"I'd like to do that. But first, there's one more song I'd like to sing. I practiced it for this occasion." She walked over to the piano then Sara nodded to Izac, who took her signal and came to the piano. When she asked if he'd play the song they'd practiced together. He whispered, "I'd love to."

Sara began by saying, "Alvaro will know this song well. It's from the movie *Streets of Fire*. I believe we first fell in love because of that film, what, just a few weeks ago. This is the last and final song—"Tonight Is What It Means To Be Young"—in this wonderful, unexpected film, and I'd like to sing it. It's my very first time singing alone to an audience. This is, I believe, the perfect occasion for another first time. I'm singing it both for Alvaro and for my dad. I'm also, of course, singing it for all of you."

Callie handed her a microphone. The lights came down, except for one spotlight that Will had focused on Sara. Her head was down, getting her bearings. She listened as Itzac beautifully played the familiar lyrical introduction. When Sara raised her head, her eyes were bright, and her face was radiant. When she began to sing, softly slowly, she captured the crowd, and then she took off, singing like she'd never sung before. People clapped and cried out as she sang this intense, powerful, stirring song.

Sara's singing was compelling, carrying everyone along in her intense, stirring voice, gently mesmerizing the crowd, and then with a stunning flourish, she was done.

In the tumultuous applause, Alvaro swept Sara into his arms.

Cash cried out, "Let's see some salsa dancing!"

Itzac and Andre joined in the cheering for dancing.

Callie signaled the musicians, who began playing.

Alvaro led Sara by the hand to the dance area. He took her in his hands, and moved her gently, gracefully around the dance floor—Alvaro, a superb dancer, led masterfully, moving her beautifully in sync, forward step together, back step together, forward step together. One, two, three, hold four…five, six, seven, hold eight. There was an intuitive connection, a series of swirls, sidestepping, general walking away then effortlessly coming together…then something magical happened…Sara flew through the air as he swung her in a circle, holding only her wrists and hands. She landed gracefully leaning backward, her head almost touching the floor as Alvaro held her waist, spinning her in yet another circle, and then she was in the air again. The crowd went wild, crazy, as she flew down lightly into his arms.

◆◆◆

It was three thirty in the morning. The other guests had left. Callie, Cash, Sara, Alvaro, Andre, Lew, and Itzac sat around the maple prep table in the kitchen. They were coming down from a wonderful, unforgettable evening. They were sipping fine Armagnac. Callie had even given Lew a little taste.

"Lisa thought my family was magnificent. Her word," Lew said.

"She's right," Sara nodded.

"I like her," Callie offered.

"I'm glad, though honestly, among my friends, having your mom like your girlfriend is usually a negative." He tasted the Armagnac, made a face.

"I'm glad it still counts for something."

Lew turned to Sara, "How are you doing in this unusual family?"

Sara smiled, she really liked Lew. "You're smart to ask. Truthfully, I'm crazy about all of you."

Alvaro added. "She's not kidding. I hear about all of you a lot." He covered his mouth but couldn't hide a yawn. "So, it's three thirty in the morning. Do you guys ever get tired of talking?"

Lew answered. "Never, and I mean never."

Cash laughed. "Okay. It's bedtime. He stood, hugged Andre, Itzac, then Alvaro. Finally, he took Sara in his arms. She put her arms around him and started to cry.

She stepped back, wiped away her tears. "Dad, I hope it's okay when I cry. I'm doing that a lot around you. Honestly, it's good for me."

Cash turned toward her, with a warm smile. Callie came and put one arm around each of them.

The Macher stood, raised his glass. "To our new family. I begin in Yiddish." He looked to Andre, who nodded.

Callie smiled at Cash, she couldn't help it. Cash was next to her, his arm around her waist. Sara came back with Alvaro. They stood beside Cash. Sara reached out and held Cash's hand.

"*A mentsh tracht und Gott lacht.*"

"A person plans, and God laughs," Andre translated.

"Cash, a *Choshever mentsh.*"

"Cash, a man of worth and dignity."

"Callie, a *vundern zikh.*"

"Callie, a wonder, a marvel."

"And then the unplanned happens. An unknown, twenty-five-year-old daughter arrives. Sara, our new family member."

"*L'Chayim.*"

"To life."

"*L'Chayim*," said in unison around the table.

ACKNOWLEDGMENTS

The author would like to thank: Tyson Cornell, Jacob Epstein, David Field, Guy Intoci, Brendan Kiley, Patricia Kingsley, Robert Lovenheim, John McCaffrey, Ron Mardigian, Bonnie Hyatt Murphy, Tom Murphy, Dorothy Escribano Weissbourd, Emily Weissbourd

SPECIAL ACKNOWLEDGMENTS

Brendan Kiley is a reporter at the *Seattle Times* who has covered a variety of subjects (arts, culture, presidential conventions, drugs and drug policy, and much more) and now writes long-form articles for the paper's *Sunday* magazine.

Brendan has done outstanding detailed research for all of my books. He has also been a very valuable sounding board for discussing plot issues that arise in the course of writing the books. He has made a meaningful contribution to all of the books he's worked on.

Jauretsi Saizarbitoria is an advisor on Cuban culture, informed by her own personal time living in Cuba. During her time there, she performed several duties including working with journalists, film production, and travel services, offering a deeper intimate look at everyday life on the island.

She skillfully guided me through, and taught me about, all things Cuban—including, but not limited to, culture, neighborhoods, architecture, tourism, customs, airports, hotels, restaurants, prisons, etc. Her expertise was very valuable in writing this book.

Lisa Fyfe did an exceptional job creating the cover for *Rough Justice*, as well as for the first Callie James title, *Danger in Plain Sight*.

CPSIA information can be obtained
at www.ICGtesting.com
Printed in the USA
LVHW030737130922
728208LV00004B/4